THE GIRL AND THE SILENT NIGHT

A.J. RIVERS

The Girl and the Silent Night

TWAS THE NIGHT BEFORE CHRISTMAS...

Jonah

Then

THE EXCITEMENT OF CHRISTMAS NEVER GOT OLD. HE WAS AN ADULT now, but that didn't matter when the calendar turned to December and it officially became Christmas season. He got the same flutter when he thought about the holiday that he did when he was little. The magic was still real. It was the one time of year when he and his brother could be children again. They didn't think about the pressures of the rest of the world, of adulthood, of all the changes that were happening around them so fast it was sometimes hard to breathe.

This time of year, they only thought about Christmas.

They still spent the night at their parents' house for a few days before the holiday and insisted they didn't fill their stockings or put their presents under the tree until they were asleep. It was silly, but he never tired of the way their mother's eyes sparkled when they reminded her, or the nostalgia that filled their father's face when he told them it was time to get to bed just like he had when they were just little boys. The parents enjoyed it just as much as their twin sons. They had no grandchildren yet, so all the sugar, spice, and joyful merriment of the yuletide season went directly to Jonah and his brother, Ian.

This year was the first time there was a reminder that would someday change.

"There's no way that's going to fit," Mariya said, giggling as she cradled a mixing bowl in the curve of her hip and mixed the dough inside.

"It's going to be fine," Ian's voice insisted from somewhere in the depths of the dark green branches. There was a distinct grunt behind the words, and he made a spitting sound like he was trying to get sap out of his mouth.

Jonah laughed at his brother, stepping back to hold the door open further. Ian said that was his job. Jonah offered to help him carry in the massive pine they'd cut down themselves, but Ian was determined to do it himself.

"Just open the door," he told him. "Hold it open and I'll handle the rest."

He was showing off. Not that Jonah could blame him. Mariya laughed again and the sound fell over him, tingling on his skin like fresh snow. It was the first year she was spending Christmas with the family and the seamless way she blended in said it wouldn't be her last. Soon her last name would be Griffin and she would welcome in the next generation.

She turned to look at Jonah, her wide blue eyes glittering with her silken smile. Her thick eyelashes lowered and she focused on stirring again. The soft pink of her cheeks made warmth spread through his heart and the blue of her eyes made him lose himself in the depths of clear crystal ice.

They'd touched him first. He wouldn't let go of that, not ever. She saw him first, met his eyes first, smiled at him first. But he was patient. For now, that smile was enough.

"Help me," Ian finally relented through the shaking of the branches stuffed into the doorway.

"I thought you could do it on your own," Jonah teased. "You said all I needed to do was hold the door open, and I seem to be doing that just fine."

"Help me with the damn tree," Ian grumbled.

"Ian," Mrs. Griffin scolded. "It's Christmas Eve."

"Sorry," the branches of the tree seemed to say. "Help me with the joyful tree."

Mariya laughed.

"Remind me again why we got our tree on Christmas Eve," Jonah said as he grabbed hold of the trunk of the tree and started trying to wrangle it through the doorway.

It was far too big. If they even managed to get it through the door, they were likely going to have to crush the top just to make it fit into the space. But it had looked great out in the forest when they found it. Both of them had gotten too wrapped up in the spirit to think about such trivial details as whether or not it would actually fit into the house.

"To make it more special," Ian replied.

Jonah wasn't so sure about that justification. It seemed like a tremendous amount of work for only one night. But his mother and Mariya had been working all day making food for their family tree-trimming party, and his father was on his fifth trip up to the attic to bring down the decorations. It did have a certain element of urgency and thrill to it.

They finally managed to get the tree inside and stuff it into the stand. The very top of it leaned forward against the ceiling, the branches awkwardly folded, and it took up a decent portion of the room, but there was no denying it was a good tree. The smell of the branches filled the entire space, bringing to mind all kinds of memories and nostalgia from years before.

"It smells wonderful," Mariya smiled, wiping her hands as she came into the room.

It was as if their minds were linked. She could feel his thoughts.

Jonah reached his arm out for her and stepped into it, letting him wrap his arm around her waist and pull her in. Ian fought his way out from behind the tree and stood on the other side of her, taking her hand. He leaned in to kiss her and she rested her head on his shoulder.

"Look this way!"

The three turned to look over their shoulders at Mr. Griffin. His huge camera was poised at his face and they barely had the chance to smile before he snapped a picture of them.

"Merry Christmas!" their mother announced, coming into the room with a platter mounded with cookies.

"Merry Christmas," the three chimed back.

Mariya looked up at Ian. "Merry Christmas." She kissed him softly, then turned to Jonah. "Merry Christmas."

Her lips were soft and warm on his cheek.

"Merry Christmas."

Now

"Merry Christmas, Mariya," he whispered, running his fingers over the image of her face.

The texture of the picture was different there. Rather than the smooth texture of paper, it was rough from the many years of his fingertips touching the bridge of her nose and the softness of her lips.

The cold wind whipped up and he pulled his collar up over his neck. In front of him, the bay window in the living room was dark except for the glow of lights on the Christmas tree perfectly framed in the center of the panes. It wasn't quite as big as that one years ago, but he was sure the same ornaments were nestled in the branches.

He moved across the lawn with comfort, familiarity. The blades of sleeping, frozen grass were new, but the dirt beneath them knew the press of his feet. The porch was different. It hadn't been there that

Christmas when they'd dragged the massive pine into place. The screen door hadn't been in place. But he knew that front door.

This wasn't the first time he'd been here in the last few years. But it was the first time he walked up the steps in the shimmer of the multicolor lights. It wouldn't last. He couldn't stay. But he paused to let the memories flow over him and pretend, if only for a second, that they were real again.

He was finally home for the holidays.

PROLOGUE

I started investigating her death before it happened.
She helped me.
She gave me what I needed.

Then

Lakyn Monroe was accustomed to not having much space.

It was a common misconception that she had always lived in some sort of bubble. That her fame kept her distance from everyone else and that she existed with a buffer between herself and the real world.

The truth was that her fame was something she was still getting used to. It wasn't the slow-burn type of fame that came with being a child performer who happened to make the crossover or an actor who started in just small parts and gradually climbed up.

Instead, she'd sparked into fame almost overnight. She'd gone from nothing to everything, and so often it still felt like she was stumbling over her own feet just to catch up.

No one saw that. No one knew just how hard she worked just to look like she had it all together. They saw the fame. They saw her jump into the back of limos and luxurious cars and thought she was in her private oasis.

They didn't see how often she was crushed into that seat by her agent, her manager, her mother. Reporters. Producers. Anyone who wanted a little piece of her. They took her space so they could get close enough to take that piece.

She'd gotten used to not being able to breathe on her own.

Instead, they all drew the breath out of her into themselves, then breathed it back, stoking her, making the flame bigger, making the embers glow.

That night, it was different. She couldn't breathe, but she was starting to feel like the men filling the space around her didn't want her to. They weren't breathing for her. They weren't trying to waken the embers. They were trying to snuff them out.

She didn't know the name of the man next to her. She didn't think anyone had said it. And even if they had, she chose to focus on the others to retain it. It wasn't an accident that she was in this car. She put herself there. It was intentional, willful. She'd agreed to meet with the man who hadn't even stood from behind his massive desk when she'd walked into the room.

She hadn't expected much else from him. In all honesty, his cool, collected personality, the air of subtle manipulation that came from acting superior by default rather than by overt action, was exactly what she anticipated. She knew what she was getting herself into.

This wasn't a friendly visit. Not that it was meant to be wrought with animosity or any type of danger, but she didn't expect to be welcomed with open arms. After all, she was dragging these men into the light they wanted to avoid. The man behind the desk in particular.

Judge Sterling Jennings.

Lakyn knew he was corrupt. That wasn't even a question. It wasn't a matter of whether he was involved in the framing and false imprisonment of an innocent man—a brilliant, if odd, man, who'd been sitting in a cell for years waiting for his true story to be told. It was a matter of what exactly he had done.

She knew the story was there. And she was going to be the one to tell it. Xavier Renton wouldn't continue to waste away in a cage for something he didn't do. Not if she had anything to do about it. And she knew the judge held the missing answers. She just had to find them.

That was where her true flame burned. Everyone wanted her to be the starlet: the false eyelashes, bright lipstick, glossy hair, glossier voice. She was the perfect canvas to them. They could take her and transform her into anything they wanted her to be.

And she had asked for it, they reminded her. She wanted to be in the spotlight. She wanted people to look at her, to watch her, to admire her. It was why she put those videos up on the internet for everyone to find. There was nothing scandalous about them. Lakyn was just intrigued by the camera and the ability to make herself seen. She'd always been fascinated by the idea of all those people out in the world, people she would never cross paths with, living their own completely separate lives.

For as long as she could remember, she'd wanted to close those gaps. She'd wanted to make connections there was no reason to make. She didn't buy into the idea that every person came into the world alone as a separate entity and would live out their existence that way. She didn't believe there was no connection among humanity and that people couldn't touch each other's lives. She wanted that touch. She believed in the link of breath, of heartbeats, of the simple reality of being human.

The camera let her dip her fingertips into that connection.

She roamed the parks she adored and told anyone watching what she was experiencing. She rode rides with the camera like she was riding alongside viewers. She ate like they were sharing a snack. She brought them along with her.

She didn't realize with every video, she fragmented herself. Pixels became tiny droplets of her that blew out of screens and gathered in waiting palms. Some drank her up. Others dried their hands of her and clicked away. Still others bottled up those droplets. They collected the frozen crystals and the heated steam. Those droplets became their medium and their leverage.

They could craft her into anything they saw simply by luring her with what they held. She sought herself out again; they promised to gather all the pieces and build her again. They sprinkled the ground with those droplets like leaving breadcrumbs for her to follow. And she did. She followed them from the computer screen to the TV screen and they were laying the path to the movie screen.

But she didn't know if she wanted to follow them there. At the same time they were trying to make her bigger, she was starting to pull away. She'd found her passion in helping others. It sounded trite and even predictable, but in her, it was authentic. Others might say they wanted to use their notoriety and fame to make a difference in the world, but Lakyn truly did.

She wasn't all altruism and selflessness. Becoming the world's darling might not have been her life's greatest passion, but she'd never say it didn't have its perks. There were obvious benefits to the fame she was suddenly tossed into, and she didn't turn her back on it. But she was drifting further from that, wanting more and more to scrape away the murky layers of missing persons, crime, and tragedy, and find what was really beneath. To bring some light into the lives of those scarred by darkness.

It was how she found Xavier Renton. It was how she learned of the group called The Order of Prometheus. And it was how she became convinced Judge Jennings was at the core of the darkness coiled tight beneath the town of Harlan.

She wanted to meet with him and hear what he had to say. She couldn't ask him straight out what he had done, of course. But she could lead him. She could twist him and turn him until he revealed enough that he said what he hadn't ever meant to say.

She didn't know how much of that she had accomplished yet. They would need to have more conversations. There were many threads and she had to find the right one to pull.

Which put her in the back of this car. Pressed up against the man she didn't know. The one who looked at her as if she wasn't there.

They were supposed to be bringing her home. When they'd told her they'd made the arrangements for her to meet with the Judge and would send a car for her, the two halves of Lakyn Monroe went to battle.

On one side was the part of her that was still nothing but a girl sitting in her house fumbling around with internet videos, trying to find what would click. That was the part of her that said she should never get into a car with men she didn't know. That she should always have her own car or someone she knew driving her. That this was dangerous.

On the other side was the part of her that was everything. She was the bright light, the new star, the face that came to mind anyone thought of young talent and fame. She was famous because she was famous. People saw talent in her that she had never displayed. They saw potential in her she never intended on exuding. She was something to everyone. Positive or negative.

That was the part of her that was accustomed to drivers and arranged rides. Who rarely got to drive herself anymore and was more familiar with having a bodyguard lurking behind her than a boyfriend or close friend walking beside her. That part insisted that this was normal. That she did it all the time and it was nothing unusual.

Both parts of her recognized it was dangerous.

Neither part thought that meant enough to stop her.

She had to do this. She couldn't back away just because she thought something could go wrong. She had already gone so far and done so much. She had the pictures and recordings of the temple she'd broken into under the guidance of Xavier's impenetrable mind. She'd already collected enough that she believed she could get people to see what she saw when she looked at him.

Betrayal.

The case against Xavier seemed strong, but also very neat and convenient. It was fascinating and drew her in when she'd first read about it, and as soon as she met the man who had now lost eight years of his life to the prison system, she knew something truly horrible had happened. Not just to the man brutally murdered in Xavier's garage, but to Xavier himself. Someone put him behind those bars. And they did it on purpose.

He told her he didn't commit the crime. It wasn't a begging, beseeching plea of innocence like most convicted murderers put out to anyone who would listen. He didn't cry. He wasn't desperate. He didn't cling to her and cry out to be heard and understood. That was what was compelling about him. He simply said he didn't do it.

He wasn't dismissive or careless about it. It was often difficult to understand what he was saying, but even when she struggled to string the words together, she could sense his emotion. It was his best friend who was murdered. The man who was there through every step of his life. Xavier struggled without him. He was adrift without him. He didn't fit into the world even with him, and when Andrew Eagen was no longer there, it was like he'd been dropped into another universe and expected to know how to survive.

But he didn't fling himself at her feet or beg for her to hear him. What was happening to him was his reality. She didn't understand that. She didn't know what he meant or what that felt like. But she knew he wasn't speaking out for himself. This wasn't about getting himself out of jail or getting some form of compensation. He wasn't angling for people to know him or for his story to sweep the world. He wasn't trying to get the truth known for his own needs. It was for Andrew. It was for the simple, basic purpose of proving what was real.

And she was going to fight for that for him.

That fight got her here. At first, nothing seemed too out of the ordinary. The conversation with the judge was unremarkable and she'd learned little that helped her. She tried to remember as much of it as she possibly could, though. There might be something she would be able to say to Xavier that would mean something so he could guide her to the next step.

Now that feeling was waning. The press of the man's thigh beside her felt like an inconvenience of space at first. Now it was oppressive. The warmth inside the car kept increasing as heaviness pressed down around them. Something was wrong.

She watched out the window as the car hurtled along the road into the night. Everything around her was familiar. She knew where she was. It wasn't far from home. Maybe they were going to bring her back.

Only, the turn came and went. No one said anything. No one even acknowledged where they were going.

This wasn't going to end well. It was in the pit of her stomach and the deepest well of her heart. It was in the back of her mind and the tips of her fingers. This was over. They had no intention of bringing her home. They had no intention of her leaving wherever they were bringing her.

She would fight for every second. It wasn't going to be easy for them.

But unless there was a miracle, this was the last night of her life.

Lakyn wouldn't give them her fear. They had no right to it. No claim to it. She knew they wanted it desperately, but it was something she wouldn't let them have. She might not be able to stop the car. She might not even be able to stop them from whatever they had planned for her. What she could do was make sure someone knew.

Not giving away any of the thoughts crawling up into her mind, she kept her expression casual, her breathing steady, her eyes soft and unbothered as they continued on with the road to her house at their back. Her fingers moved carefully so the man beside her wouldn't notice when she pressed the button to start her phone and to mute it so no sounds came out. He didn't notice when she seamlessly pressed the sequence of commands that connected her to the number that had become the most familiar over the last few weeks.

She didn't wait for an answer. It wasn't going to come. All that mattered was the machine listening. It took her words and held onto them.

It held a piece of her where the men couldn't get it. The only thing that mattered was that someone heard it. That would keep them from having total control.

If someone heard, then these men wouldn't have their secret anymore.

With the phone recording in her pocket, Lakyn tried to gather details about what was around her before she spoke. She had to choose her words carefully so it would seem like she really was speaking only to the men with her. They needed to think they were smarter than her. That they had total control. That she hadn't figured it out.

"I thought you said you were taking me home," she finally said.

It didn't cause any suspicion. None of the men looked at each other or gave any kind of response. It was exactly what she wanted. And what she needed to move her plan to the next step.

"You took a wrong turn back there. You should have turned right to go to my house, but you turned left," she said.

"It's fine," the man beside her grumbled. "We know where we're going."

That wasn't reassuring, even if it was meant to be. Lakyn got the impression the man thought he was being clever, that he was saying something that sounded comforting when he was actually threatening her. She didn't let on that she could hear it in his voice. That she knew they weren't going to find another turn or take a detour that would bring her back to her house.

She wished she could close her eyes in that second. If she could just let her eyelids down for a brief moment, she would be able to see her house again. The cute house with the soft pink walls in the bathroom. When she'd first bought it, the agent mentioned the walls, said they would be easy to repaint that room into something more neutral. Or even a bold on-trend color.

Lakyn liked the pink. There was something about it that made her think of her grandmother, even though she was certain her grandmother's house never had a pink bathroom. That thought brought the sting of tears to the backs of her eyes. She fought it, keeping herself calm, refusing to allow any of the men in the car to see her emotion.

"Oh. Well, that's fine. It's easy to make mistakes out here on all these twisty back roads." She lifted her voice just slightly. She didn't want them to notice how much more loudly she was speaking, but she needed to make sure her voice was getting picked up by the machine. "I should have listened to my sister. She told me to always have a snack in my purse. I'm getting really hungry and I'm probably an hour away from home."

"You'll be fine," the man in the front seat said. The man they called Laurence.

He was the one she was supposed to trust. The one she thought was bringing her in closer and funneling the judge and all he'd done to her. Now it felt like it was actually the other way.

She looked around again, making a show of peering out through the windows like she was taking stock of the land around her.

"Do you think the farmers ever get confused about which farm is theirs? Everything looks so similar out there. We just went by four separate wheat fields and two cornfields before these tracks. Don't you think that gets confusing sometimes?" The car suddenly swerved off the main road and Lakyn grabbed hold of the door to hold herself steady. "Why are you turning left again? You should be turning right to go to my house, not left."

The thought flickered through her mind that her hand was right next to the door handle. She considered grabbing hold of it and yanking the door open, just flinging herself out. It would take some time for the car to stop and get back to her, giving her a chance to get away. But at the speed the car was moving, she would probably be seriously injured when she hit the ground.

That was if she could even get out. She had a strong feeling this was not a compulsive decision on the part of these men. They didn't just suddenly decide they were going to abduct her. Because that was what this was. It had taken some time for her to really wrap her head around that reality and come to terms with it, but that was her reality right then.

She'd been abducted and was truly at the mercy of these men. They would have taken steps to make sure they could hold onto her. It started with insisting she put on her seatbelt before they got started. In that first second, it just seemed like a cautious middle-aged man giving her the same kind of warning he would give his children before he drove them somewhere.

Now she realized it was a step in keeping her under control. He'd essentially had her trap herself. There was a slim chance she'd be able to release the buckle and get out of the belt if she moved carefully enough, but even that didn't give her much hope. She was certain they'd taken into consideration that possibility. The door would be locked, the child lock activated so she couldn't just open the door and get out.

There was nothing she could do but continue to rattle off every clue she could think of to say, enunciating each word carefully so whoever heard the message first would know where to go and what happened to her.

"Where are we?" Lakyn asked, forcing herself not to sound scared, but confused and curious. "I don't think I've ever been out this far. I'd like to come back sometime when there's more light so I can see it better. We passed by a sign two roads ago. Did you see what it said?"

She was hoping they would answer. She doubted they would. There was no reason for them to. But that was precisely why she thought they might. It was a cruel game, but not an unusual one. Not when it came to those relishing the feeling of someone else's life sitting in their hands. If they thought there was nothing she could do with the information, it would do no harm sharing it with her. It would be like giving a tiny bit of rope, a tiny bit of breath, seeing no reason not to prolong those moments just after life, but before final death.

But there was no response. The car took another turn and started to slow. It felt like something was coming. She didn't know exactly what, but the path was ending.

"When I agreed to speak with the judge, I didn't think I was going to get a leisurely drive out of it, too. This really has been lovely, but I need to get home now."

Everything around the car was dark. Only the headlights cutting through let her see the outlines of the trees and the rolling fields. They went further, seeming to leave reality and enter memory. This was a place that used to exist, not one that was meant to still be a part of anyone's life.

But there was someone there. There was something still existing out in the darkness. A glimmer of light in the distance. And another closer. The car slowed and Lakyn could see the light in front of them was another car. The doors were closed, but the overhead light glowed, illuminating the shapes of people inside.

"Why are you stopping?" Lakyn asked. The breath was starting to catch in her throat and heat burned in her cheeks. The fire swelled in her chest. Not for performing. Not for others. But for herself. "I don't want to be out here with you. Where are we? Who's in that car?"

The wheels came to a stop and the car pressed forward for just an instant before settling back into silent, painful stillness. This was it. It wasn't time to pretend or to play. The time had come to fight.

"Come on, Lakyn. Get out of the car. It's a beautiful night. I want to take you for a walk in the cornfield."

They got out of the car and stood to either side. The man beside her slid out through the other door and for an instant, it was only her and the heavy air inside the car. They'd taken the keys with them. She couldn't scramble into the front and try to drive away.

"No. I don't want to take a walk," she said, lifting her voice again. "I'm not going into that cornfield. I've never liked mazes. You need to bring me home. I don't want to be here. Bring me home, Laurence."

People often wonder what their last words will be.

Those were hers.

Once the phone clattered to the floor and the hands tore her from the car, letting the seatbelt break tear against her rather than unhooking her, there was no more need for words. There was no one left who would care to hear them.

After that, there were only screams.

They weren't cries for mercy, pleas for the men to rethink what they were doing or to be gentler. They weren't full of sadness and fear.

They were primal. They ripped out of her, guttural and uncompromising. Every one of them was a link, interlocking into a chain that would hang heavy around these men's necks for the rest of their existence. She knew what they were doing. She knew there was nothing she could do about it. But she wouldn't give herself over easily. If they wanted her, they would have to rip her out of herself.

She would fight. Not because she thought she would live. She would fight so they would never forget her dying. She would hang on them, mark them.

She would never let them go.

Lakyn had no way of knowing the men weren't the only ones to hear her. Someone was watching as they reduced her to strands of hair and broken bones, torn flesh and streaks of blood. Far from there, hidden in the shadows of the night, a woman listened to her screams and watched until the fire burned out.

Soon

There was someone watching her.

There were a lot of people watching her, but there was something different about this one. Marlowe could feel intent eyes on her as she danced among the flashes from cameras and people calling her name.

She tried to ignore the eyes, to smile and laugh like they weren't there. She only cared about the other people. At least, that was what she wanted them to think. She didn't want any of them to know how hard her heart was beating or that the only thing on her mind was where she'd left her pill bottle. She'd taken it out of her purse, she remembered that. It would have fit if she was bringing the larger bag she'd chosen first, but then she changed her mind.

This outfit was better. It had more sparkle and shine. The color looked good against her skin. And it showed plenty of it. But the bag that went with it was so small. Barely big enough for a condom and some self-respect, as Brittany always joked. Not that it really applied to Marlowe. She didn't have the time to date indiscriminately. Or to party every night like a lot of girls her age.

But tonight was her night. Everyone there was celebrating her. Even if they didn't know they were when they got to the club that night, they were there for Marlowe.

The event coordinator at the club made sure it wasn't hard to watch her. The platform was roped off with black velvet to stop anyone from climbing up to her, creating an altar where they could admire her from any corner. And that's where the eyes were. The corner. She knew they were there even when she couldn't see them.

The lights flashed frantically to the beat of the music, flickering off the sparkles on her dress, glittering on her skin. When she closed her eyes, she could still see them. A hand touched her back and a drink was pressed into her palm. It barely cut through the dryness in her mouth, but she didn't want to stop dancing. Not yet.

If she stopped dancing, she'd have to pay attention to the thudding of her heartbeat. She'd have to think about the pill bottle she'd left behind because it didn't fit into the tiny purse. So she danced. She closed her eyes and didn't think about anything else. She soaked in the sound of her name and the flash of the cameras. She reminded herself that this was what it was all about. It was why she was here. It was what she wanted. What she had always wanted.

But her heart didn't stop pounding. The sweat didn't stop beading at the base of her neck and sliding down her spine. She grabbed for another cup and drank it down. She wished she'd carried the bigger purse.

The eyes were getting closer. They felt like they were all around her now. Not the people calling her name. Not the ones taking pictures and tossing them out to the virtual world as proof of something: proximity, or shared experience, or moments that would be talked about for weeks. These eyes didn't care about anyone else knowing they were there. They only cared about Marlowe.

She grabbed hold of the arm closest to her.

"I have to go."

It didn't really matter who she said it to. They were all within the black velvet ropes. They'd been given access to the altar. There was no need to wait for a response. She wasn't asking permission. It didn't matter to her if they wanted her to stay or if she hadn't finished everything she was supposed to. She hadn't taken all the pictures people expected or said the things they were waiting to hear. But she needed to leave. She needed to get away from the lights and the sounds and the eyes.

A buffer of silence fell over her when she stepped outside. She could still feel the tremble of the music on her skin. She could still feel the fear of something in the footsteps behind her chasing, even when she was standing still. The driver pulled up in front of her and her security guard opened the door for her. He peered inside quickly before stepping back to let her in.

He always did that. He tried not to let her see it. He didn't want to frighten her, to make her think he was checking for anything that was going through his mind, already fully formed. But she knew he did it. The same way he would go into her apartment before she did and pretend he was just turning on the lights for her. Or the way she'd seen him dip his head slightly toward a cup of coffee before handing it to her, breathing it in.

Marlowe climbed into the car and waited for the guard to close it. Behind her, she could hear the party still going on. It didn't stop because she left. But they noticed. They already knew she was gone and the energy was shifting. The door would open soon and someone would come out into the quiet.

An hour later she was thinking about them again as the air whipped across her face. It was colder up here than it was on the sidewalk. But she didn't care. It was the last thing on her mind. Somewhere out there in the city, the club was still open. The music was still playing. The people inside were dancing like there was no tomorrow.

For Marlowe, there wouldn't be.

By morning the blood pumping in her temples would be ice on the pavement.

CHAPTER ONE

Now

TWISTING MY WRIST AND TILTING BACK JUST SLIGHTLY PUTS THE spouted glass measuring cup in my hand at the perfect angle to pour a thick ribbon of glaze over the pan of cinnamon rolls on the table in front of me. I tuck the phone in my other hand against my shoulder and pin it in place with my ear, so I can use my now-free hand to grab a rubber spatula. In meticulous, perfect strokes, I scrape every last little bit of the glaze from the sides of the cup onto the rolls and spread it out.

I've made enough of these rolls in my day to have the glazing technique down to a science. That is, of course, if Sam isn't there to stick his fingers in the glaze as it hits the rolls and Xavier isn't slowly easing a spoon under the flow to catch it. And Bellamy hasn't already started unraveling one of the rolls from the pan to eat it.

As it is, I'm alone. After everything that happened over

Thanksgiving, Bellamy stayed with me for a few days to process it all. With Eric finally back at work after his ordeal in the gladiator pit, I didn't want her to have to be alone to work through it. I'm not going to say I know what she's going through. Or even that I can imagine it. I've been through my own losses, but that means I know how different every one of them is. Just because you've experienced losing someone you care about doesn't mean you can instantly commiserate with other people.

Losing my grandparents wasn't the same as losing my mother.

Greg's murder wasn't the same as Eli's.

She went through not only losing several friends she has known for decades, but also having to come to terms with the reality of why she lost them. She's in a space that no one should envy. The hollow, airless realm of trying to reconcile anger, loyalty, love, and disgust all at the same time, all for the same person.

There's nothing I can do to take that from her. I can't even really share the space with her. I didn't know them the way she does and I didn't have the same attachment or reaction. All I can do is sit right outside her bubble and let her know she's not alone. We've gotten good at doing that for each other over the years.

But for today, it's just me. Tomorrow morning I'm heading back down to Harlan, but I figured while I was here I would throw together some cinnamon rolls. That turned into two batches, one to bring back with me and one to bring to Janet and Paul across the street. Then a third to bring to the guys. Then a fourth for the freezer for any cinnamon roll emergencies that might come up.

And another batch for that, too.

So I'm surrounded by cinnamon rolls in various states of doneness and feeling like I'm catering for an entire Christmas feast. Baking trays are piled up on every surface and I'm covered in flour. I'll have to convince Sam to get one of those massive double ovens soon enough. With the amount of cinnamon rolls he goes through, though, I don't think it'll be a hard sell.

"Do they smell good?" Sam asks through the phone pressed against my shoulder. Even after all these years and all these cinnamon rolls, he still sounds like an excited kid when I make them.

I chuckle. "They're bread, sugar, and cinnamon with an obscene amount of butter. Yes, they smell good."

"Obscene amount of butter?" he asks. "That's my favorite measurement."

"Don't I know it."

"Are you doing the powdered sugar glaze or the cream cheese frosting?" he asks.

"Some with each," I tell him. He groans and I laugh again. "Alright, husband. As much as I would love to stand here with this spatula in my hand and talk doughy to you, I think you told me when this call started that you didn't have a lot of time to chat, but wanted to update me on what's going on."

"Oh," he says. I can almost see his slightly crooked boyish smile crook the corner of his mouth up and his green eyes sparkle. "Yeah. You distracted me. I told you that they found Rocky dead in his prison cell."

"Right," I say, switching back to holding the phone in my hand so I can put the measuring cup and spatula in the sink. "The drug dealer who said he doesn't know anything about Marie. What was his name again?"

"Gerald Collins. I thought it might have been a hit. You know as well as I do that drug dealers don't always fare terribly well in prison. Even the higher-ranking ones. Sometimes prison is the one place where enough people think they can get to them they are actually in more danger than on the streets. Considering what I knew about Collins and the things he's in for, I figured that was what caught up with him."

"But I'm guessing that's not what you found out," I intuit.

"Correct as always, my dear. I spoke with everybody I could get into a room with and it turns out, no one knows what happened to him. He was found with a bed sheet around his neck, dangling from the side of the bed. It was tied to the opposite side and it looks like he fell off the top bunk face first so it caught him. But he also had a puncture wound in his belly and another one in his throat."

"I'd say it's a bit challenging to hang yourself after that."

"To put it mildly," Sam says. "Both of them were deep enough to cause unconsciousness within fifteen seconds."

"So, someone helped him. It still could be a hit. Unconventional, maybe, but a group of guys could have done it," I suggest.

"Not to someone that big. Rocky was huge. No way that many inmates could have gotten into his cell without anyone noticing."

"Did they find anything? Any indications at all of who might have been involved?" I ask. "How about security cameras?"

"The cameras on that floor of the prison were malfunctioning that night," he says.

"Of course they were. And I'm sure that has nothing to do with the situation at all."

"Considering the only other bit of evidence, if you can even call it that, they found is a discarded guard uniform, I would say it's safe to say it does."

"A discarded guard uniform? Who does it belong to?"

"There was no name tag or other identifying marks, and all of the guards were able to produce all the pieces of their uniforms," he tells me.

"Perfect." I let out a sigh. "It sounds like whoever offed Rocky is taking a page out of Jonah's playbook."

We still don't know how my uncle escaped from prison. It's been nearly a year and the investigations are still no closer to pinning down exactly how he managed to get through the tightly secured facility and out into the world with not only no one realizing he was gone for several hours, but then not being able to trace how he did it at all.

A woman named Serena, one of his associates, was supposed to be there to help him. But she was killed before she could, setting off a whole other chain of investigation that ended up in me finding a serial killer who'd left a long trail of destruction in his wake, including kidnapping both Dean and Eric and making them fight in underground gladiator pits. The specific method of how Jonah escaped is still a mystery, but an even bigger one is all the tangles and complex webs he weaved across so many underworld players and organizations.

"Do you think he might be willing to give you some insight into it?" Sam asks. "If you're not asking specifically about how he escaped, maybe he'll give you some hints about something like this."

"I really doubt it," I sigh. "He's not at all interested in getting caught and sent back to prison. But I'm willing to ask him. The worst he can do is say he won't tell me."

Both of us know that is far from the worst Jonah can do. But it feels better telling myself that.

It takes Jonah longer to call me than it usually does when I reach out to him. That makes me nervous. I try not to spend too much time thinking about what my father's brother is doing when I'm not talking to him. It makes it easier to keep myself sane and not go completely off the rails attempting to hunt him down when I don't try to imagine where he might be or what he might be doing. What destruction he might be planning and who he might be hurting.

That's why I always prefer when he calls me quickly. If he calls me within a couple of minutes of me putting out the signal that I need to speak with him, I feel like maybe he's just sitting around. He's not in a prison cell where he should be, but maybe he's just in hiding. Hunkered down and waiting.

It's harder to believe that when I have to wait. I'll put out the sign, commenting on an article with the specific phrase he chose, to let him know I want him to call me. The article has changed since we first came up with the arrangement. Jonah sent me a message with a link to a new one and a new phrase to use. It keeps it less obvious when the comment section isn't just a repetition of the same seemingly meaningless phrase.

I've used that change to make the delay worry me less. Maybe he just doesn't remember the article that he chose.

In the realistic part of my mind, I know that's not the case. Jonah is methodical. He doesn't forget.

So for every minute that I'm waiting for him to call me back, I'm wondering what it is that's keeping him from noticing the signal. What's keeping him from seeing it and picking up the phone to connect with me? I want to know and I don't at the same time.

He finally calls me back right before it starts threatening my sanity.

"I need your help," I start, before he can launch into any of the platitudes he usually starts to lay on me.

He's still trying to get under my skin. He's still hoping he'll be able to get beyond everything I know and start twisting my own thoughts and beliefs into his vision of the world. From even before my birth, he had plans for me. There was a brief moment when I thought he was doing better. He admitted his brother Ian is my father, something he would never say. I thought it meant the spell he had over himself was broken.

It didn't take long for that bit of hope to burst like a soap bubble. All shiny and buoyant, then gone. He's still the same. He might have managed to come to terms with the reality that he isn't my father, but that doesn't mean he doesn't still hold a sense of ownership over me. He still wants me to be by his side and run the world under the control of his organization Leviathan.

Every time we speak, there's an undercurrent of those dreams in his words. It's long-game manipulation and I can't deal with it right now.

"What is it, Emma?" he asks.

I can hear the pleasure in his voice at the thought that I'm coming to him for assistance. He likes the connection. He wants something more to link us than my desire to slap handcuffs on him and toss him back into prison. I'm choosing to ignore it.

Instead, I explain the situation with the disappearance of Sam's cousin Marie, and the mysterious death of the drug dealer thought to be linked to her.

"You want to know if I know how the drug dealer was murdered?" Jonah asks.

"Yes," I say. "It doesn't make sense. There's no video evidence. It couldn't have been inmates. The uniform belongs to the prison but they can't figure out what guard it might belong to. Which, to me, sounds like someone from the outside did it. Or someone from the inside who wasn't supposed to be there. And that brings me to you. I thought you might be able to give us some insight into how that could happen."

There's a brief pause.

"You don't think I know what you're doing?" he asks.

I sigh. "Yes, I know what this sounds like…"

"It sounds like you are, yet again, trying to get me to explain to you how I arranged for my timely release," he says.

"Escape, Jonah," I snap. "You weren't released. You escaped. And considering you were supposed to be in there for enough lifetimes that the warden's descendants will have to use exponents to write the 'greats' and would still be inheriting your bones, I think 'timely' really seems like you're playing fast and loose with the language."

"But you want to know how it was done," he counters.

"Of course I do," I say. "But right now, I'm asking because we're trying to figure out what happened to Marie."

"I can't talk about that, Emma. I can't tell you about how I got out."

Very familiar anger starts creeping its way up the back of my neck.

"You said you were going to tell me the truth," I say. "You promised to be honest with me."

It still feels strange to have the word "honest" have anything to do with Jonah and actually mean it. But I've found I have to believe it. I have to set aside my immediate biases, and probably what is the most logical and realistic approach, and be willing to accept that this man is capable of being honest. If I can accept that, I will be open to what he has to tell me. But it also means I have to open myself to being pissed off when he stops being honest.

"I promised I would be honest with what is mine to tell," he says. "And the way I got out of prison is not just mine to tell. One or more other people were involved, and it's not up to me to tell their story."

It's not the first time he's said this to me, and it pisses me off just as much as every other time he's said it. But there's nothing I can do about it. As much as I would like to think I can just reach down his throat and rip out everything he knows, that approach isn't going to work out for me. I'm at the mercy of what he is willing to give me. And right now, it seems like that's not much.

CHAPTER TWO

"And they've gone over all of the security footage?" Dean asks me. "They know who went into the facility and came out all day?"

"All the security footage they have access to," I confirm. "It seems some of the cameras mysteriously malfunctioned during the time Gerard Collins was murdered."

"It's convenient how that seems to happen," he notes.

"I thought so, too," I say. "Unfortunately, anytime you're dealing with technology, there is the possibility that there will actually be a malfunction. It could be a legitimate glitch in the security system or downtime with the program that uploads the footage. Sam spoke to a couple of people at the prison and they said it's not the first time their cameras have had problems."

"In that section of the prison?" Dean asks.

"It happens all over the facility," I tell him. "At the time when those cameras weren't working, there was another bank of them not working on the other side of the building as well. And a couple on the outside. Of course, the ones on the outside could make it seem like it was purposeful to have the cameras not work at that time. But they're not in the same locations and there are others that were working that recorded exits and entrances, the parking lot, all of it."

"And nobody suspicious came in or out?" Dean asks.

"No," I shake my head. "Everybody captured on those cameras is supposed to be there, when they're there. None of them are acting suspiciously." I let out a sound that somewhere between a sigh and a growl of frustration. "I can't believe I actually called Jonah and asked for his help."

"It makes sense," Dean muses. "As far as anytime you might call an escaped convict in hopes that will assist you with something makes sense. After all, you want to know how the security in a prison facility could be breached, and he's the only one who could tell you that."

"I could," Xavier pipes up.

"But he won't tell me," I point out. "I even said it had nothing to do with him and I didn't expect him to tell me how he escaped from prison. That I just wanted him to give me any ideas or things that jumped out at him about the circumstances, and he wouldn't even do that."

"Because he doesn't want you to take that information and be able to piece together how he escaped from his prison," Dean says. "He knows you aren't stupid. And he probably also knows you never think about one thing at a time. You might have been genuinely asking about how Collins might have been murdered, but you would have tucked that information into the back of your mind and used it to think about how Jonah escaped."

"I can't help it," I admit. "It drives me crazy that I can't figure out how he managed to get out of there. There's no logical reason at all that he should have been able to get past so many inmates and so many staff and so many physical barriers. How exactly would he get out of such a maximum-security prison?"

"So was Alcatraz," Xavier offers. "People have gotten out of there."

"Allegedly," I say. "They never found those men."

"Which means they didn't find them in the prison," Xavier says. "Or on the grounds."

"But they very well could have immediately drowned in the water right off the island," Dean says.

"Or have been eaten by sharks," Xavier adds. "But it wouldn't have happened in their prison cells. They still escaped. They got out."

"That's true," I admit. "And people know a lot more about how they probably did it than we know about Jonah, and it's still considered a huge mystery. I just really don't want it to be decades from now and people still be talking about this and trying to understand it. I need to figure out how he did it so it doesn't happen again. Not with him. Not with anyone."

"I could do it," Xavier says.

I nod as a sigh slides out of me. "I know, Xavier. I know you could have escaped."

"No, I can figure out how he did it."

"What do you mean?"

"If you want to know how a snake got into the hen house, you don't just shine a flashlight around looking. You get down on the ground on your belly and see how the snake sees. So, put me on the ground. Let me see how he might have slithered."

Dean immediately shakes his head. "No. No, Xavier. That's not happening."

"What?" I ask. "What's not happening?"

"He wants you to put him in the prison," Dean says.

"What?" I ask, shocked by the suggestion.

"If I'm there, I can see what he saw. I can experience what he experienced. It'll become my reality and I'll be able to change it," Xavier shrugs. "Emma, I know you could arrange for me to be put in there as a fake inmate. They'll come up with a backstory for me and everything. Or, they could let me come up with my own backstory. That would probably be a better idea. That way it would be more compelling because I would know all the details and it would be better if I know the details of my own life. Because, you know, they say you're not supposed to ask other inmates why they're in. But people do. They ask all the time."

"I can't ask the warden to put you in prison," I protest.

"Yes, you can," he says. "We just went over that. It's been done in other investigations and there's even that reality show where people are put in to research the conditions. All you have to do is come up with a story for me, a crime I committed, length of my sentence. Figure out where they would have transferred me from and why, and plop me down on in there."

"No, Xavier, I mean I can't do that to you. You already spent eight years in prison for something you didn't do. I can't put you through that again," I say.

"I didn't commit a crime then," he shrugs. "The biggest difference would be people would know I didn't this time. We wouldn't be able to tell the guards or the other inmates. That would create an experimental environment that was inauthentic to the genuine circumstances. Of course, it is next to impossible to exactly recreate what happened when Jonah escaped due to the fact that he escaped. His escape fundamentally altered the environment itself as well as how others interact with the environment.

"The guards will be watching more carefully, and the inmates will be more suspicious. But I'm smarter and more resourceful than Jonah, so I thought maybe it will balance out. You're probably worried about me saying things like that because it makes me sound full of myself, but I'm practicing my prison attitude. I'm going for arrogant this time."

I'm almost shocked speechless for a long moment. "You're not going for anything this time because you're not going undercover in the prison. I'm not going to let you go through that again. You said it yourself that when you were serving your sentence you wouldn't even consider trying to escape because you were supposed to be there and you didn't want to become a criminal," I say. "What if that's how you started feeling this time?"

"I wouldn't," Xavier says. "Because it wouldn't be my sentence. It would be Leland Amherst's sentence. Twenty-five years to life for murder after the bloody death of his brother during a dispute over their circus performance proceeds. During what was supposed to be a friendly meeting to discuss the issues, Leland beat Grady over the head with a baseball bat and then put him in with a trained elephant to make it look like he was trampled. If it wasn't for that damn piece of bloodied straw found in the tread of a boot Leland put outside his trailer, they never would have known."

Dean and I stare at Xavier for a few wordless seconds.

"Who?" Dean asks, his voice drifting up high.

"Leland Amherst," Xavier says.

"He made him up," I tell Dean.

"What?"

"He made him up. That's who he wants to be in prison. Only, there are a couple of things he hasn't taken into consideration with his story."

"Oooh, layers," Xavier says, his eyes sparkling a little. "What didn't I consider?"

"One, a story like that would have been spread all over the news and everybody would have already heard about it. Two, it was an episode of *Murder, She Wrote*. And three, you aren't going to prison, so you won't have anyone to tell the story to," I say.

"What about Gregorio Montenegro? Masked wrestler aimed for stardom. The only thing standing in his way was Shane 'the Pittsburgh Banana Split' Neihouse. Until a temporary tattoo laced with ricin spelled his doom mid-frog splash."

I look over at Dean. His eyes close briefly and he gives his head an almost imperceptible shake.

"We'll cut back," he says. "There's just so many shows now."

My eyes slide back over to Xavier. "The point is, I'm not going to do that. Your years in prison were horrible for you and there's just no way I can make you go through that again."

"It wouldn't be the same," he says.

"I appreciate it, Xavier, but no. There has to be another way."

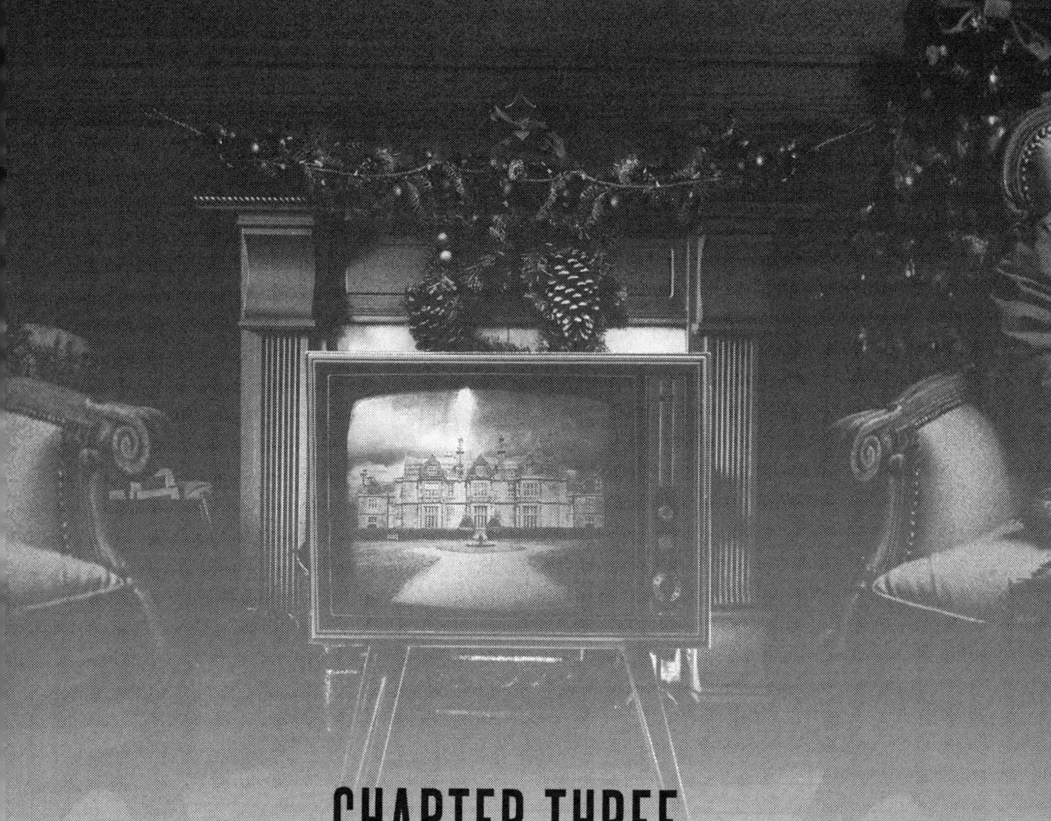

CHAPTER THREE

My phone rings and I take it out of my pocket to glance at it.

"Hold on," I say. "I've got to take this. It's that producer."

"Ask if she needs any extras," Xavier calls as I walk out of the room. "I could play a scarecrow."

"You hate scarecrows," Dean tells him.

"Frederic Mulligan could overcome it."

"Who?"

I don't hear the rest of the conversation because I close the door to the library behind me as I answer the phone.

"Hello?"

"Agent Griffin?"

"Yes."

"Hi, this is Delta King. How are you today?"

"Doing fine."

"Fantastic. Good to hear."

It's the same exchange we've had every time I've talked to this woman on the phone and it has just as much sincerity and warmth in it as when the toll taker asks how you're doing as she tosses coins over her shoulder and is already looking at the next car. I could probably say just about anything right now and she would move right on with the conversation. *My leg is caught in a bear trap. I've contracted consumption and am currently on my way to the sanatorium. The shark I'm attempting to ride doesn't like his bridle and is giving me trouble. Fantastic. Good to hear.*

"What can I do for you?"

"I'm just calling to confirm that you will be available tomorrow," she asks.

"Yes. I'm in Harlan now."

"That's great. Call time is eight. I'll see you at seven. Do you know how to get to the old Moore cornfield? Next to the…"

"Pumpkin patch. Yes. I'm familiar with it," I say.

Images of working our way through the cornfield with Xavier at the helm, torn between loyalty to historic accuracy and the pop culture answers he knew were the ones that would actually progress us through the twists and turns, flood my mind. Those images make me smile. But not the ones that chase after them.

Beyond the cornfield and the pumpkin patch, there's a path that leads through the woods past vignettes of infamous murderers and scenes of horror. But that doesn't bother me. It's beyond the path, over a road that was never meant to be used and through a gate meant to keep people out and curious eyes from knowing what was further in the woods. I know what's there.

I can still see the abandoned amusement park with its dilapidated buildings and crumbling paths being overtaken by weeds and grass. The broken-down rides left to rot where they stood when the last guest stopped laughing and walked away. When the gates were locked behind them with no intention of anyone walking through them again. I can still see the swings that once lit up in bright multi-colors as they swept riders through the night sky.

And I can see the silhouette of Xavier dangling from one of them, the strap tied around his chest sliding up to catch him by the throat.

I know the cornfield. And I know the one Delta King and the rest of the people involved with the show she's producing are trying to create.

"Good," she says. "There's a parking area set aside. It's clearly marked. Please be sure to use it so we don't contaminate the rest of the set."

"I promise I won't skid my husband's squad car into the middle of the scene," I say.

She lets out a canned laugh. "See you tomorrow. Let us know if you need anything or if there's anything you'd like to have on set."

She hangs up before I would have been able to answer her even if I had something to say about it. I shake my head as I head back into the living room. I'm not sure why I agreed to do this. Actually, I know why I did it, I just wish it didn't feel as important as it does.

"A brace on my back and hoes in my pants," Xavier's saying as I walk into the living room.

Dean looks up at me. "His scarecrow strategy."

"Ah."

"Using hoes…"

"The gardening implement," I say with a knowing nod.

"Yes. Attaching them to the wooden post behind me and using them as supports for my feet would be thematically appropriate and more difficult for the viewer to detect because a hoe is already an anticipated element of the farming landscape. Therefore, it would be logical and expected that it would be present."

"Makes sense to me," I shrug, tossing my phone back onto the table.

"What did she say?" Dean asks.

"Just that I'm expected on set at seven in the morning. She asked if I knew how to get to the old Moore cornfield," I say.

"I don't understand why they are using a different field," Dean says.

"If they are going to bother to come all the way out here rather than just shooting somewhere else, why are they bothering to pick a different field?"

"I don't know," I say. "I know the real field is still considered a crime scene and is involved in an open investigation. Until all members of the Order are accounted for, dead or alive, and all of the victims are identified, that field isn't going to be accessible. Especially not for a made-for-TV true-crime series. And I guess they want to shoot as much of the surrounding area as they can to give it the most authentic feel possible."

"They are really going for the whole documentary thing, aren't they?" Dean comments.

I let out a sigh. "Apparently. You know, I think it would have been better if they just embraced it and made it a TV movie. Just glossy it up and make it as showy as you want. Slap 'inspired by' at the front and just let it be a big production. Calling it a documentary feels . . ."

"Icky," Xavier offers.

"Exactly. It's like they think if they call it a documentary they can get away with more."

"Or they won't be accused of trying to profit off a death," Dean says.

"There are entire networks on TV dedicated to profiting off any number of murders. And Lakyn Monroe's murder is one of those that is going to capture the popular imagination for a long time. People are still fascinated by her. A beautiful, smart, successful young woman who tries to give back to the world by helping the wrongfully accused, only to put herself right in the path of real killers. They eat it up.

"Cast it with pretty people, add some dramatic dialogue and a lot of lens flares, and it will all but print money. I'm not averse to the true crime genre. I like watching those shows. I just don't like it when people who are clearly trying to create entertainment rather than informing people about the actual crime make more of what they are doing than is really there.

"If you want to make a TV show, go for it. But if you want to make a documentary, you use real locations and people that were actually involved rather than giving actors roles. The fact that there's a script really bothers me."

"Why?" Dean asks.

"They aren't their words," Xavier says. "No one knows what they actually said. Or what they were thinking. Or what they did. Well, Lilith Duprey does, but I don't think it would be the best idea to try to get her involved as a script consultant."

"Definitely not," I nod. "She has finally started to regain some sense of normalcy. As normal as it can possibly feel to live in a mental health facility where you'll spend the rest of your life, I guess. But that's better than where she was. And it means she can feel like her life is worth something more than what Sterling Jennings and the others forced her to do. Getting her to recount all the details of that night so they could be transcribed into a script would probably not be the best choice for her stability and well-being."

"Speaking of consultants, though, why did you agree to be one?" Dean asks.

"And why are you being brought in so late?" Xavier asks. "Haven't they already shot a lot of it? I would think if you were supposed to be a consultant for a project, you should actually be involved."

"I am involved. They've asked me a ton of questions, I've had a couple of video chats, and I'm going to be on set for the next several days of shooting."

"Half of it has already been shot," Dean points out.

"I wasn't part of that half of the story," I shrug. "That part is all about Lakyn when she was young and how she came up through the entertainment industry to be as popular and successful as she was. I don't come around until she's missing. And I'm doing it because I still feel really protective of that case."

"So do I," Xavier points out.

"So, you should understand that I need to make sure they're doing it right. I know they have a certain degree of artistic license, but it can't go too far. Lakyn Monroe can't become just another story by people who weren't a part of it and weren't there for people who have no idea what really happened. When things like that happen, the messed-up stories spread like wildfire and can cause serious problems. That's why I'll be there. To answer questions, tell stories, and hopefully help them make something real out of this. Or at least stop them from completely destroying what is real."

"Who do they have playing Lakyn?" Dean asks.

I notice Xavier's posture tense just slightly. It's not enough to assign an emotion to it, just enough to show a shift.

"It's a girl named Marlowe Gray. She's young and pretty new in her career but seems to be picking up speed pretty quickly. She was in a few things within the last year and a lot of people are already calling her the next it-girl. I wasn't aware there were still 'it-girls', but there it is. She looks similar to Lakyn. Beautiful. Dark hair. According to everything I can find about her, she started out in dance classes, did some school plays, a couple of community theater productions. Apparently, her father was a musician but died when she was a baby. She was discovered through a social media post pretending to audition for her favorite TV show," I say.

"It sounds like they actually picked a pretty perfect person, then. Sounds a lot like Lakyn."

"I guess you're right."

I wait for Xavier to jump in, but he stays quiet.

CHAPTER FOUR

Sometimes the changing of the seasons catches me off guard. When I'm in the middle of a case that's taking up my energy and attention, I'm not as aware of what's going on around me and stop really noticing when we switch from one season to the next.

I know we're in winter now. A week ago, the little chosen family I've put together gathered at Sam and my house for Thanksgiving. That means by the time the turkey digested, it was officially Christmas for all of us, whether we were ready for it or not. I'll be the first to admit I wasn't fully prepared for the first Thanksgiving I spent with Xavier, when I got a crash course in his seasonal rules and needed to learn the vital importance of drinking eggnog and eating candy canes before the sun came up on Black Friday. We still don't know what sugar plums are. But his traditions have become my traditions, and that means the little desk calendar in the back corner of my mind is very aware that it is December, and we are fully in winter.

But it wasn't until just a couple of days ago that the weather decided to catch up. It was a far warmer fall than the last couple of years and that always makes it harder to really sink into the next season. Tonight, as I lie in bed struggling to sleep, I can already feel the chill around me. I'm buried down deep in the blankets, but Xavier gets migraines and Dean gets nosebleeds if the heater is up higher than sixty-three degrees no matter how cold it is, so there's no real coziness waiting for me on the outside of my bed cocoon.

I suppose it's all worth it for the lessened possibility of blinding head pain and blood everywhere, but I swear there are times when I have gone to the bathroom in their house and thought it would probably be warmer if there was still an outhouse in the backyard.

I've been considering just staying here for the rest of the night, but I know that will just mean staring at the ceiling and wondering why there are lights that keep coming on in the house. I can see them under my door as they come on, stay for a few seconds, then turn off only to be replaced by another one off to the side.

The positioning of my room in the oddly shaped mansion Xavier designed for himself gives off the same vibes as a box seat at the theater. It's angled so it looks out over various portions of the house, meaning I could be seeing lights from any number of spaces. Which just makes it more confusing. Not concerning, so much. Just confusing.

If I was at home, saw lights like that, and didn't feel Sam's feet wrapped around mine at the end of the bed, I'd figure he was up scavenging through the kitchen for whatever nocturnal nosh was inspired by his dreams. If I didn't feel those feet, however, I'd have my gun in one hand and my phone in the other. It would be a crapshoot what kind of emergency the responders would actually walk into.

But that's because my house, as secure as it is, is a hell of a lot easier to get into than Xavier's. Even with the various locks and security systems put in place by my loving and sometimes overprotective husband, there are ways to get inside without making too much of a scene over it. That's been proven several times already.

Xavier's house, on the other hand, is a veritable episode of Scooby-Doo with a dastardly score of Indiana Jones stuffed right in the middle. His brain works too fast and too much to be satisfied with just normal thoughts and pursuits. What he envisions or doesn't have, he simply creates. And when it comes to his house, that means a variety of gadgets from the simple and surprisingly useful button beside each bed that gets two slices of toast going first thing in the morning, to the far more dangerous and complicated devices I can only describe as booby traps. Like the large bust sitting on a pedestal in the corner of a hallway that is actually attached to a spring-loaded device that propels it forward right at head level when trigged.

And by triggered, I mean someone walks in front of it without knowing to first hit the button hidden in the corner of a gilded frame around a truly horrible painting of a woman holding a cat positioned on the wall about twelve feet from the pedestal.

Fortunately, that particular little monster is in an area of the house that's rarely used. Unless a person wanting to break in gets the clever idea to access the house by climbing up the trellis attached to the small balcony leading into floor-to-ceiling windows just down the hall from said trap. And that is only one of the various devices and tricks Xavier installed around his house in the years before he was sent to prison. Even more fun are the gadgets he intended to be useful or fun that turn out to be terrifying, like the hallway studded with wall sconces that spontaneously light when pressure sensors in the floor activate kerosene lamps and tiny blow torches embedded in the walls.

We avoid that hallway.

But this is why I don't have much concern that the lights are an intruder meaning us any harm. Chances are the traditional security system consisting of several locks, an alarm, and cameras would have stopped them already. And if not, they would have been brained with a bust or lit on fire by now.

Which means there's one most likely explanation.

I muster up the courage to climb out of bed and wrap myself in a blanket to ward off the cold. Stepping outside my room, I see the light to my left flip on. A few seconds later, it turns off and Xavier crosses in front of me across a foyer, then enters the room to the right and turns that light on. He's pacing. And saving energy.

"Xavier?"

He stops in the middle of the foyer, the brief moment between one of the rooms being lit meaning he's standing in darkness so I can barely see him.

"Emma?"

"Would it be okay to turn a light on?" I ask.

"Sure."

I turn on the foyer light and see him in his pajamas and a bathrobe, a mug gripped in one hand.

"What's that?" I ask, gesturing to the mug as I walk up to him.

He glances at it. "Warm milk."

"You don't like warm milk," I say. "You won't drink it because you say it feels like it's coming straight out of the cow and that's inappropriate for anyone but a baby cow."

"I know. But it's supposed to help you sleep."

I look down into the mug and see that it's completely full. He hasn't even taken a sip.

"I think you have to actually drink it for it to do you any good."

He nods, looking at the mug again with a faintly sad expression. "I'm always hoping that because my brain knows the intended effect, just having a mug of it close by will create the power of suggestion."

"Would you rather have some cider?" I ask. "I saw there was a bottle from the orchard. I could heat up some cinnamon rolls to go with it."

He nods again and I take the mug from him. It's cool to the touch. He's been pacing with it for a while now.

In the kitchen, Xavier slides onto one of the stools at the island in the center of the room and watches me put a pot on the stove and fill it with apple cider. I add a few warming spices to it, then go into the refrigerator where I stashed the batch of unbaked cinnamon rolls when I got here. With the oven preheating and the smell of warm apples starting to fill the room, I lean against the island and look at Xavier.

I don't need to say anything. If he's not ready to talk, he won't, no matter what I say. When he's ready, he'll start. The cider finishes warming and I pour it into two mugs, sliding one over to Xavier. The oven beeps to tell me it's gotten up to temp and I slide the rolls in. There's a bowl of cream cheese frosting, the topping of choice for both Dean and Xavier, in the refrigerator for when they are finished.

"I still see her, Emma."

I stand up from the open oven and ease the door closed.

"Lakyn?"

"Not all the time. Not as much as I used to. But she's still there," he says.

"I know."

"Sometimes I'll hear things that she said to me or think of something I should have told her that might have helped her. I wonder if there was something I could have done differently."

"Xavier, you can't think like that."

"Of course I can. And I do. I should have said more. Or less. Or something else. Dealing with her was having a giant game board in front of me and I had a regular die and a twenty-sided one and a deck of cards and a spinner. And I had to move pieces but only if my letters spelled the right word and all the hippos ate their marbles without closing their mouths too soon and bouncing one of them into the mousetrap knocking over the whole block tower without collecting $200. And maybe I should have rolled a different number. Just one different turn and she might still be here."

"And the Order would never have been uncovered. And more people would have died."

"I know. And for that, her death was worth it."

"That's not what I'm saying," I say.

"I am. Lakyn's murder wasn't a loss, it was a sacrifice. She had to die, Emma. But I still wonder. I've carried that around. All our conversations.

Everything she was trying to help me with. Everything she couldn't help me with. It was something that I was willing to carry and now everybody is going to see it. They're going to see her and talk about her. They're going to say her name and remember what she sounded like. They'll watch her videos and see her pictures and talk about how she could have been so amazing. She'll be more now than she was then."

I don't know what he's getting at. He's trying to tell me something. But I don't understand if it's a good thing or a bad thing. Xavier has always spoken positively about Lakyn. He considered her a friend, which is more significant coming from Xavier than it would be for most other people. But there is a distance in the way he talks about their relationship and what she meant to him. Obviously, he valued her and trusted her, at least to a point. He appreciated the effort she was putting in to trying to get him exonerated.

But there wasn't the level of affection like there is with Dean or with me. Or even with Sam. He didn't cry for her the way he cried for Millie. She was kind to him. She was doing her best to help him and he felt like he had somebody in the world when she was around. But if someone was to ask him if he misses her, I doubt he would say that he does.

So I don't ask him. It's easier not to try to understand the complex way he sees other people. I've learned that with Xavier, reality isn't what we know. It's what he knows. What is happening to Xavier at that moment is his existence. Looking ahead and behind are both very hard for him and he rarely does it.

That includes the way he thinks about the people in his life. A person can have value and importance to him in the moment, but as soon as they are no longer a part of his regular life, he doesn't think about them. He doesn't miss them or feel pain when they aren't around. He might reminisce about them or recall memories with fondness, but that doesn't bring up the same compulsion to contact that person or try to see them again.

It's not that he's callous or unfeeling. Or even arrogant, Leland Amherst aside. He just has a very limited capacity for genuine connection and lasting affection. I know it's different for me. For Dean. For Sam. Even for Bebe. I don't think he would blink if Eric was not part of his life anymore. Or Bellamy. Occasionally he might notice they aren't there and think about them, but it wouldn't be a stumbling block.

He doesn't ever say it, of course, but I think that's the realm where Lakyn exists for him. He doesn't categorize people or explain to me how he feels about anybody who's in his life. It's not something he thinks about or would even consider. It's his normal.

Right now is one of those moments, though, when a person who usually resides in that nebulous place in the back of his mind where they exist but aren't acknowledged rises up closer to the surface. But I don't think it's really Lakyn that he's thinking about. It's someone more important. Someone he does miss.

"But what about Andrew?" I say.

It's not a question. It's acknowledging what he's thinking. A slow nod tells me I've found the path he was directing me to. It's the one leading to thoughts he can't quite put into the kind of words other people would understand.

"Everyone will be thinking about Lakyn. And they should. What she did was brave and beautiful and strong. People will say her name and will remember her. But Andrew . . ."

"I'm sorry, Xavier."

"You have no reason to be sorry. You didn't make the decision not to name him or tell his story in the show."

It was one of the questions I asked when they first approached me about consulting for the mini-series. I wanted to know the focus, what they were planning on telling, and how. Delta wasn't able to give me the kind of full answer I would have wanted. Not that I really thought she was going to give me a play-by-play, but one thing she did say was that Andrew's murder would be downplayed.

"They didn't want to put emphasis on his death because you were exonerated," I say. "You didn't kill him, but according to the courts, there is no resolution to what happened to him. They didn't want to bring conjecture into it."

"But they're willing to make up what she said? What I said?"

"They have recordings of your meetings. And some messages."

"I can accept that they don't want his death to be a big part of the show. Like you said, no one really knows what happened. No one but the Order, anyway. And I wouldn't want that to be the only reason people know him. But he shouldn't be forgotten. They shouldn't pretend he didn't exist. He did."

"I know he did," I whisper. "And he was important. I promise you, I will make sure they know him. I'll make sure they say his name."

CHAPTER FIVE

"I DON'T WANT TO TRY TO GET THROUGH THAT HAPPENING AGAIN," Xavier says.

I'm unraveling a cinnamon roll and using chunks of it like tortilla chips to scoop up more cream cheese frosting as I sit curled in the corner of the couch. Xavier and I moved in here a mug of apple cider and half a cinnamon roll ago. It's warmer here than it was standing over the tile floor of the kitchen, but I'm still curled up and covered with the blanket.

I feel like I might have missed part of a conversation Xavier thinks he's been having, but that's not all that unusual. Most of the time he loops back and picks up the parts of the talk he forgot to say out loud. This time, he examines the frosting on his cinnamon roll and glances at his mug of hot apple cider like he's contemplating taking a coffee and donuts dunk approach.

"Through what happening again?" I ask.

He looks over at me. "Andrew's death."

"I don't understand," I say. "I don't think you can go through Andrew dying again."

As soon as I say it, I realize that's not really the truth. I've been forced to work through the same death more than once. But I don't understand how that could be what Xavier is worried about. Andrew's death was documented and verified. In part by Xavier himself. This isn't a situation that could be a faked death or mistaken identity.

"But I could go through my closest friend dying again," he says. "Andrew helped me with everything. When he died, I had to learn to live, to function without him there to help me. This might come as a surprise to you, but that was a struggle for me."

Stone cold straight face.

"I remember you telling me that," I say.

"Now I have Dean. I can't lose him, too. I can't go through that again."

"You won't," I say. "Dean isn't going anywhere."

"You can't promise that, Emma," he replies. "You can't be sure what's going to happen. What if we never find out what happened with the Emperor?"

"He's dead, Xavier," I say. "He had a heart attack and has taken up residence in the family plot at Oak View Cemetery."

"But it wasn't just him. He had other people working for him and they might not be pleased that Dean made it out alive. We still haven't figured out what happened to him. Which means it could happen again. Or someone else could go after him," Xavier says.

"That's true," I admit. There's no point in trying to use platitudes to comfort him. "There's no way for any of us to know what happened or to guarantee that it won't again. Or that something else won't happen. But you have to let go of that in order to keep living. I know that's hard for you. But you have to be willing to live, even with not knowing what's going to happen or knowing there is a risk. Because that's how you know when life is really worth it: when you are afraid of losing pieces of it." I pause for a second. "This is where you would usually have some snappy sentiment for me."

"To get to the sunflower seeds of life, you have to be willing to crack some shells," Xavier offers.

I smile. "I like that one."

I don't know if it actually means the same thing, but I'll take it. And to be honest, I didn't clarify that the snappy sentiment had to have anything to do with what we were talking about, so that one's on me.

∽

"Not sleeping again?" Dean asks a couple of hours later when he walks past the room on the way to the kitchen.

"Not at this precise moment, no," I mutter, continuing to read through the papers in my lap without looking up.

"Earlier?"

"None of those moments, either."

"You're hanging out with him too much."

"You're one to talk," I reply.

He heads for the kitchen and comes back with one of the cinnamon rolls.

"They're better if you microwave them for about ten seconds," I tell him.

He leaves again and when he comes back, the roll is on a plate and I glance up to see the cream cheese slightly melted.

"You have to be on set in just a few hours," he says.

"I do," I nod, then look over at Xavier where he fell asleep on the couch and I covered him with a blanket. "He's terrified of losing you, you know."

Dean gives me an inquisitive look. "Xavier? What do you mean?"

I nod. "He's afraid of going through the same thing with you that he did with Andrew. The fact that we don't know what happened to you the day you were taken for Salvador Marini is really getting to him. Even though Salvador is dead, not having the answers scares him. He's afraid without knowing you're in danger."

Dean sits down and stares at Xavier for a few seconds. I don't have any childhood memories of my cousin. I don't know if he ever went through an awkward phase or who his first crush was. I never scurried under tables with him on holidays while the adults had their boring conversations. That's because I didn't even know he existed until a few years ago when a horrific case put him in my path. Even then, we didn't know the role we played in each other's lives. We didn't know the uncle cut out of my life is the father he never knew.

But that doesn't mean he isn't important to me, or that I don't know him well. Everything we've been through together put us on a fast track to the close relationship we have now. It's close enough to know the sometimes cold, hard exterior chiseled by a dark past and the horror of war shield a similar fear of loss. The way he's looking at Xavier holds all of that.

"I don't know what else we're supposed to do," Dean says. "Every time Noah comes to talk to us it seems like we're going over the same things. The investigation into that new arena we found didn't give us any new details. Mark Webber is still in the hospital in a coma. We don't know if he's the same guy who I fought that night or if he was only there to fight Eric."

"I know," I say, giving him a break so he can let out a breath. We were lucky to have found an ID on the guy who nearly beat Eric to a pulp. "I know it feels like we're constantly going back to square one, but that's our only choice. Noah is doing everything he can."

"I know he is," Dean says. "Which makes me feel like I'm the one who's missing something. It's my fault we don't know more."

The detective I met while working on the disappearance and murder of Lakyn Monroe, along with two other deaths from around the same time, Noah White, has been investigating Dean's abduction alongside us for the long months since it happened. He hasn't given up. And neither will I.

"It's not your fault," I tell him. He shakes his head, a dismissive expression crossing his eyes. "Dean, listen to me. It's not your fault. You weren't supposed to remember any of it. That was how it was designed. Eric doesn't remember most of what happened, either. And the surviving men who fit the M.O. weren't able to give clear descriptions of what they went through, either."

"But they remember more."

"Your blackouts aren't something you can control. They didn't start because of anything that you did, and you can't start or stop them. You know that," I double down.

"It doesn't mean I don't hate myself for not being able to give more details."

"Your abduction was not random," I say. "It wasn't spontaneous or something they just threw together. That was planned. It was orchestrated. This is much more than the blackouts. Something happened that made you not remember."

"But there's no indication anything happened," Dean says. "I didn't have any puncture wounds anywhere, so I wasn't injected with anything. And trusting isn't exactly one of my most prevalent personality traits, so I highly doubt I would just hop in the car with someone and accept a snack and drink."

"But it had to be drugs of some kind. I don't know how they got it into you, but they did. You are far too strong to just be overpowered. It would take a couple of men to do that and you wouldn't go quietly. It would have alerted Xavier. Whoever was helping the Emperor somehow managed to get you in the car and to the gladiator arena without you knowing or fighting back, and without Xavier having any idea what was going on," I say.

"We just need to figure out how."

"I think first we need to know who. If we can figure out who, we'll know how... and why."

CHAPTER SIX

At some point after my conversation with Dean, I fell asleep and when I wake up on the couch covered with another blanket, I'm worried I overslept and I'm not going to be able to make it to set. A quick glance at my phone tells me I'm not too far off, but if I really rush, I can make it.

Showering, brushing my teeth, and shaving my legs at the same time is really all the multitasking I think I can accomplish without things getting weird, so I get them done as fast as I can. Taking a blow dryer to my hair is a few minutes I really don't want to give up, but I don't want to walk out into the early morning December chill with wet hair even more. Mascara and boots, both black, finish me up and I'm on my way.

By the time I run into the kitchen, there's already coffee waiting for me and a small plastic storage container full of Xavier's favorite trail mix. Peanuts are a vital part of his regular life, helping to counteract an excess of sugar that could trigger his anxiety due to his heart condition. But he discovered that eating trail mix in small amounts throughout the day when he's not going to be at home keeps him even, and to boot it's more interesting than just a handful of peanuts, though that remains his go-to in the event of really needing something.

After tinkering around a bit, Dean found the perfect balance and now large containers of the blend are kept in the kitchen at all times. I thank them both and promise to let them know if anything interesting happens on set before running out of the house and jumping into the car.

I don't really have high hopes for this being a thrilling experience. When the producer first got in touch with me, she explained they were interested in sharing more of Lakyn's story with the public and wanted to make sure it was authentic and accurate, which I appreciated. Me being a consultant for it meant ensuring the details of the investigation were handled properly and coaching the actress playing me. That's the part I think they want me for the most. It always looks good to have the actual law enforcement personnel involved when doing any kind of dramatization of a crime.

And with as much publicity and public focus came down on me surrounding Lakyn's case, I think they're hoping to capitalize on that a bit. I don't love the thought of being trotted out as a marketing device if that is on their mind, but it goes back to why I told the guys I'm doing this in the first place.

Lakyn deserves her story to be told. So does Millie Haynes. And Lilith Duprey. And Lydia Walsh. None of them can be told without the others. I want to make sure in focusing on Lakyn they don't forget the rest existed. They were there. They were tangled in the same web that killed them. All for different reasons and by different hands, but inextricably linked.

I slide into the marked parking area just under the wire and head for what looks like a toll booth set up at the end of the lot. The tall, heavyset man inside looks at me for a second like he's preparing to tell me to leave, then recognition flickers across his eyes.

"Emma Griffin," he starts.

I nod. "Yes. I'm here for the..."

"Filming. Of course. We've heard that you were going to be involved. I just want to say I'm honored to have you a part of it."

"Thank you," I say, a touch confused by the sentiment from someone who seems to be essentially a security guard making sure only authorized people access the set.

He searches around inside the booth for a second, making a sound like he's trying to stall me while he finds something. A few seconds later he comes up with a badge hanging from a lanyard.

"Here you go. Once things get going, you'll need this to move throughout the production area. Everyone is gathered down at the craft services tent. Delta and the director, Mac Mayhew, will be waiting there."

I thank him again and slip the lanyard over my head as I walk past the booth and onto the short dirt road that leads to the old cornfield. Ahead of me, a large white tent covers several tables crowded with people. I can see hotel pans heated with Sterno and baskets of fruit and pastries. Most importantly, I can see a coffee maker.

I've already gotten through the cup Dean made for me and I have a feeling I'm going to need more to get through the day. I walk straight into the tent and get a cup of coffee, then peruse the breakfast options.

Across the tent, I see a familiar face. I recognize Delta King from the picture on her email. She has a headset around her neck and a clipboard gripped in one arm as she speaks quickly with the people around her. It looks like a movie version of what a movie looks like during production, which I realized is one of the most meta thoughts I've ever had.

She glances off and notices me. She says something quickly to the men on either side of her chair, then crosses over to me. As if she remembers the need for emotion at the last second, a smile crosses her face when she is a few steps away.

"Agent Griffin," she greets me, reaching her hand out to me. "I'm Delta King."

I nodded. "Hi. You can call me Emma."

"I see you've gotten yourself some coffee. That's great. Have you eaten?"

"Not yet."

"Well, go ahead and get something to eat, we'll be getting started here soon and I'd like you to have a chance to meet everybody before we start." She looks up and off to the side behind me. Her face says she's noticed something she definitely doesn't like. She lets out a sigh and then smiles at me again. "Thank you so much for agreeing to do this. If you'll excuse me, I have to go take care of something."

She rushes off and I go back to looking over the food options. Glancing up, I notice Delta right outside the tent, standing close to a woman I recognize as Marlowe Gray's mother. She shows up in a lot of pictures of Marlowe's jobs and appearances. Right now, she and Delta don't seem to be having the friendliest conversation. I can't hear what they're saying over the voices of everyone else in the tent, but finally, Marlowe's mother throws up her hands and walks away.

I grab a couple of things to eat and make my way to one of the picnic tables set up outside of the tent. I've barely gotten a chance to take a few bites when someone slides onto the bench across from me. I look up and have a very strange moment that feels something like deja vu, but isn't quite that. I'm looking at a younger version of myself. A younger version with a lot more makeup and some extra sheen in her ponytail. But the look is right and I notice the gun on one hip and FBI badge on the other.

It doesn't take more than a glance to know it's not a real badge. There are a couple of things off about it. But that makes sense. It's just a prop. And I have a feeling I'm meeting mini-series Emma.

"You're her," she says. "You're us."

I've been around enough cults in my career to not like the way that sounds, but I smile and nod anyway. I extend my hand to her.

"Emma Johnson," I say. I shrug a little. "Griffin. Agent Emma Griffin."

She shakes my hand and nods. "That's right. You got married."

I nod. "Almost a year ago."

"Congratulations. I'm Paisley Walker. I'm you."

She gestures toward herself. I nod and point to her badge.

"Small tip? I never wear my badge on my hip. Most agents don't." I reach into my pocket and pull mine out to show her. "This way I can access it easily, but I'm not going to lose it and people are less likely to focus on it as soon as I approach them."

She nods and takes the badge off to put in her pocket.

"Can you tell me more about what it was like to investigate this case? What was it like to discover her body?"

"Well, I didn't discover it. Other people knew it was there. I just found where they'd left her."

"We're going to be filming that scene today and I wanted to go over with you how I should react. What did you do when you saw her? Did you jump back? Did you scream?" she asks.

I take a bite of the egg biscuit sandwich I chose from the buffet and shake my head.

"No," I say. "That wasn't the first body I'd seen. Not by far. And when I went into the field, I had a strong feeling I would find her, so it wasn't startling."

She nods like she's taking it all in. She looks like she's going to ask another question when Delta King shouts for everyone's attention from the front of the tent. She gestures toward me.

"By now you probably know we have a special guest with us today. The real Agent Emma Griffin will be acting as a consultant for the remainder of the project. Please welcome her." They applaud and I wave awkwardly. "We're going to be getting started in just a few minutes, so please finish up your breakfast and be ready in ten." Everyone goes back to eating and she crosses the tent to me. “Oh, good, I see you’ve met Paisley.”

“I have,” I nod.

“If you’re finished eating, I’d like to introduce you to a few more people before the first scene starts rolling.”

I take the last bite of my sandwich and follow it up with a swig of coffee.

“I’m ready.”

CHAPTER SEVEN

We walk out of the tent and head for a collection of trailers.

"I'd like you to get a chance to meet Marlowe before things get busy today. She's a really impressive actress, especially for her age. It would be nice if she learned to be on time and was a bit more cooperative, perhaps, but I guess that comes with the territory."

I'm surprised by the assessment of the girl I haven't even met yet. But I suppose people in this industry tend to be on the blunt side. We walk up to a trailer with a name plate on the door emblazoned with "Marlowe Gray" and Delta knocks on it.

"Marlowe? Good morning. You missed breakfast." There's no response and she knocks again. "Marlowe? Come on out, I have someone I'd like you to meet."

There's still no answer and I can see the expression on Delta's face get nervous. She reaches into the pocket of a black utility belt around her waist and pulls out a key. She starts to put it in the door, but before she can, the door opens and Marlowe's mother looks out at us.

"Meredith," Delta says, the name coming out with a big gust of breath.

"Delta," she says. "I'm sorry. I didn't hear you knock."

That seems like an odd response to me. Delta didn't say anything about knocking, which tells me Meredith did hear the knock and was just doing something that stopped her from opening the door immediately.

"Meredith, this is Agent Emma Griffin. She's the FBI agent who solved Lakyn Monroe's death," Delta says.

"Oh, Paisley's part," Meredith says. "Hello."

She extends her hand and I shake it. "Good morning, Mrs. Gray."

"It's Coolidge, actually," she corrects me. "But you can call me Meredith."

I nod but don't say anything else.

"Marlowe missed breakfast again," Delta tells her. "Is she ready to get started?"

"She's not here," Meredith says. "I actually came looking for her."

"Maybe she's on set already," Delta says. "It would definitely be a first, but I can be hopeful."

She walks down the steps of the trailer and starts across the field again. Ahead of us, I can see an area dotted with cameras and lights and assume that's the primary set, the recreation of the field of bones. It's eerie to see it this way. Again, I know why they can't use the actual field, but it feels so odd to make a fake version out in another abandoned field, especially one so close to where everything actually happened.

We're moving at a fast, determined pace toward the set when a girl in her late teens, possibly early twenties, leaves the set and starts toward the craft tent.

"Brittany," Delta calls. The girl doesn't even lift her head, and Delta lifts her voice a little higher. "Brittany!"

The girl looks up, and when she notices Delta, she hurries over, stuffing her phone into her back pocket as she comes.

"Sorry, I was posting," she says. "Good morning."

"Morning, Brittany. I want you to meet Agent Griffin. She's…"

"I know who she is," Brittany cuts her off with a nod. "I've followed some of your cases. It's really great to meet you."

"Thanks. It's nice to meet you, too."

I don't know who she is, but I have a feeling that's going to be a frequent occurrence on this set.

"Is Marlowe already on set?" Delta asks.

Brittany nods. "She was just a few minutes ago. I was taking some pictures, so I don't know exactly where she is right now."

"Okay. Thanks, Brittany."

The girl flashes a smile and starts away from us, reaching into her pocket again for her phone.

"Social girl," I say as we start toward the set again.

"She's Marlowe's best friend, but she also handles her social media and her virtual fan club," Delta explains.

"She doesn't do her own social media?" I ask.

Delta laughs a little, shaking her head. "Marlowe is too busy to speak to the people who are actually around her. She doesn't have time to interact with virtual people. But having good visibility is critical for building careers these days. She has to stay relevant and connected with her audience, or she won't gain traction. So, Brittany handles that for her. She talks to the fans. Posts pictures and video updates."

"But everyone thinks it's actually Marlowe," I note.

"A little bit of movie magic," Delta says with a wink.

That's definitely one difference between the girl playing Lakyn and the woman herself. Lakyn did things like that on her own. She really did stay connected to people.

We get onto set and she points out a few more people, including the director and the actors playing the members of the Order. The man playing Sterling Jennings looks so much like the actual judge it makes my stomach turn a little.

"The casting director did a good job," I point out.

Delta nods. "I want everyone in the story to be recognizable as much as possible." We look around for a few moments and she shakes her head. "Where is that girl?" Looking to the side, she seems to notice someone and gestures. "Fred."

I look over and see the security guard from the parking area.

"Good morning, Delta," he grins.

"Fred, this is Agent Griffin," she says. "Emma, this is Frederic Hellman, Marlowe's manager."

"Oh," I say.

Delta looks confused at my expression and Frederic smiles.

"We've met," he says. "Briefly, in the parking lot."

"I thought you were the security guard," I tell him. "I'm sorry."

He laughs. It's a cheery, booming laugh. "That's alright. I was in the booth and didn't clarify who I was, so you can't help but make the assumption."

"You were in the parking lot booth?" Delta asks.

"I dropped something out of my pocket last night after filming and called to see if it was found. Lewis said he found it and had it at the booth for me. He wasn't there when I went to get it, so I was looking for it."

"Did you find it?"

"No. But I'll go back and see him a little later."

"Have you seen Marlowe? Brittany said she was on set, but I haven't been able to find her," Delta tells him.

"I just saw her. She was walking that way," he says, gesturing to the side. "Seemed like she was trying to get into her character. She had her phone out and seemed to be talking under her breath."

Delta nods. "Mac was telling me she's nervous about filming the scenes today. I'm sure she's just trying to get her mind around it."

"You're doing her death scene today?" I ask.

"Yes. Her death and some of the early investigation. We mostly filmed in order thus far, so she only has a few more days of filming before all of her stuff is finished, but this is what she was most anxious about." She glances down at her clipboard, then back at me. "Speaking of which. Would you want to see some of the footage we've already shot? None of it is edited yet or anything, but you can look at the rough material."

"Sure," I shrug.

"Great. After filming tonight, we'll go to the production office and I'll show you what we've been doing." She steps slightly to the side and cranes her neck like she's trying to see something in the distance. A look that's somewhere between relieved and aggravated comes to her face. "There she is."

She takes off in the direction she was looking, but I stay where I am, looking around at everything happening. It looks a little chaotic, like everybody is doing too many different things for it all to come together into one cohesive thing. But I remember what Delta said about all the different scenes set to film today and wonder if more than one of them could be going on at the same time.

It's a strange feeling standing here looking at the corn and hearing the laughter and careless chatter of everybody around me. It's not the actual field, I remind myself. It's just an old, abandoned cornfield that has nothing to do with what happened. But that's what it's meant to be. The juxtaposition feels off.

Delta comes back up to me with a pretty girl I recognize as Marlowe Gray following slightly behind. She wipes her nose with the back of her hand and runs her fingers through her hair, her eyes focusing to the side rather than at me.

"This is the woman I was telling you about," Delta says to her as they get close. "Agent Emma Griffin."

"Emma," I smile, holding my hand out.

Marlowe's gray eyes are the perfect embodiment of her last name, but when they meet mine I see a storm. She shakes my hand and nods.

"Nice to meet you."

Her hand falls away from mine and she rubs her nose again. I try not to latch onto the gesture. It's far too easy with my investigative background to pick up on tiny details like that. But this isn't an investigation.

"The crew is finishing getting everything ready for the shots and the car is on its way, so before we get started, I was wondering if you could come with me," Delta says. "I want to show you the field."

"The field?" I ask.

"Yes. We used photographs of the scene to try to recreate it, but you're the only one around here who has actually seen it."

CHAPTER EIGHT

Walking into the cornfield, I immediately notice that except for one large path seemingly cut directly through it, the field looks like a tangled mess. Broken stalks on either side have spread debris on rocky dirt. In a few places, I notice precise rectangles of cleared area.

"What do you think?" Delta asks.

I look around. I was hoping this was just the entry part of the field and she was going to bring me to another spot.

"This is it?" I ask.

She looks from side to side like she's surprised by the question. "Yes. Is there something wrong with it?"

"You said you saw pictures of the field," I say.

"Some news footage, yes."

"So not pictures of the field itself. No crime scene images?" I ask.

She bristles slightly, her spine straightening and the expression on her face tightening.

"We weren't given access to the case files," she admits. "We asked, but the detective wouldn't permit it."

"Detective White?" I ask.

"Yes," she says. There's a note of bitterness in her voice and I feel like there's more to this story than just her not liking my assessment of the field. "I contacted him and informed him about the project and that I would need access to all the available information, including crime scene photos for the set designer to utilize and he refused."

"He isn't consulting on this, is he?" I ask.

"No, he isn't."

"Did you ask him?" I ask.

She draws in a breath. "No. When I was envisioning how to present the story, his portion didn't seem relevant to the narrative I'm creating."

That is a lot of words I don't think I'm comfortable with, but I keep myself calm.

"He's the sheriff who headed up the investigation for Lakyn's disappearance and death, as well as the deaths surrounding her investigation and the Order of Prometheus."

"I understand that, but I feel zeroing the focus in on Lakyn herself and your involvement in the case is far more compelling. Detective White will be mentioned, of course. But he won't be a primary element of the story."

"Okay," I say with a single nod. "I suppose that's a way to approach it."

"Is there something wrong with how the set is dressed?" she asks.

I glance around, trying to decide where to start with my assessment.

"This is an abandoned cornfield," I say. "And except for the random road cut through it, it looks like an abandoned cornfield."

"It's supposed to," she says. "And keep in mind it is December, so the set designer and his team had to do a considerable amount of work locating cornstalks that still look like it could be February. There's a separate section designed to look like October for when you found the body and started the investigation."

"Oh, no. I understand that. And I commend you for that attention to detail. The issue is the field where Lakyn was found wasn't abandoned. It was meticulously cared for."

"It's been described as a field on unclaimed land that hasn't been used by a farmer in several generations," Delta frowns.

"That's true," I nod. "The defunct farm where the field is located is a section of land that has no true owner. At least not one who is listed. But it's not unoccupied or abandoned. From the outside, the field might look like no one has been in it in a long time, but when you get inside, especially toward the back where the bones were, you realize how carefully it was maintained."

The media coverage of Lakyn's death and the field of bones had been intentionally sparse in some of its details, not wanting to delve too deep into some of the more gruesome and disturbing aspects, as well as not giving up details potentially crucial to the case against the members of the Order still to be brought up on charges. Their disappearance before any of them could be arrested made the case far more complicated and necessitated keeping some things confidential to protect the integrity of the eventual case.

Which means this woman may never have heard of Lilith Duprey.

"I thought it was a dumping ground."

"It was a graveyard," I correct her. "The bodies weren't just tossed out of a car. Some of them, including Lakyn, were killed here. Others were brought and buried. It was intentional. But the graves didn't look like that," I tell her, gesturing toward the rectangles in the tangled undergrowth. "Most of them were undetectable, which is why it took so long to excavate the area."

"Most of what's being filmed in the field today is going to be Lakyn's death, which is at night. I intended on having your character start your investigation, but I can put that off so that some modifications can be made to the field. We'll change and film more scenes with the inmate character."

She adjusts her headset and presses a button to connect to someone on the other end.

"Xavier," I correct her.

"I'm sorry, what?" she asks, tilting her face toward me like she's pulling away from the conversation waiting in her earbud.

"Xavier. You said the inmate character. His name is Xavier."

She stares at me blankly for a few seconds like she's waiting for me to say something else.

"Right," she nods. Her hand goes to her earbud. "Hey, yes, we need to change the shooting schedule. Is Austin on set?" There's a pause and she nods. "Perfect. Make sure he's ready to do his interior shots. I don't know how far we'll get in them and I'll have to call in a couple of other actors, but if they are available I want to be able to do everything. Just in case, his jacket is with Props. We're starting with B-roll of Marlowe and Paisley. Great. We'll be over there in just a second."

She looks back at me. "Alright. That will give us some time to fix things around here as much as we can on such short notice."

She says it as if I designed the set myself. But I don't argue. She asked me to come here to consult and I am currently giving her a consultation.

For the next several hours I grit my teeth through watching them film random shots of Marlowe and Paisley acting as though they are doing mundane daily things. Sitting under a tree reading. Making notes in a notebook. Pretending to have phone calls and sending endless text messages. Staring into the distance. A lot of staring. Marlowe typing furiously and scanning through random web pages I can only imagine will be obscured with creative lighting and camera angles if actually put into the final piece.

After every shot, Paisley looks over at me as if looking for my reaction. A few times I interject with comments, but for the most part, I just watch. I'm not sure what the point of these shots is, but this would be why I actually take down criminals rather than making movies about it.

We break for dinner and I've just sat down when Paisley joins me. She looks down at the salad in the center of her tray and the little plates of various vegetables and potatoes surrounding it.

"I've been having a really hard time keeping up a vegetarian diet," she mentions.

I take a bite of the mashed potatoes on my own plate. "Have you recently decided to be vegetarian?"

"For the series," she says, as if that's an explanation that makes sense.

I try to figure out what that could have to do with anything, but I can't.

"Why?" I ask.

"It's a character choice," she says.

"But I'm not a vegetarian," I reply, displaying the chicken breast I'm getting ready to eat.

"I just feel that an FBI agent who has committed her life to solving murders and protecting those who have been victimized would have a compassionate soul. Vegetarianism fits in with that," she says.

I blink at her a few times.

"But I'm not a vegetarian," I repeat.

She shrugs and spears a piece of steamed broccoli with her fork. I'm not sure what to make of that.

After dinner, it's time to film the death scene. I've been waiting all day for it, but I wouldn't necessarily say I'm excited to witness it. I know her death is the central pin of the series and many viewers are likely going to be anticipating being able to see the director's version of what happened. But it feels exploitive. Recreating her death doesn't add anything to the series but a few minutes of gore porn and I don't understand how that fits into Delta's apparent vision to honor Lakyn.

I ask her about it as we make our way down to the stretch of road being used for the footage before they arrive at the field.

"Seeing her death will be cathartic to viewers," she tells me.

I'm stunned. "Cathartic? Watching a fictionalized version of a death you didn't witness and no one has video evidence of is somehow going to help people who didn't know her process the emotions behind Lakyn's death?"

"Without the horror of how she died, the rest of the story doesn't have the same weight," Delta says. "It's important to the entire narrative."

For what feels like the thousandth time today, I bite my tongue.

CHAPTER NINE

Marlowe has her phone out again before the shot. She reads something that obviously upsets her, then hits the button to turn the phone off. Brittany rushes up to her and she hands her that phone before the prop master hands her the phone she'll use during the scene.

The men playing Judge Jennings and the other members of the Order who were there the night she died go to the car they'll use to film that portion of the sequence. I wonder how they will credit those other men. We know that Judge Jennings was in the car. It's the one detail Lilith shared with us from that night. She could see the judge while they murdered Lakyn. But she never told us who the other men were and there's been no way to prove it.

All we know is there were two others in the car.

They get in and then Marlowe makes her way over. I have a visceral reaction to seeing her climb into the back seat. It must be like the feeling people have when they're watching a horror movie and yell to the character not to run outside into the woods in her underwear, or to not think the attic is a secure hiding spot. I feel the compulsion to tell Marlowe to stop. To not get in the car.

But I'm not really telling Marlowe. I'm trying to tell Lakyn.

I've thought about this moment many times. I've wondered what went through her mind when she agreed to get in the car with the men. Was there anything telling her to stop? Did anything in her gut tell her this wasn't a good idea? Her car had been dumped far away from where her body was found. But why wasn't she driving it that night?

They get in the car and the rig designed to make it move without the sound of an engine disrupting the audio moves forward. It's going slowly, but Delta assures me it will look much faster when the footage is edited.

"At this point, Marlowe is saying the actual words Lakyn did during the drive. Obviously, we can't show the entire thing in real time. It was more than an hour. But we've taken out the most interesting bits for her to say,"

"The most interesting bits?" I ask.

"Yes. Marlowe and I sat with the script writers and went over the transcript of the call and agreed on the pieces that sounded best."

"The transcript?" I frown. "You don't have a recording of the call?"

"No. I didn't think it was necessary to go through requesting that, especially when we weren't allowed access to the crime scene photos or the case file."

That grates on me. Nothing could ever embody the tension of that night as well as the sound of Lakyn's own voice. I've heard that recording so many times. I know it word for word, and I've often tried to imagine what she was feeling when she was saying those words. I wonder at what point she realized how dire her situation was, if she knew she was going to die and just wanted someone to find her, or if there was a small part of her that hoped someone would hear the message in time and be able to rescue her.

This is the only way she can tell her story.

And I know for a fact the audio has been released to other outlets. A couple of true crime shows have already been made about her, though they were fairly bare-bones and only gave a wide overview of what happened, focusing more on her life and then her disappearance than what happened after.

As we stand there, I notice Frederic hovering off to the side. He looks distracted, like there's something else on his mind and he can't quite make himself focus on what's going on in front of him. It's somewhat of a surprise to see him there. I didn't think most actors had their managers on set with them all the time. But I also didn't think the mothers of performers over the age of eighteen would hang around on the sets either, yet Meredith is standing a few yards from me. Her arms are crossed over her chest as she stares at the car. It backs up and starts up again.

Frederic looks at the director where he's sitting in a lift chair that moves with its own rig alongside the car. I'm curious about the budget of this production. It strikes me as being closer to the independent end of the spectrum. Their research is clearly lackluster, but they have access to impressive equipment and a large crew.

I ponder the chance that this is a passion project for someone who Delta approached with the idea and who is willing to pour money into it without caring so much about what comes out of it as long as there is a profit. Which there will be. I know that. It doesn't matter much what they produce at the end, people will tune into it in droves, wanting to be a part of the phenomenon. Wanting to have one more piece of Lakyn.

Out of the corner of my eye, I notice Frederic's focus shift briefly to Delta, then to Meredith. When neither of the women reacts to him, he takes a couple of steps backward like he's trying to slink away from the set without anyone noticing. He turns sharply and walks away at a quick pace.

A moment later, the car stops and everyone inside gets out. Marlowe looks slightly the worse for wear, but Brittany rushes up to her with a bottle of water and rubs her back. She shows her something on the screen of her phone and grins as Marlowe offers a smile and nods. As soon as Brittany walks away, Meredith cuts behind where Delta and I are standing to stop her in her tracks. Her hand wraps around Brittany's arm and it looks like she is insisting on seeing what she showed Marlowe.

Brittany shows her the screen and Meredith smiles and nods much like her daughter, but there's a different slant to the way she reacts over Marlowe. Brittany touches the screen and looks like she is scrolling. Suddenly, the smile fades from the older woman's face and she points at the screen. Her head snaps to look at Brittany, who shakes her head and shrugs like she doesn't know something Meredith is demanding of her.

Meredith looks at Marlowe and starts over to her. Marlowe notices her coming and cocks her head to the side. Meredith gestures for her daughter to step to the side with her. They have a rushed, furtive discussion. Almost more of an argument. I can't hear anything they're saying, but it almost sounds like Marlowe is mentioning something about 'her pills'. Her mother is shaking her head no and insisting she drink the water.

The conversation escalates, but before the two of them can progress into a shouting match, Mac, the director, intervenes and leads Marlowe in the other direction. Delta walks away from my side to stop Meredith as she apparently heads back to where she was standing before. This time they are close enough for me to hear them.

"Meredith, I've asked you before not to do that. This is a set. You can't just walk onto it," Delta says.

"That's my daughter," Meredith retorts.

"Yes. I understand that. But she is an adult. You are here out of courtesy, but if you're not going to follow the rules, we're going to have to ask you to not come to set."

"Are you threatening me?" Meredith asks.

"It's not a threat. I'm simply letting you know that we have to keep the production moving and you can't interfere with it that way."

The women glare at each other for a moment before Meredith walks around Delta and heads in the direction of the craft tent. The interaction was startling. It's obvious there's an underlying conflict and that Meredith's presence isn't necessarily welcome. It makes me wonder why she's there—if the courtesy is for Marlowe or for her.

"That's done. Time to move into the cornfield," Delta announces, directing everyone around her as if the tense conversation hadn't just happened. I have to give it to her, the woman is efficient. It was another indication that perhaps this isn't the most professional level of sets. They did that take in one shot.

Everyone makes their way to the wide path made into the middle of the field. Lights shine from enough of a distance they could conceivably be moonlight, allowing the corn itself to disappear into the darkness. Just like Delta said, the stalks won't be visible in the shots from this scene, especially after all the footage is edited.

Mac gathers Marlowe and the actors playing the Order members together in a tight cluster several yards away from everyone else and leans toward them as he talks in a hushed tone. The actors nod, then separate and get into their positions for the scene.

I feel myself getting more anxious as the seconds count down to when the scene will start. I don't want to watch it, yet I feel like I can't look away. I wasn't there the night Lakyn died. I didn't even know who she was at that time. I didn't know who she was until after she'd already gone missing. That was when I first heard her name and first started wondering what might have happened to her.

Even though I know there's nothing I could have done, I still feel a strange sense of responsibility toward Lakyn. I feel like I need to watch this so I can know they are doing her justice. Even though I didn't see it. Even though I have no idea what really happened. As ridiculous as it might sound, there's a part of me that feels like I'll know if they get something wrong. Like something deep inside will tell me if I watch and see them completely botch the scene.

With the exception of actually seeing her body out there in the field, contained within the metal cage Lilith put over her, and the somewhat limited information I was given after the autopsy, I know next to nothing about what she actually went through that night. By the time I found her body, there wasn't any evidence left.

I have my guesses. Lilith didn't want to talk about what she witnessed the last time I asked her, and I highly doubt that opinion has changed dramatically. But from what we found with her body, the condition of what was left of her clothes, and the slight amount of physical evidence that was gleaned during her autopsy, I have a vague idea of some of what she went through.

I still don't think it's necessary to show her death. If the point of this series isn't to glorify the violence and horror of her actual death, then it's not necessary to attempt to recreate it. But if they have to, if that's part of the vision this filmmaker is insisting on beaming out to every screen that eagerly tunes in, it feels vitally important that it show the truth.

CHAPTER TEN

THE DIRECTOR SILENCES THE SET AND CALLS ACTION. THERE IS NO big, booming voice yelling the word, though. Just a slate, a countdown, and someone yelling loud enough to be heard in the next county that they're rolling. A slightly perceptible nod from the director is all it takes for the scene to begin. In a split second, chaos erupts.

I know it's not real. My brain tells me I'm watching actors. The fact that I'm surrounded by other people and see cameras gliding around capturing every angle tells me I'm watching actors. The churning in my stomach says it's real.

Marlowe's tormented screams fill the sky. She digs her heels into the dirt and claws at the men dragging her by her dark hair along the path just like she's truly fighting for her life. Everything in me wants to run out there into the fields and stop them. My fingers twitch and tingle, wanting to grab for the gun that isn't on my hip. No live firearms on set. It was emphasized to me multiple times since I agreed to be a part of the project.

Because there will be prop weapons on set and firing those weapons is a part of several different scenes, having a real gun with live ammunition is just far too dangerous. There have been tragedies that started just that way. A real gun. Live ammunition. An unknowing actor thinking they were just using a prop to act out a scene unintentionally really shooting someone.

But my compulsion is still to reach for it. I want to shout out to them to stop. I want to dart in and protect the women they are hurting. I have to remind myself they aren't actually hurting her. What I'm seeing is not a glimpse into the past. It's pretend. But it brings a new layer to my ongoing connection to Lakyn Monroe and her brutal death.

When I was first investigating her murder, there were times that I tried to imagine what might have happened to her. It's part of unraveling every mystery I encounter. Anytime there is a murder, I attempt to recreate the details in my mind. If I can try to see what the victim went through, it can help me to identify where I might find crucial clues, or how I'm going to further the investigation and ensure those who are responsible don't get away with it.

But those re-creations happen in my mind. I'll talk my way through them. Sometimes sketch them out or make charts and thought webs out of them. That brings me closer and yet keeps me at enough of a distance. Right now, I've been dropped down into the middle of it. I can't control what I'm seeing or how long it will last. I can't just stop it on a single detail and delve into it or wash it away.

This is unfolding in front of me at an unstoppable pace, making my thoughts spiral, until I see something that stops the squirming discomfort and puts me firmly back into agent mode.

Marlowe is really fighting.

This isn't her channeling Lakyn and trying to show what the last terrifying moments of her life were like. She is really trying to get away from one of the men who has her tight by the upper arm. The man who also has his hand down her shirt. He laughs as she struggles and even from the distance, I can see Marlowe's emotions spiraling into fear, anger, and disgust.

"Stop!" she screams, but that only seems to make the men more eager. "Get off me!"

I start toward the director, but before I get there, he's already on his feet, stopping the scene.

The man quickly pulls away from Marlowe, taking his hand from her shirt and stepping to the side like nothing happened.

"Marlowe, I appreciate your enthusiasm in the scene, but the script doesn't call for any dialogue at this point," Mac says. "There will be music and we want to focus on the sound of your screams and struggle rather than any spoken words."

"Did you not notice that jackass feeling her up?" I demand.

The director turns around to face me. He looks both offended and confused.

"Excuse me?"

"Marvin had his hand down my shirt," Marlowe snaps, trying to catch her breath. "That isn't part of the script, either."

"I was just getting into my character," Marvin protests. "This was Lakyn Monroe. If they were dragging her out into a field and had her at their mercy, you know they didn't just kill her and leave."

There's a disgusting implication coursing just beneath the surface of those words. He can't bring himself to say it, and that only shows his intention more.

"Yes, they did," I say.

Marvin looks over at me and something in his face clouds. "You don't know that. Wasn't she basically a puddle when you found her?"

My skin crawls at that description.

"The word you're looking for is rape," I say. "Sexual assault. And it wasn't a part of this. That wasn't why she was killed and it's not the way these men operated. They didn't kill her for no reason and there was no room for sick pleasure in the process."

"I told you to stop," Marlowe adds, finally finding her voice. "I tried to get away from you."

Marvin scoffs. "We're doing a scene pretending to drag you into a cornfield and kill you. Of course, you'd say to stop."

"She never said it in rehearsals with the fight choreographer," the man playing the judge says.

"And you never shoved your hand down my shirt," Marlowe fires back.

They start bickering, but the director holds up his hands. "Alright. That's enough. Marvin, I'm going to give you the benefit of the doubt that you were just making a choice for your character and it happened to be very much the wrong choice. Don't try to pull anything like that again."

"Seriously?" I ask. "You're going to let him get away with that and just keep going like nothing happened?"

"He said it was a character choice," Mac says. "He got swept up in the moment and went too far. He won't do it again. We're going to re-set and start from the top."

"Just like that? You're just going to do it again? He does that and you're just going to let it go, like nothing?"

"Look," he says in a mixture of emotion that I can't decide is either condescending or just simply frustrated, "we've already shot a considerable amount of footage with his character. Removing him from the project for one small infraction that we can't prove had any intention beyond an attempt to deepen his character would do irreparable harm to the series," the director says.

"What about Marlowe?" I ask. "You're so concerned about doing irreparable harm to your series, but what about her? The woman who just got felt up in front of you?"

The director gives me a look that says he's losing patience with me and has no interest in this conversation continuing. He really does care more about the production than he does the human beings who are a part of it. He draws in a breath and looks at Marlowe.

"Marlowe? Are you alright?"

A dozen pairs of eyes turn to her. She's trapped in the heat of them, and I can see the pressure crushing down on her.

"You really think asking her in front of everyone is going to get you an honest answer?" I ask.

"I'm fine," Marlowe sighs. "It was just a bad choice. I overreacted."

"And I'm sure Marvin will be more cautious in the decisions he makes moving forward," Mac says. "So, that's settled. We're wasting time, so let's go ahead and reset and get started again."

I'm right at my boiling point, but it's obvious there's nothing I can do about it. I walk away from the edge of the set and watch them go back to the beginning of the scene. This time, it's not as intense. I'm too invested in watching how the men treat Marlowe for it to seem as real.

They go through the full scene, then the director calls the actors over for a few notes before saying they're going to do it again. Marlowe looks stressed and exhausted. She starts up again, but part way through this scene, she stops and holds up her hand.

"I just need a second," she says.

"Are you okay?" Delta asks. "Do you need some water?"

Marlowe nods and Delta hands her a bottle.

"Thank you," Marlowe tells her as she takes a deep swig. "Just give me a minute. I'll be okay."

"Do we have any other water?" Delta asks.

A few members of the crew look around and realize they don't. The producer mutters a frustrated string of profanities and starts toward the craft tent.

"I'll get it," I offer.

"You don't have to do that," she says. "We supposedly pay people to do that."

"I know," I say. "But I have a feeling you'll be more beneficial here than I will. And I was thinking about grabbing a snack anyway."

"Are you sure?" she asks.

"Yeah. It's no problem."

She steps up a little closer to me. "I'm sorry about all that with

Marvin and everything. Sometimes tempers can get heated on sets like this, especially when the piece deals with… intense subject matter."

"I can imagine," I say. "I'm sorry I reacted like that."

"It's alright. That's what you do. It's why you're as good at your job as you are. You just have to trust we're good at ours." She smiles at me as if trying to soften the scolding. "You'll get used to it."

I smile at her and nod before turning away to head for the water. The smile disappears as soon as I'm heading in the other direction. I don't think I'll ever get used to this. I hated to apologize for coming to Marlowe's defense, but it's also clear she didn't want to be defended. And that's her choice. If she decided that she didn't feel like it was intentional or that she wanted to let it go for the benefit of the project moving forward, it's not up to me to make that decision for her. It's not my place to try to control her perception or force a reaction or response out of her.

It feels colder away from the set and I pull my coat around me more closely. I'm thinking about bringing a scarf for the next night shoot as I walk past the trailers and notice something that catches my attention. There's a light glowing in Marlowe's trailer.

I know for a fact it isn't her, and that light wasn't on when we wrapped dinner and headed for the street and field to do the night shots. Curiosity tugs me toward it. As I approach the front steps, I can hear something moving inside. I climb up to the door. Remembering how her mother stormed away from the set, I wonder if it could be her again. Something inside crashes and I reach for the handle of the door.

As soon as I open it, I see it isn't Marlowe's mother inside.

CHAPTER ELEVEN

"Agent Griffin," Frederic starts, clearing his throat and straightening up from where he was bent down gathering a stack of books off the floor.

I'm guessing that's the crashing sound I heard.

"Didn't find what you were looking for at the parking booth?" I raise an eyebrow.

He cocks his head slightly to the side. "The parking booth?"

"Earlier when Delta asked why you were in the parking booth when I got here, you told her that you dropped something out of your pocket and the security guard put it in the booth for you, so you were looking for it," I say.

"Oh," he says. He shakes his head, offering me what looks like he's hoping is a convincing smile. "No. I was just trying to find Marlowe's… script."

It doesn't sound like he was trying to find something to say to make up an excuse. It's more like he was starting to say something else, but changed his mind and used 'script' as a placeholder instead. My eyes flicker down to his hands to see if he's holding anything. Both of them are empty, but there's something behind him on a small table. He's standing in front of it so I can only see a flash of color to his side before he adjusts his position, further obscuring it.

"I didn't realize she would be in need of her script when she is already on set," I say.

I ask the question out of curiosity of what he's going to say, how quickly he can explain himself, rather than because I don't understand why she might need to review the script. His expression flashes blank for a moment, then something clicks in his eyes.

"Since they changed the order of the scenes being filmed, she wanted to go over what she was going to do next and how she should prepare. She's especially concerned about impressing you now that you are on set," he says. "The work that her character does with your character is such an important part of the entire project, so she wants to make sure she handles it as well as possible."

I give a couple of slow nods, then a slight smile. "I'm sure she'll do just fine. Well, I was on my way to the craft tent to get some bottles of water for the set, for Marlowe, actually, so I should go do that. I just wanted to make sure everything was alright in here since I heard that crash."

"Oh," he says with a hint of an awkward laugh. "Yeah, I knocked over some of Marlowe's books. She insists on having a stack of them with her in every trailer. I can't remember another young performer I've represented who has been like that."

I'm not sure what the point of that statement was, but I nod anyway and start back out of the door. I pause on the top step and turn back around to face him.

"You know, she's right down there with the director and producer. I'm sure they would have access to a copy of the script," I say.

Frederic's face pales slightly and I leave before he can respond.

I collect a case of water and lug it down to the set, dropping it down onto the ground beside the chair emblazoned with Marlowe's name. Almost instantly, Brittany rushes up to wrangle one of the bottles from under the thick plastic packaging. Marlowe comes up slowly after her and accepts the open bottle her best friend hands out to her.

"Are you going to be alright?" Brittany asks. "Do you need a break?"

"I'm fine," Marlowe tells her. "I just needed some water."

"Are you sure? You've had a really long day. I could stand in for you if you want to just sit out for a couple of takes."

It's the first time I've really noticed Brittany's appearance. Her hair is pulled back away from her face, but it's nearly the same dark color as Marlowe's. Her eyes are brown compared to Marlowe's intriguing gray, and her mouth is not quite as full, but they look similar enough that if Brittany was to step into the role for a scene, as long as the camera didn't focus directly on her, she might not be noticeable.

Marlowe is midway through a deep sip of water and pulls the bottle from her lips with a tightened expression.

"I'm fine," she repeats in a more insistent tone. She looks over at me and gives a subtle raise of the water bottle toward me. "Thanks for getting these."

"No problem," I nod. She starts away. "Oh. Frederic should have your script down to you in a minute. He was looking through your trailer for it."

She turns back to me and quickly covers the quizzical look in her eyes. "Great. Thank you."

By the time filming is finished for the night, I'm cold, tired, and ready to go back to Xavier and Dean's house. It's not until I'm starting toward Delta to say goodnight that I remember I'm supposed to watch the rest of the footage with her.

"Ready to go?" she asks as she approaches.

"Sure," I say.

"Great. Let me just tie up a couple of things and I'll meet you over by the production trailer."

"The production trailer?"

She gives me directions and I nod, then head over. Standing at the bottom of the steps of the trailer, I watch the people who were on the set filter out toward the parking lot. A couple of the guys are laughing and jostling each other around, and some of the other actors were bundled close together in conversation. Still others have disappeared out of the real world into their virtual existence and are walking without looking ahead, their faces trained on their phones as if in terror of what they might have missed while they were working.

Then comes Marlowe. She's walking with a driven, determined stride toward her trailer. Brittany is trying to keep up, managing to stay beside her for a few steps, then falling behind and jogging to catch up. She has her phone in her hand and keeps holding it out in front of Marlowe, gesturing toward something on the screen. A couple of times, Marlowe looks over at it, but the tense expression on her face doesn't change.

Out of the corner of my eye, I see a figure come around the corner of the production trailer. I look up and see Meredith take a step toward me, then stop short. She, too, is focused on a phone, and it's like she thought I was someone else and is surprised to see me.

"Agent Griffin," she says.

"Hello."

"I was looking for Delta."

"She's coming. She's still down on set talking to the crew."

"Oh," she says, giving a long gaze in the direction of the cornfield, then bringing her eyes back to me almost sharply. "What are you doing here?"

She sounds protective. Bordering on defensive.

"Delta wants to show me the footage that has already been shot," I say.

"All of the footage?"

"I'm guessing that would be many hours, so probably not. But she wants me to get an idea of the project so far," I tell her.

She nods, and by the look on her face, I have a feeling she's asked for that privilege before and was denied.

"What do you think so far?" she asks.

"Of the mini-series?" I ask.

"Yes. It's pretty amazing, right? It's going to be huge."

I give a bit of a shrug. "I can't really make an assessment of that yet."

The hint of a smile that had come to her lips disappears. "What do you mean?"

"I have only seen part of what was done today. I didn't do a script review. And, honestly, from what I've seen, there's a lot of work that needs to be done. Whether that's done in filming or editing, I don't know, but there are some issues. But Delta seems like a smart woman who cares a lot about this project. I'm sure she'll make sure it's done well," I say.

"What kind of issues? I think Marlowe has been brilliant."

"I'm sure she has. I'm just talking about the story. But that's why I'm here. This is a completely different industry. They can't be expected to know the ins and outs of what I do and what happened any more than I understand everything they do," I say.

"Good," Meredith says, nodding. "This is going to take her career to a new level, you know. It's going to solidify her image as a multifaceted actress capable of handling impactful, award-worthy roles. She's going to skyrocket from here."

She's an ambitious mother, I have to give her that. I don't agree. I don't argue. There would be no point in either. There's nothing wrong with Marlowe's skills as I've seen so far, but that doesn't mean I think she's going to burst into stardom because of a made-for-TV true crime mini-series.

"Hey, Emma," Delta says, sounding slightly out of breath as she hurries toward me. "I'm sorry. I got held up going over a couple of minor rewrites for tomorrow's scenes. You could have gone inside."

"It's unlocked?" I ask.

"Yeah," she says. "There's almost always an editor in there working. Come on. It's cold out here." She glances over at Meredith like she has just realized she's there. "Is there something I can help you with, Meredith?"

"I want to see the list of people Marlowe authorized to access the set," she says.

"Why would you want to see that?" Delta asks.

"Because I want to know who is able to come visit her when she's working. Maybe you haven't noticed how on edge she's been, but I think it has to do with someone who came to visit," Meredith says.

"I have noticed that," Delta acknowledges. "But I'm not jumping to any conclusions. And I'm not going to give you that information without Marlowe giving me permission to. She was allowed to authorize people to come to the set and visit her in her trailer during slow times and visit the set during breaks. Just like the other primary actors. It's a little perk of being a star. But they are her visitors to choose. She's an adult. She can have whoever she wants here as long as they don't cause a disruption, and no one has."

Meredith looks over at me, then back at Delta, and flashes a tight, false smile.

"Okay. Well, as long as you don't think anyone has bothered her," she says, backing up slightly. She glances back and forth between us. It looks like she's waiting for an invitation to stay with us, but Delta doesn't extend it. "Goodnight."

Delta shakes her head but doesn't comment as she leads me up the steps and into the trailer. The rush of heat is at once soothing and makes me realize just how cold I actually was. It's like when you are so hungry you don't even realize it until the second you put a bite of food in your mouth, then you're ravenous.

My skin feels for an instant like it's been flash-frozen before starting to thaw. Delta calls out to someone she calls Fox and a hulking man with thick facial hair and sparkling, friendly eyes ducks out of a back room.

"Hey," he calls over. "All wrapped for the night?"

"Yep," she says. "Footage should be up. This is Emma."

"Griffin," Fox says excitedly, coming toward me with the same energy as a bounding puppy. "The FBI agent. The real one."

I can't help but laugh as he shakes my hand. "That's me."

"I can't believe you're actually here." He looks at Delta. "Do you have any idea how much of a badass this woman is?"

Delta stammers a little, shooting me a look that says she probably knows absolutely nothing about me other than my involvement in Lakyn's case. It doesn't offend me. I'm fully aware the average person doesn't fanboy over crime.

"It's alright," I say to Delta, who gives a hint of a shrug, then I look at Fox. "Thank you."

"Are you only here for today?" he asks.

"No, I'm going to be here a few more times," I tell him.

"Emma is consulting on the details of the crime and the investigation," Delta explains. "And I thought she might like to see some of the other footage we've taken." Fox continues to stare at me, and Delta's eyebrows lift with expectation. "Fox?"

He jumps a bit. "Sorry. Yes. Footage. Do you have anything specific you want her to see? I doubt she wants to sit here for the next couple of days watching everything from all the different cameras." His eyes drift over to me. "Do you?"

There's hope in that question, but I have to dash it by shaking my head. He nods with understanding and I laugh again.

Delta gives him a couple of key moments she wants me to see and asks him to bring up the rough edit as it is so far.

"Want some coffee?" she asks when he heads into the other room to get everything ready.

"No, thanks," I say.

"Good for you," she says. "I can't get away from the stuff. It's the only thing that gets me through the late nights sometimes. Especially in the cold."

She walks over to a machine on a nearby table and pulls herself a tall paper cup of coffee. It smells like some generic roast probably bought by the industrial bucketful to fuel the crew, but Delta doesn't seem to mind in the least. I can absolutely feel her on that. There are times when the need for coffee in any form is far more important than minute little details like flavor and drinkability.

A few minutes later, we're in front of monitors watching clips of raw footage. It's interesting watching the story coming together in little bits and pieces. It's almost like seeing a moving visualization of a puzzle gradually being made. It's not linear, but I recognize most of the moments, most of what I'm seeing. There are some bits I have to ask about or Delta pauses to explain to me, mostly glimpses into Lakyn's life meant to highlight her as a person and what was happening in her life leading up to the chain of events that ended with that fateful phone call and her death.

I notice she skims through considerable chunks of some of the footage and I ask her what's in those sections. She shrugs.

"There were a couple of scenes that were hard to get nailed down because the guys were squirrely that day."

"What do you mean?"

"They were just goofing around and being ridiculous. They kept making each other laugh and playing little pranks."

"I would think that would drive you crazy," I note. "You want to get this project done and they are wasting your time like that."

"It does," she nods. "Unfortunately, that's pretty common when you're working with young actors or people who are inexperienced. The casting director didn't want to go with anyone too well known for the series because it would feel over-produced. Marlowe is the biggest name in it and she is meant to be the primary draw because she is the main character. Everyone else is fairly new to the industry. That way they become their characters to the people watching, rather than them envisioning those actors in other roles or as characters they're more familiar with."

"That makes sense," I nod.

I watch a few more scenes building up Lakyn's life. I don't have much feeling toward them or input about them. Since I didn't know her or about anything going on in her life before her disappearance and death, I don't know how accurate those portrayals are or if they are highlighting important moments in her life. There are a couple that I vaguely remember from during the investigation when I was trying to find out more about her. This was when people thought she had just disappeared, that she may have run off with someone.

They talked about an older boyfriend, someone she left with because she wanted to start a new life. I'll admit I believed them. When I first heard about her case and was tasked with finding her, I thought she probably just ducked out of life because she didn't feel like dealing with it anymore. She was young, beautiful, wealthy, and extremely famous. She had the entire world open in front of her and could do anything she wanted. It would be more than easy for her to just slip away.

But I was wrong. I don't mind admitting that. I never do. Being wrong is part of being human, of being FBI.

Delta stops on another clip of footage. This one with Paisley.

"These are the first scenes she shot as Agent Emma Griffin," she tells me with a playful sideways smile.

She seems to be warming up a bit. I've gotten past the robotic, ultra-controlled exterior to someone more approachable.

I watch Paisley's performance as me and am stunned to see how many times they went through the same few seconds' worth of a scene. All it was meant to show was her walking into a room, but she did it over and over again.

"Why did she keep redoing that entrance?" I ask.

"She said she needed to find her motivation," Delta says.

"To go into a police station?" I raise an eyebrow. "I'd think the motivation for that would be fairly clear."

"You'd think. But she wanted to show different emotions and energies."

Paisley certainly goes through a full range of both as she continuously enters and exits the room. In some, she looks angry. In others, distracted. In others, she's on her phone. In one, she walks in sobbing and throws herself down on her knees.

"Wow," I comment in reaction to that display.

"Yeah, that one was particularly invested." She shows me a few more scenes, including some of the footage from tonight. When she's done, she looks over at me and opens a hand toward the screen like she's presenting what I just saw. "So? What do you think so far?"

CHAPTER TWELVE

"It's a mess," I say to Dean when I get home and find him still awake. "She showed me the footage so far, and I don't know how they would get a single decent episode of anything out of it, much less a whole mini-series."

He's sitting in the parlor, reading a book under the light of a bright gooseneck lamp. He looks over the edge of the book at me.

"What's wrong with it?" he asks.

"Everything," I sigh, flopping down into a chair near him. I cringe and shrug. "Alright, not everything. The concept is sound. It's a compelling case. I'm not going to pretend it's not. And Marlowe really is talented. But it seems like everybody else has forgotten they aren't just filming a horror movie somebody threw together during a screenwriting class and thinks it's brilliant."

"Maybe you just need to give them a little bit of wiggle room," he offers. "You're really protective of this case because you know it. You were there. Xavier was there. These people weren't. Give them some grace, Emma. They aren't going to get everything right. Remember that weird day when the crime channel showed episodes of five different series that were all about the same murder?"

"And they all had different details and told the story differently," I say. "I know."

"But they all got the general idea, right? And it wasn't necessarily that any of them got things wrong. They just focused on different aspects and trimmed out others. It's how they chose to present it, and that's okay. Of course, there's also the need to find actors who are far more attractive than the real-life person they are playing." He says that last part with a grin.

"That's true," I acknowledge. "A critical part of making one of those series. Not easy with Lakyn, though. But Marlowe is about as close as they could get. Followed closely by her best friend."

"Her best friend?" he asks.

I barely even noticed I'd made the comment, but now that he asks about it, I tell him about Brittany and the strange resemblance I noticed.

"Maybe that's why they're so close," he suggests. "I remember when I was in middle and high school there were some girls who looked kind of alike and loved to play it up by wearing the same outfits and doing their makeup a lot. They would be little twinsies with each other all the time."

"Well, I guess at that age you're looking for just about anything to help you connect with someone else," I say.

"What about you?" he asks.

"I didn't do a whole lot of connecting over looking like other people," I shrug. "I preferred things like interests and hobbies."

"No," he says. "I mean what about the actress playing you?"

I open my mouth to answer, then close it when I realize I'm not sure how to answer.

"Her name is Paisley," I finally say. "She's quite a bit younger than me. Pretty."

"What's wrong with her?" Dean asks.

"What do you mean?" I ask.

"You have that look."

"What look?"

"The one people get when someone has a crooked wedding cake with flowers in the wrong color buttercream. Or an ugly baby," Xavier says as he comes into the room and sits down on the couch.

"What look is that?" I ask.

"You know something's wrong and it's bothering you, but you can't say anything about it because it would be mean," he says.

I glance between him and Dean. "Is that one of my more common looks?"

Dean looks like he's trying to find the right words to piece together an answer.

"Yes," Xavier says bluntly.

"Oh." I contemplate this for a second. "Well, good to know."

"So, what's wrong with her?" Dean asks.

"It's not that anything is wrong with her," I say. "She's just... a lot. I guess. She sat with me at the meals and talks about her role and the decisions she's making for her character."

Dean looks as taken aback as I felt when she started making the comments.

"Decisions she's making for her character? What does that mean?"

"She decided to adopt a vegetarian diet. Because she thinks an FBI agent would be compassionate enough not to want to eat animals."

"But you're..."

"We had that discussion."

Dean makes a contemplating sound. "That's definitely a choice. But what's really wrong with her?"

"The same thing that's wrong with all of them. They seem so flippant. Like this is just a fun story she's a part of. It just doesn't feel like they are taking it seriously."

"Again, Emma. Give them time."

"I know," I say. "I am. I'm going back tomorrow."

CHAPTER THIRTEEN

Before

THE ASSORTMENT OF NOTES SELECTED IN THE DRAWER BEDSIDE table look like just mementos from an inmate facing a lifetime of confinement with no relief. An inmate who found a compassionate ear and unwavering friend.

Perhaps, an inmate who had lost touch with reality along the way.

But she knew there was so much more to it than that. Xavier had entrusted Lakyn with the notes because there was something specific he needed her to do with them. These weren't just ramblings. They weren't just a random selection of words scattered on paper or drawings that popped into his mind. She already knew how brilliant he was. That he'd been crafting and improving his home since it had first been designed, and it was filled with gadgets and hidden features only he knew about.

But these drawings weren't descriptions of those. This was the place she needed to go. He told her this building, something he called the

Temple, would hold the answers she needed to earn his release. Or at least get him another trial. If he could just have another trial, he could prove he wasn't guilty. He could replace his lawyer and make sure he had one who would pay attention to what he said and not accept the obvious corruption of the judge. That would be the first step. He would need to make sure they replaced Sterling Jennings as the judge in his case. Another judge would see the truth.

He could make sure they knew every detail as to why he couldn't possibly be responsible for Andrew's death.

But that wasn't going to be enough, and he knew it. Just being able to show it was improbable that he could have been the one who murdered his admitted best friend was a step, but only a step. It would help, but it would leave an inconvenient reality. A lack of resolution.

People don't like hanging ends. They especially don't like murder cases that end with the only one accused walking out of the courtroom exonerated and no other person left to blame, no one to hold accountable. There are people who will walk onto a jury already chomping at the bit to declare a guilty verdict simply because they believe no one could get so far as being put on trial for murder if they didn't do it. Juries are instructed to consider only the facts and the law, to take an impartial eye to the proceedings, but in reality, what some people want to do is to punish someone—anyone—for a crime. Facts and law be damned. And when a suspect is presented before them, no amount of evidence or argument can ever be enough to counter the overwhelming desire for punishment.

Which meant Xavier had to make sure everybody in that courtroom knew there were other suspects. Not just one. An entire group, an organization with chilling practices and a core of brutality and victimization beneath its surface of success and prestige. He described them as existing outside of the realm of the world, but not quite somewhere in another world. They moved through society undetected. Even the people in their lives who were closest to them didn't know about their secret.

Being a member of the Order was an honor and a

responsibility. Being a part of this particular chapter carried with it something else. To join this chapter meant being willing to accept a call. One day the goal of the organization wouldn't be to lift someone up and find ways to improve their lives, boost their wealth and success, and elevate the ones around them.

It would be to kill them.

And they all accepted it. They all took on that element of it as an honor and a privilege just like everything else. When they were brought into the fold, they were protected. They were offered power and access to the world beyond their imaginations. They could do more than they ever could have before, dream up what they wanted to accomplish, to change, to influence, to destroy. And it was done for them.

They were the ones to take Andrew's life. Xavier didn't know exactly why. There was a reason. A specific one. He knew that. The Order didn't kill for fun. They weren't in it for the thrill. They killed as a tool, a means to the end of their choosing.

Xavier told Lakyn the only way they were going to be able to prove what they had done, and what he hadn't, was to get proof of the Temple. They needed to be able to show everyone who had any control over his fate what these people could really do. Especially the Judge and the Sheriff who held his fate in their hands. The ones who kept him on edge.

He told her they peeled the glue away from his edges when they were near him. They poured fabric softener and lint onto the Velcro that kept him attached to the world and watched his grip loosen.

Lakyn didn't know what he meant. She didn't know what much of what he said meant. But she didn't believe he was insane like he'd been portrayed. She didn't believe he was dangerous.

She did believe he was incredibly intelligent, vulnerable, and not guilty of the crime for which he was convicted.

And she was the only one who was going to be able to help him. So, she would do as he said.

Her nerves were starting to build up as she tied on her boots. But mixed with the nerves was excitement. She had never done anything like this before. It felt significant. Like she was doing something real. Even if she didn't fully understand what she was doing or why, it was so much more than anything expected of her. So much more than people thought she was capable of doing.

Taking the bits of information and fragmented instructions, she drove through the darkness to the massive building hunkering at the edge of town. It used to be a church. The shape was distinctive. The air of worship and restraint still hovered around it even though it had been many years since the congregation called it their home.

But the closer she got to it, the more that feeling was tainted. Ribbons of indulgence slithered through it, ruining the sanctity that once filled the space. It was a mockery to have them meet within these walls.

She found the entry point Xavier described, wondering if he'd ever gone inside this way or just knew it was there. The darkness around her felt alive. She listened to her breaths against the feeling of being watched. She filled her mind with the sound of the air rushing in and out rather than the shiver of eyes on her skin.

In and out. In and out.

Her boot slipped when she first pressed it to the stone to launch her up toward the window. It sounded explosive in the quiet and Lakyn went still. She waited for someone to come. For a light to burst on and trap her. But nothing happened. She drew in a fuller breath, stretching out her lungs until they hurt, then let it out in a long stream until they ached just as much from being empty.

The next step stuck. She climbed up and in moments, she was inside. The eerie feeling of the Temple descended on her. Part of her felt like she could still hear the activities that went on inside when it was a church. Laughter. Singing. Prayers. Crying. Milestone moments for the people who made this place the center point of their lives. Born to the baptismal, married at the altar, mourned beneath the pulpit. The life cycle happened here, and it was still echoing through the halls, even after the people had left. The building didn't forget important moments like that.

Now that she was inside, part of her wanted to explore. The fear that had coursed through her was still there, but she was starting to thrive on it. She'd been afraid before and let it hold her back. She'd been told she wasn't able to do things because of fear, or that if she was afraid she shouldn't try. She should stay with what she knew, with what she was good at, with what people admired her for. Don't stray from that. Don't try anything else. Don't let yourself trip and fall because you tried too much.

Now she used the fear to fuel her. This was for Xavier. She was afraid because this was worth doing. Because it wasn't just about her. Because for once, she might be able to do something that mattered.

Her hands shook as she walked down a dark hall and found the office Xavier described. She took out her phone and started taking pictures.

Before

The wind that touched her skin was cold and sharp. Marlowe could feel hidden snow in it. Forgotten rain, breath, stolen body heat, all turned to ice that nipped at her when she stepped outside. She pulled her sweater closer around her, trying to bury herself back in it. It felt like she was protecting herself from more than just the chill.

But not her body. She was safe. Nothing would touch her. Not for fear of ruining what she had to offer. What she was worth.

The voice behind her used to make Marlowe turn, but it didn't anymore. She'd heard it enough times that she didn't need to look when it came.

"Did you really think I wouldn't notice? That you would just be able to get away with it?" she asked.

"What do you mean?" replied the voice.

Now she turned, letting out an incredulous scoff.

"Please don't play that game with me. Don't pretend you don't know what I'm talking about. It doesn't change anything."

Sudden long strides toward her pushed her back a step until she was pressed against the wall. Heated breath rolled down the side of her neck from the gritted teeth positioned just in front of her ear.

"No one will believe you."

The cold air rushed over her again and she slowly sank down to sit on the cold ground.

When she was finally able to drag herself to her feet, she rushed inside, wanting the door between herself and the rest of the world. She could have someone there with her in an instant if she called. An empty hookup plucked randomly from the legion of fans willing to do anything and everything for her. A security guard tasked with standing outside the door to stop anyone who might try to come in, or right inside just to fill up more space in the cavernous apartment.

It seemed like a good idea when she got it. Staying in her trailer or a hotel for weeks wasn't something she relished. Hotels could be a nice diversion, but they felt so impersonal after a while. The apartment wasn't exactly hers. It came furnished and she'd only added a few little bits and pieces here and there. But it was far better.

But now she felt the loneliness inside of it. She liked the chance to close herself off, but when she did, it seemed to swallow her. She didn't want the empty hookup. She didn't want the security guard. She didn't know who or what she wanted, but whatever it was, it wasn't there.

She went to her bedroom and opened the drawer, digging through the stack of clothes inside to find the bottle buried deep beneath them. It was smaller than the bottle that sat on top of the dresser. The one people knew about. At least, some people. She popped open the top and tilted two of the vibrant pills into the palm of her hand. Without even leaving the side of the dresser, she popped the pills into her mouth and swallowed them down with nothing.

She'd learned to do that when the need to get her pills inside her fast superseded the discomfort she'd experienced when taking pills as a child. Back then, when she was young enough that even taking a pain reliever that wasn't liquid or candy-flavored and chewable was a big event, she went through cups of water and would often cry trying to get a pill down. It was difficult and painful, frightening to be prescribed anything when she was sick.

Somewhere in the apartment, her phone started ringing. Marlowe squeezed her eyes closed and gripped the edge of the dresser. The ringing seemed like it was getting louder until it was the only thing she could hear.

She wanted to scream, if only so there was something else to hear. But she held it in. Like she always did.

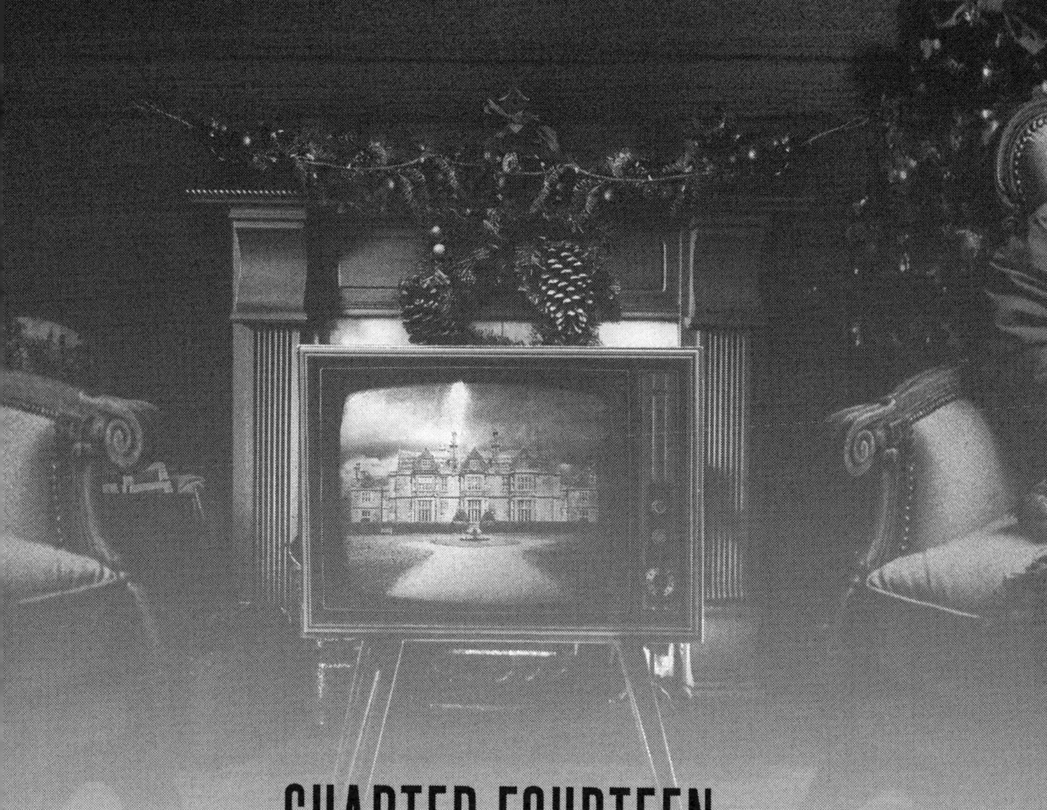

CHAPTER FOURTEEN

Now

DELTA SITS DOWN WITH ME AT BREAKFAST THE NEXT MORNING. She only has a cup of coffee in one hand and a croissant in the other. It's like she can't commit herself to eating an entire meal. Something might come up that would need her immediate attention, so she takes the guerilla approach to breakfast instead.

"The set designers are working on improving the field this morning," she tells me. "Hopefully they'll be done in time for me to be able to do some shots there later today. We want to get some basic footage of the field from different angles and with different levels of light so that it can be interspersed with the actual scenes."

As she's saying this, one of the guys walks past the table. He stops and backs up, his attention obviously piqued by what he caught of the conversation.

"Are you talking about the cornfield?" he asks. "I heard some of the crew has been out there since before sunup making some changes to it."

"That's right. They're making a few improvements."

"Perfect," he says when the words are barely out of her mouth. "I was just thinking last night, maybe there could be an extra scene after Lakyn's death with all the bones."

"What do you mean?" Delta asks.

"Okay, so what if she didn't die right away? No one really knows for sure, right?" he asks.

"Yes, they do," I tell him. "She was beaten to death before the men left the field. They didn't just leave her out there."

"But that's just a guess," he counters. "I mean, I've researched this case. They say they don't know exactly everything that happened to her, and some people think she might have actually been alive and suffered there for a while before finally giving up. And I think that's the more interesting way to tell it. Like, imagine this. There's her big scene with the guys. It looks like she's dead. The audience thinks she's dead for sure.

But she's not. There are some shots of the field, some shots of life going on around her, maybe them moving her car, whatever, whatever, and then, the big reveal." He pauses for dramatic effect. "She's still alive. She's just unconscious. She wakes up with a big gasp and realizes how much danger she's in. Maybe she doesn't know how badly she is injured. He thinks the guys are still there in the field. She needs to get away.

So, she starts dragging herself across the ground, trying to escape. She can't stand up. Or maybe she tried a couple of times and falls over. All the time, she's crying and gasping for breath. The whole thing. Then, she collapses again further in the corn stalks. Her eyes open and all around her, she sees weird shit. Maybe there's a skull staring back at her. She tries to get away, but she's delirious and thinks the bones are animating and coming in after her."

"Like zombies?" Delta asks.

"Kind of. But not really. Because they wouldn't have all their skin and stuff. Oh, but maybe they could. That could be really gruesome.

There had to be some people who were killed right around the same time as her and dumped there, right? So they would be, like, partially decomposed, but not all the way. She could run into one of them and it could stand up and come after her like a zombie. So, she's completely terrified and ends up dying from fright."

He's grinning like he thinks he's just come up with the greatest idea to have ever graced cinematography. I'm holding myself back from making any comment, trying to let Delta be the one to stop this nonsense. Fortunately, she's looking at him with just about as much disdain as I'm feeling.

"Thank you for your input, Barry. But I really think that we are going for more of a realistic approach than a horror movie."

He glares at her. "Fine. But it would be better my way. You'd get a lot more people watching if you added something more interesting to it."

He walks away and Delta looks back at me, shaking her head slightly. "I'm sorry about that. Anyway, I was going to say that the shooting schedule today has a lot of scenes with your character. Obviously, some of them had to be fictionalized… oh, perfect timing. Here's Paisley."

I look over as the actress comes to sit down at the table. She's wearing a floral sundress and has her hair curled down around her shoulders.

"Good morning," she says. "I'm really excited about the scenes today. I think you're both really going to like what I'm going to do with the character."

"What you're going to do with the character?" I ask.

"I've been meditating on what she's going through during these scenes and what might be influencing and motivating her so I can know how to behave, my non-verbal communication, how to deliver the lines. All of it. I think I've really captured the personality how I want to portray it."

Delta doesn't seem to be listening to her. Instead, she's looking at what she's wearing.

"Did wardrobe give you this?" she asks.

Paisley looks down at her dress and smooths one hand down it.

"No. But they asked us to bring a few of our own things in so that what we were wearing didn't always look brand new. This is one of the things I brought."

"What were you supposed to be wearing today?"

"Jeans and a sweater," she says. "Just like in every other scene. Except for when they give me a suit."

"That's because that's what I wear," I point out. "Unless I'm going to headquarters, court, or a press conference. If I'm working, I'm most likely in jeans and a comfortable shirt."

"It's just bland. There needs to be some visual interest," Paisley says. "Something to keep the watchers engaged."

"The story itself is what's going to keep the audience engaged," I tell her. "They aren't watching to admire you. Besides, a dress like that doesn't even make sense. Keep in mind it was October when I started investigating her death. That's a summer dress."

"You weren't outside every moment of the investigation," she argues. "There had to be times when you were inside. Especially when you were interacting with the detective and trying to get him to see things your way."

"Excuse me?" I sputter, hoping she isn't saying what I think she's saying, but knowing full well she is. "Are you implying I would dress like that to convince Detective White to do something for me?"

"I'm not going to say that outright," she replies. "But, look, you are a celebrated FBI agent, right? You've solved a lot of crimes, some that people said couldn't be solved."

"Because I'm good at what I do," I counter. "I went to school. I studied hard. I have skills and I use them to analyze crime scenes and human behavior until I can break down a crime to who did it."

"Right," she nods. "But all that thinking and figuring things out isn't exactly entertaining. And it just doesn't feel right. I think adding a little bit of sex appeal and showing that extra resource that can be used when solving crimes will make it much more interesting to viewers."

"Paisley," Delta sighs, pinching the bridge of her nose. "You need to put on what wardrobe told you to." The actress starts to protest, but Delta stops her. "And don't be late to your call."

Paisley glares but doesn't argue as she gets up and flounces away.

Things don't improve when filming for the day starts. Rather than staying at the same location, we're transported in several production vans to a building that's standing in for the jail facility where Xavier was housed during his appeal. Today's scenes are supposed to show when I met Xavier and our early interactions, then discovering Lakyn's body.

But we don't get that far.

Paisley slams her hands on the table in front of her and leans across it, shouting. She grabs a piece of paper out of the hand of the man in front of her and balls it up, throwing it to the side as she demands he speak clearly.

"Stop," the director says. "Just stop. Paisley, what are you doing? That's not in the script."

"I'm experimenting. I want to make the scene more believable. I don't understand why I'm just sitting here listening to this," Paisley groans, gesturing at the actor playing Xavier.

"What do you mean?" Mac asks with a slight wither in his voice.

"He doesn't make any sense," she complains. "No one talks like that. And I'm supposed to just sit around and listen to it? Over and over? And pretend like it means something? I don't think my character would do that. It doesn't feel authentic. The direction I want to take the character is edgier, more relatable. I think it's a major leap to think a hardened FBI agent would tolerate standing around listening to this blather and pretend it means something. Either my character needs to react more, or the dialogue needs to be rewritten to make more sense."

She crosses her arms over her chest defiantly.

"I disagree," Van, the script supervisor on set says. "The dialogue doesn't need to make more sense. If anything, it could be amped up."

"Excuse me?" I ask, shocked at his suggestion. "Those things he's saying, those are actual words that Xavier Renton said."

"I know," Van says. "We were able to access the audio recordings from the meetings. We know exactly what was said. But nobody else knows that. We can keep a lot of it, but I think that he's being too subtle. I think we need to really lay on the crazy. Show how out of touch he is. I can add some lines in here, but you can just make it up. Ramble. Babble. I don't think you should sound coherent in anything you say. Really make it so that the Emma character has to work for figuring out what you're talking about if anything."

"You're going to make it worse?" Paisley asks, obviously offended her suggestion fell flat. "This is absurd. No one would just let someone like that sit in a room with a normal person without some sort of protection."

"That's true," Mac notes. "Is his jacket available?"

A moment later a prop manager comes out onto the set and I'm on my feet.

"No fucking way."

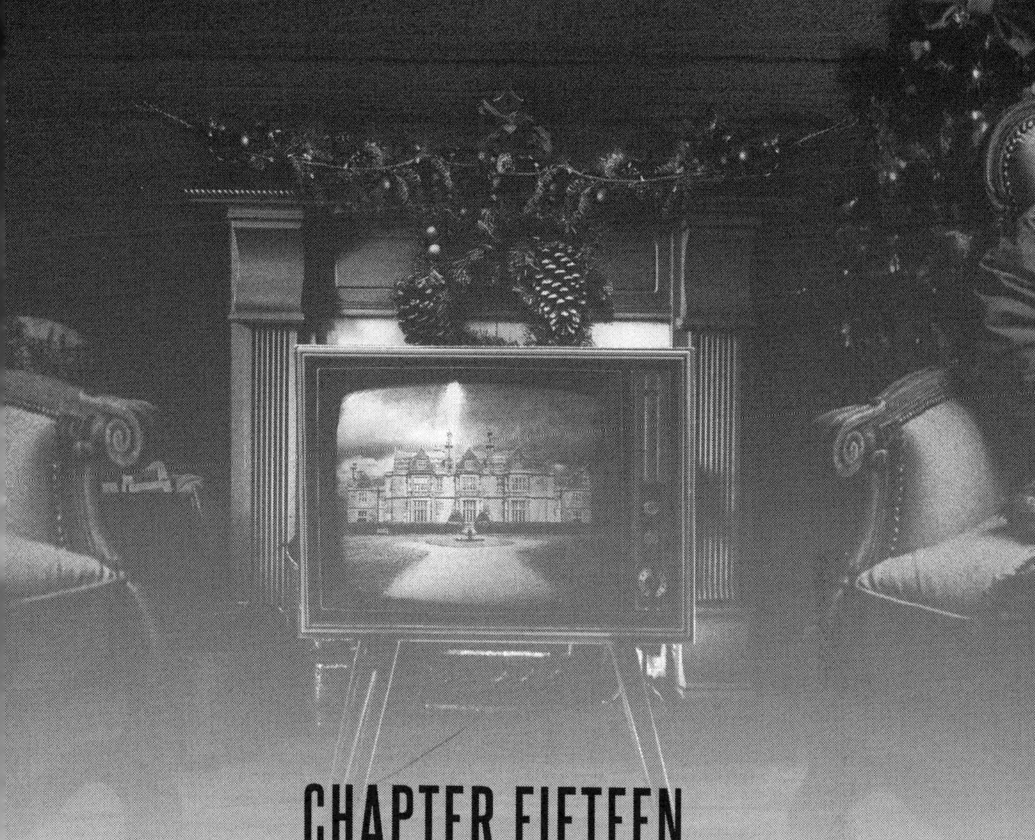

CHAPTER FIFTEEN

"IS SOMETHING WRONG, EMMA?" DELTA ASKS.

I stare at her, incredulous that she's actually asking me that question when we can both clearly see what's in the prop master's hand.

"You're seriously telling me that is the jacket you've been talking about?" I ask, pointing at the straitjacket being held out to the actor.

Delta's eyes go over to the jacket and then come back to me. She nods almost imperceptibly.

"Yes," she says. "What did you think we were talking about?"

"Something in tweed? An inoffensive gray inmate-issue zippered hoodie? Not a fucking straitjacket!"

"I don't understand what the problem is. He's a psychiatric inmate. It doesn't take that big of a leap of the imagination to think he probably spent a good amount of time in one of these. Besides, I'm the one who they're asking to wear it and I don't mind. If there's anyone who should be bothered by it, it would be me," the actor playing Xavier chimes in.

That's enough to push me right over the edge. I've been doing my best to hold it together, to not show what I was feeling and what was going through my head while I watched the production. I've been keeping in mind what Dean told me. This isn't real. It's a fictionalization. A dramatization. People don't actually expect what happens in these to be absolutely accurate.

But this I can't take.

"No," I declare firmly with a shake of my head. "You don't get to be bothered by it. You are an actor. You're a typical human being with normal functioning who fits into the world around you without any issue, who has been cast as a man so extraordinary you couldn't even fathom him. He is the only one who is allowed to be bothered by that concept. He is the only one to speak about it.

"But since he's not here, let me illuminate you. Xavier Renton was not a psychiatric inmate. That term alone is exceptionally problematic, but I'm not going to get caught up in semantics. I'm sure what you are trying to say is that he was under psychiatric care. The research team should have told you that is not true. The facility Xavier was in when this happened was not a medical facility. It did not categorize inmates based on mental health and did not provide mental health treatment or care. He was not labeled as psychotic at any point and would have never worn a straitjacket. Ever.

"And I want to make something exceptionally clear to you. Listen to me carefully," I enunciate. "Xavier is not crazy. He is not broken. He is not damaged or 'off' or nuts. There is nothing wrong with his mind. The only thing that is wrong with him is a structural problem with his heart that was cruelly manipulated in order to cause amplified symptoms of anxiety, panic, and unpredictability. He was subtly and undetectably tortured into always feeling right on the edge of collapse while also being alone, confused, and completely unsure of what the future might hold for him.

"Imagine suddenly finding yourself in a strange land full of people who speak the same words that you do, but you struggle to understand what they mean by them. You can't communicate with them effectively. You don't know where you are and can't navigate yourself. The tasks that the people around you think are simple and basic are confounding to you and make you feel out of touch, and because you are an adult, you're ignored and even made fun of for not being able to do them correctly.

"Imagine this is your basic reality, but there are also moments when you will simply suddenly not know where you are or what's happening. You'll look around you and not remember why you were in a place and not be able to figure out what you are supposed to do next. The thought of someone speaking to you or touching you is so unnerving you go out of your way to avoid it, even making your life harder for yourself in the process. Like you're in a grocery store and in an instant, you feel like you can't remember what you're supposed to be doing.

"You know what a store is. You understand the concept. But suddenly you're plagued with the sense that you're doing something wrong. That you aren't privy to some unspoken rules or guidelines to how to shop, and that you're automatically going against them. That you're in the way or that everyone around you is staring at you, judging and qualifying what you do, what you say, what you pick up. You can't remember how to find anything or what aisle anything would be in, so you start going up and down every aisle a few times, picking up a couple of things when you find them, then doubling back and retracing your path over and over.

"Maybe you start talking to yourself to try to calm down and work your way logically through what's happening. You're not hearing other voices or thinking there's someone with you. You are fully aware that you are the one saying these things and it's because you need to move your mouth, to use your voice, to hear something reverberating around in your head other than the voices of everyone around you going about their lives.

"Now imagine there is only one person in this world who you feel understands you or cares about what you think and feel. Your best friend. He makes it possible for you to interact with the world and to live without a constant feeling of terror and confusion. He handles basic tasks for you that have been previously unreachable, like driving, grocery shopping, paying bills, calling to order a pizza. Things everyone else takes for granted. This person makes you feel like you can actually live your life. Like you're safe. He translates the world for you, filters it for you. And translates you for the rest of the world.

"Then he's gone. Not gradually. Not because you decided you didn't need him anymore or that you could handle things on your own. Not even because you fought and decided he shouldn't be a part of your life anymore. He's gone because someone murdered him. Brutally. Horribly. In your home. Then, you are blamed for it. You have no one. You are alone in a world you don't understand being blamed for something you didn't do, and because no one can understand you, you're labeled as crazy and you can't even defend yourself. You end up in prison, isolated and tormented by the very people who are supposed to be taking care of you.

"After eight years of that, someone shows up who is willing to try to meet you halfway. She believes you. She knows you didn't commit the murder and wants to help. Then she's gone, too. This time, no one can even explain what happened. You have to advocate for yourself and try to make someone listen knowing full well you could spend the rest of your life suffering in prison for something you had nothing to do with. That is what Xavier went through."

Everyone in the room is silent. They stare at me, then their eyes start to drift to each other like they're waiting for one of them to be the first to speak.

"Thank you, Emma," Delta finally breaks the silence. "We obviously made a mistake with the straitjacket and we'll remove that from the series."

"I'm not finished," I tell her. "Since it's something they had access to, I'm sure you've all heard the audio of Xavier talking to me. You know what he sounds like. It's what makes people jump to putting labels on him like 'crazy' or 'nuts'. Because they don't understand him. He's speaking the same language as you and yet he's not, and there isn't a single one of you who is willing to try to see it that way. Just because the words he says aren't the ones you'd choose doesn't make them any less legitimate.

"Xavier isn't like anyone I have ever met before. More importantly, no one is like Xavier. He is unapologetically who he is, and who he is happens to be the most unbelievably intelligent, creative, insightful person I've ever encountered. What makes him different doesn't detract from his life. It adds to it. He sees things in a way that no one else does. He smells, hears, feels, tastes, and sees what other people never get to.

"You heard him talk about peanuts during our first conversation. Right? It sounds like an abstract personality-gauging activity. That's what I thought it was at first, too. He was trying to tell me more about himself and find out about me at the same time. And that was what he was doing, but there was more to it. That is the piece of information I used to figure out what the warden was doing to him. That one comment, something most people would completely discount as being from the rambling mind of an insane man, was what told me to pay attention to his behavior after peanuts. He would go from on edge, shaking, edgy, and frantic, to calm and cooperative, after he ate peanuts. The effect was exaggerated when he'd been pumped with sugar the way the warden hurt him. No one knew what he was saying.

"But when he was given peanuts, he became more coherent. He calmed down. Because of the salt. He knew peanuts made him feel better. He knew they settled the effect on his heart, so it didn't feel like it was going to explode. That was what he was telling me.

"I will never fully understand Xavier. It's simply something I'm never going to be able to do because my brain doesn't work the way his does. But I will keep trying. And every single time I get the tiniest glimpse of the way his mind works, of the way that he perceives the world, I feel fortunate because he doesn't bring many people close to him. He doesn't feel connected to many people. But he does have that for me. When I first met him, I thought the same thing you did. That he was just a bit unhinged and was off in his own world. Now I realize he can't ever really be in his own world. He's forced to adapt to ours.

"He has to mold himself to what this world is created to be, rather than having it rise up to meet him. This world wasn't made for him. It's an easy path for other people and climbing a mountain for him. I do my best to rise up to him when I possibly can. He's a gift."

My words seem to have sunken in, at least for the actor playing Xavier.

"Is everyone ready to try it?" Delta asks. "That should give every one of you something more to strive for. Getting that insight really should have had an impact." She looks over at me. "Anything else?"

"Yes. Paisley. You are not playing a character. This is not a person someone made up and that you get to manipulate and play around with, making her yours. That person is me. Every one of the words you're saying, you need to pretend are coming out of my mouth. Everything you do, you pretend I am doing it. There is no direction you can take your role because that is a direction that was already established. You were not a consideration and, frankly, still aren't. This isn't about you. In fact, this isn't about any of you."

I look over at Delta. She meets my eyes.

"What is it?"

"Can I have an hour with them?"

"With who?" she asks.

"All of them," I say. "All the non-extra actors."

"What do you need with them?"

"I'm going to bring them to the field of bones."

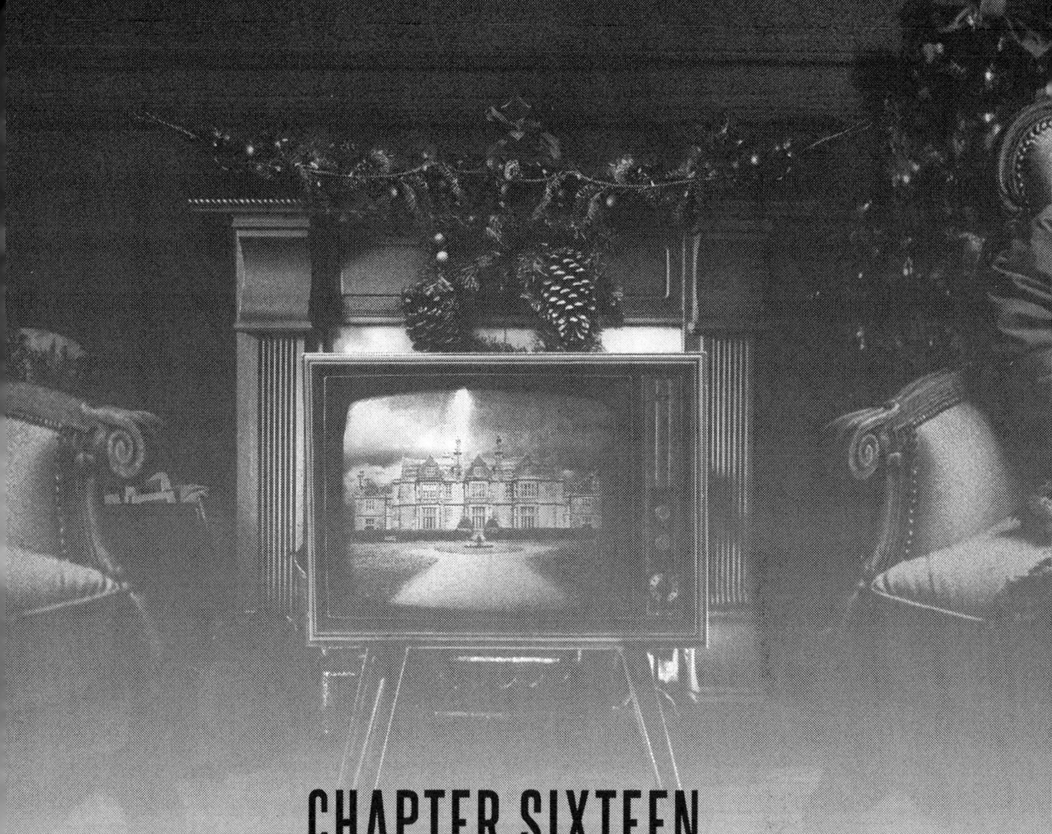

CHAPTER SIXTEEN

After

"LAKYN? WHY AREN'T YOU ANSWERING YOUR PHONE? I'VE called at least ten times. You should have been here two hours ago. We're going to go to the park without you. See you later."

"This is Mom. Where are you, Lakyn? Everyone is looking for you."

"Now isn't the time for you to start going out partying and getting blackout drunk. Your image can't take that right now. Call me. I have another part for you. It's not great, but it's something. If you ever want to get your career back on track, we need to really focus on getting you back out there. Please take my advice as your manager. This could really ruin you."

"This isn't funny anymore. It wasn't funny to begin with. Where are you? Nobody can figure out where you went after you left that production lot. At least call and tell me that you're alright. I'll give you all the time and space you need, but everyone needs to at least know that you're safe."

Lakyn Monroe has officially been declared missing one month after leaving a taping and seemingly disappearing. None of her friends or family has had any contact with her since and her vehicle has not been located. The social media queen is known for being a prolific producer of online content, but her platforms have all gone silent. Anyone who may have seen or heard from her is asked to get in touch with authorities.

The investigation into the disappearance of Lakyn Monroe has gotten nowhere, according to police handling the case. Without her car, a note, or any other indication of where she might have gone or what might have happened to her, the team investigating her disappearance feels they have few options of which direction to go next. There are some details of the investigation they say they are not disclosing to the public. As always, anyone who has any information is encouraged to get in touch with authorities. Police believe indications of her whereabouts will first appear on social media. Anyone with any connection to her is asked to keep an eye out. Watch your accounts carefully to see if you notice any changes in her platforms, comments, pictures, or anything else that might mean something. Don't assume anyone else has already reported it or that a detail might not matter.

Lakyn Monroe has now been missing for four months. The reality star, thirty, rose to fame with her vlogs dedicated to theme park touring. She since featured on several reality and competition shows. Most recently

Monroe developed an interest in social justice and has been very outspoken about issues including conviction of innocent people and prison reform. She was last seen leaving a taping of a baking competition series to be aired later this year, where she served as a guest judge. Some bank account activity continued for several days after, but has since stopped. No one has had contact with her since. Anyone with information is asked to contact the authorities. We'll bring more on this continuing story as details arise.

Then

"And she's just gone?" Emma asked. She and her cousin had just watched the news report of the missing woman and she needed to know more about her. She had never heard of Lakyn Monroe. Had never seen one of the videos that had apparently skyrocketed her to fame. She didn't understand that kind of fame. Like Dean described, she was famous for being famous.

"Apparently," Dean shrugged and reached for a slice of pizza. "Like it said, she'd gotten onto some shows and got a flash of fame. A couple people saw her leaving the lot where she filmed the baking show and she hasn't been seen or heard from since. It was just like that."

"And her car?" Emma asked. "Did they find it?"

"No. She just disappeared into thin air." He cringed. "I'm sorry."

"It's fine. But we both know people don't just disappear. No matter how much it seems like it, they're there." Emma paused to think for a few seconds. "If this girl is famous and has been missing for four months, how have I not heard about it?"

Something about this intrigued her.

"Her fame was starting to fade. That baking show was the first thing she did not on her own internet channel for a while. It seems she stopped worrying so much about staying famous and got wrapped up in a bunch of causes."

"Like the innocent people being convicted," Emma noted.

"That's the one I've heard the most about. But getting tangled up with criminals isn't quite the playful, innocently sexy appeal the theme park videos had. So, I guess even vanished she's not getting as much screen time," Dean told her.

Rumors

"I think she just ran off."

"Some man is holding her hostage. She was so beautiful. Someone is keeping her for themselves."

"She faked her disappearance so she can get attention when she shows up again."

"She was murdered. Some crazed fan." "No, a rival. Someone who wanted her fame."

"It was a serial killer."

"She had a lover and ran off to be with him."

It was clothing and bones trapped beneath a cage, but Emma knew without question.

It was Lakyn Monroe.

After

Happy New Year, everyone! Thank you for celebrating my birthday with me last night. I had a blast! This is the beginning of a brand-new year. Make the most of it! Love, Marlowe

"Have you heard from Marlowe?"

Delta didn't look all that concerned. Emma remembered the first day she was on set, when it had been mentioned that Marlowe had a problem getting where she needed to be on time. She shook her head.

"No. Not since the text message yesterday."

Delta sighed. "Alright. Thanks."

Rumors

"She's not here."

"Has anyone heard from her? A text? Call? Anything?"

"She probably spent yesterday sleeping it off and still feels like crap so she's running late."

"She needs to get here. We already lost one day with her."

Soon

"She's not answering her phone. She hasn't gotten in touch with anyone."

Now Delta looked worried. This wasn't like Marlowe. She might not get to set on time, and might not be most cooperative and easy to work with performer in the industry, but she was far from the worst she'd worked with. Marlowe wasn't the kind of drama queen to pretend she had disappeared so everyone would worry about her.

"Has anyone checked her apartment?"

"Does anyone have a key? Where's Brittany?"

"She's out of town, remember? She went to see her grandparents because she wasn't able to see them over the holidays."

"That's right. Get in touch with her. Find out if there are

any spare keys anywhere. Someone call the building manager for Marlowe's building. We need to get into her apartment."

"I know how to get inside."

Delta looked at Emma in surprise. "You do?"

"There's a back entrance. Marlowe showed it to me. It's hidden and accessible only by keypad entry, but I know how to get in. Come on."

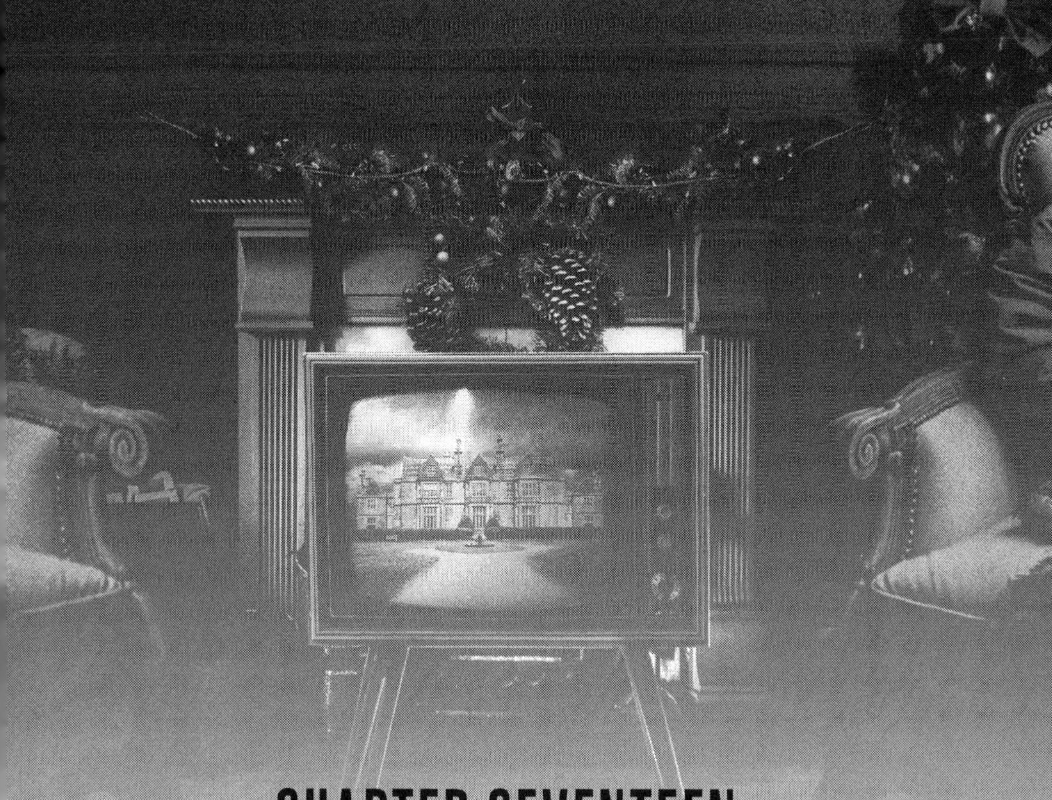

CHAPTER SEVENTEEN

Now

There will never be a time when I come close to the field that I don't feel its impact. Throughout my career, I've had countless people assume crime scenes don't affect me anymore because I've seen so many of them. They think that I'm used to it, that I don't flinch anymore.

I can see and think beyond it. That doesn't mean it doesn't impact me. I can look at a body and not see the person as I focus instead on things like the position, the injuries, the amount of blood, and any other evidence that's immediately apparent. I have to be able to see them that way. If I don't, the investigation can be compromised right from the beginning.

But that doesn't mean I don't eventually feel it. There comes a time in every investigation, after every murder, that the need for analysis fades and the recognition of that victim as a person, as a human life lost, sets in.

I carry that with me. Every victim is still with me.

I don't remember them all as clearly as the others. Some stick with me much more strongly. But they are all with me. I remember each of them. I hear their names and I can recount the details of their death, what the scene looked like.

I've always said the air around a crime scene is burned with the image of the death, that it is forever marked by what happened there. So am I.

The field of bones is a scar on the farmland surrounding Harlan. It represents the brutal tattering of many lives. And it takes up a big part of me. Not the way it looks now, quiet and tired, overgrown around the edges from the neglect that came with years untended by the woman once held captive just beyond the stalks. Bare in others where the corn was removed to aid in the excavation of the land.

I remember it the way it was. I remember the lush corn and the smooth dirt. I remember the massive black birds and the bits of flesh they carried away.

When I was first forced into therapy, I described the tense conversations with my therapist as feeling like she was trying to crack me open and search through my brain to find the bits I kept hidden away. I learned to appreciate that even if I hated having to do it.

Now, I do it to myself.

Standing close to the place where Lakyn lay for all those months, I show the cast and crew pictures of what the field looked like then. They're still saved in my cloud, a file for her death and the deaths of all the others associated with the Order never to leave the easy access of my fingertips until every one of the victims is named and every one of the guilty is brought to justice.

I tell them about the dark, twisting path I followed to bring me to this place, to the moment that I found her.

"I want you all to hear her voice. You've heard the words that she said. You've seen them written on the script and you've heard Marlowe saying them. But I want you to hear Lakyn. I want you to hear her voice so you know what she sounded like when she was sitting in that car, knowing she was most likely going to die."

I take out my phone and pull up the file that contains the recording of Lakyn's phone call. Turning the volume up as high as it will go, I skip near to the end. I hold the phone out and stand silently as I listen to her voice. It gets caught by the December air and carried out over the field like it's trying to find her again. Like it knows this is where her voice was heard for the last time.

When it's over, I look at each of their faces.

"Never once did she beg. Never once did she lose her control. She knew something horrible was going to happen to her. She hadn't been seen in a week by the time this recording was made. Did any of you know that? There's security footage of her at the bank. The same bank where Millie Haynes worked. Where she was nearly shot to death in the parking lot."

"Judge Jennings' sister," Marlowe says.

I nod. "She later died in Xavier's arms."

"That's not in the script," one of the actors says, looking over at Delta and Mac, waiting for an explanation.

"You are standing where more than two dozen bodies were left after they were murdered. Some of them still don't have identities. Many are incomplete because of wild dogs and birds. But they weren't here alone. That's something else that isn't in the script, but that you should know. Not because it's in the mini-series. Not because one of you will have to act it out or because you'll need to know it for the role you're playing. But because you need to understand what really happened here." I point out of the field in the direction of Lilith's house. "That house."

"I can barely see it," someone says.

Marlowe takes a step forward. Her eyes are misty and the expression on her face is tight. "I see it."

"The woman who lived there was held in captivity by the same men who killed Lakyn Monroe and who scattered this ground with bones. They manipulated her and convinced her to kill her husband only to realize later she'd been betrayed. The man she thought loved her and would take care of her turned on her. He held the murder she committed over her and used that power to control her. She took care of this field. She witnessed the deaths of the women who were slaughtered here and watched what happened to their bodies. Fear kept her here and kept her silent.

"Right here, in this spot is where Lakyn lay dead and where Lilith did everything she could to honor and protect her. She covered her with a cage so the animals couldn't get to her. Even though she didn't know Lakyn or who she was, she knew there was something special about her. She told me she knew someone like her, who died fighting rather than pleading, would be missed. She wanted to make sure she was found.

"Lilith finally told all her secrets. She made sure we knew about the men of the Order and their gruesome crimes. And right here, where she tried to do something good in the midst of a life wasted and tortured, is where she knelt down and slit her wrists."

A couple of the people listening to me cover their mouths with their hands. They look down at their feet like they expect the blood to rise up through the dirt again. That they will suddenly be able to see Lilith lying there.

"She killed herself," one murmurs.

"She didn't die," Marlowe says, her eyes locked on me.

I shake my head. "No. She didn't. I held my hands over her wounds until help came. They were able to save her. But she will never be the same. She'll never be the woman she was before she got caught up in all this bloodshed. But she, like Lakyn, was brave. She spoke when she'd kept silent for years. What I want you to know, all of you, is that this is not a game. This right here is not a set. You're not telling a story someone conjured up. This isn't some goofy slasher people will want to watch on Halloween and laugh about with their friends.

"This is real. It happened to real people. And I knew them. I still know them. I visit Lilith in the hospital where she will live out the rest of her life. Xavier lives with my cousin and I consider him part of my family. And in his heart is Andrew Eagen, the man he was accused of murdering. That is a name you're not going to hear in this mini-series, but one every single one of you needs to say. He was killed for no other reason than to punish Xavier for uncovering the darkest secrets of the Order and the corruption within companies owned by its members. For that, he lost his best friend, the only person he trusted, and his freedom. And for that, Andrew lost his life.

"It is the responsibility of every single one of you to be honest and respectful when you tell this story. To take this seriously and know that you are telling their story because so many of them can't anymore."

I don't know how much of it really got through to them, but by the hushed looks to each other, it seems to be enough.

CHAPTER EIGHTEEN

THE GROUP IS SOMBER AS WE RETURN TO THE SET, BUT THERE'S something brewing. I can feel how what I said changed them. At least some of them. I'm not so naive that I think it influenced all of them. There are some of the guys who aren't going to care no matter what. To them, those deaths were no different than the make-believe ones they see on TV. They can't connect to them as people because their arrogance and immaturity make them only care about themselves and the people immediately around them.

But it affected the ones who matter. They will keep the others in line. This isn't funny anymore. It's not time for play. And the ones who forget that will be corrected swiftly. But even that isn't what matters the most. The important thing is that I said what needed to be said. I spoke their names and told their stories. I made sure that they weren't forgotten.

"Alright, everyone," Delta calls out as we get out of the vans. "Let's call that lunch and we'll reconvene later."

Rather than heading for the craft table, I hang back. When I'm alone, I take out my phone.

"Hello?" Xavier answers.

"I love you," I say.

"A bushel and a peck. From the bottom of my heart. Like a sister. Forever. Like a love song, baby." He takes a breath and pauses. "Who is this?"

"It's Emma."

I can hear him take the phone away from his head and look at the screen, then put it back to his ear.

"Hi, Emma. I love you, too."

I laugh softly and hear a shuffling sound as the phone is transferred.

"Emma?"

"Hey," I say to Dean. "What was that all about?"

"He's convinced he's going to be the random phone number called by a radio DJ and be expected to play some game for a prize," he says.

"Oh. What does he think he's going to win?"

"Nothing in particular," Dean tells me. "There isn't even a station he thinks is going to do it. He's just heard it's a thing that happens and is now worried he's going to be caught unprepared and be embarrassed."

"Well, that's good life preparedness," I note.

"Xavier is a good scout."

"Always prepared," we say at the same time.

"Is everything alright?" Dean asks when I don't laugh the way he does.

"Yeah," I say. "Everything's good. I'll see you tonight."

"See you tonight," he says. "And Emma?"

"Hmm?"

"For what it's worth, I love you, too, cousin."

I close my eyes, fighting tears I can't even fully explain. "I love you, Dean."

I'm putting my phone back in my pocket when Lewis, one of the security guards, comes up to me.

"Agent Griffin," he says.

"Yes?"

"The police are waiting for you at the craft tent."

"The police?" I raise an eyebrow.

A thousand thoughts start rushing through my mind. Does this have to do with Dean and Salvadore Marini? Have they found more members of the Order? Did something happen to Bellamy or Eric?

I thank him and rush toward the tent. I worry the other people on set will see the police and get upset. I wish the security guard hadn't sent them somewhere so public, but I also can't think of anywhere else more appropriate. Especially considering he didn't know how long it would be until we came back.

As soon as I get there, I start scanning the area for uniformed officers or agents in their suits. Instead, I see just one new face among the crowd. It makes my shoulders drop with relief and a smile comes to my lips even though the remains of tears are still trying to find their way out of my eyes.

Sam is sitting in the corner seat of one of the tables at the very edge of the tent, seeming to try to absorb as much of the afternoon sun as he can. He's staring down at his phone, and I almost laugh at the way his eyes are narrowed, his eyebrows pulled tightly together.

"Is that the I'm-not-getting-any-service face or the I-can't-figure-out-the-last-number-in-Sudoku face?" I call to him.

He looks up and grins. In an instant, I'm in his arms. He hugs me close, and I bury my head in his chest.

"I heard you brought everybody on a little excursion," he says. "From the way people around here look, it seems like it was a fun field trip."

"I brought them to the field of bones to tell them about Lakyn," I say. "And Lilith. And Millie." I let out a sigh. "And Andrew."

"Sudoku," he whispers into the top of my head after a stretch of silence to give me the time to push past the thoughts.

"Nine," I tell him. "It's always nine. You never remember to add enough nines."

"You're probably right." He kisses my head again. "I told you I'd be back in time to celebrate our anniversary."

"Thank you. I'm so glad you're here. I missed you."

"I missed you. We haven't even talked about what we want to do for our anniversary. It's our first. We should plan something special. What do you want to do?" he asks.

I burrow deeper into his chest. "Lock all the doors, pull down the shades, put on sweat suits, and curl up on the couch with all our favorite food and a marathon of worthless TV? What do you want to do?"

"I am up for anything as long as I'm with you and it doesn't involve a corpse," Sam replies.

I nod. "Tough, but fair."

I hold him for another second, then step back, but run my hand down his arm to hold his.

"Why are you wearing your uniform? The security guard told me that the police were waiting for me up here. I thought something had happened," I say.

"Sorry. I'm supposed to do a video conference with some people from Michigan in a little while and thought it might make me look more persuasive if I was in my uniform."

"A video conference? You just got here."

"I know," he says. "But that's actually why I'm having a video conference. I didn't want to stay around there anymore using up my vacation and leave time when nothing is really happening. They wanted to talk about the situation and some of the details, but I figured they could do that just as easily over a video conference as they could if I was sitting in the room with them."

"So, nothing new has come up in Marie's case?" I ask.

"Not really," he tells me. "I feel like we're spinning around at a dead end. It can seem like there might be some kind of movement, but then nothing comes of it."

I nod. "I know how that is. Are you hungry? Everybody's having lunch. There's a buffet."

Sam grins. "Have you ever known me to turn down a buffet?"

We go through the line to get food and then sit back at the table where he was. It keeps us a bit apart from the cast and crew, and I notice Paisley doesn't come to join me this time. I have a feeling she'll be keeping her distance for a while.

"Who are you having the conference with?" I ask as I drizzle dressing onto my salad and poke at it with my fork to distribute it around.

"The detectives handling her disappearance and then a private investigator. I want to ask them about how Marie's disappearance was initially handled, then compare their answers to what the investigator tells me," he says.

I nod. "That's a good idea. Ever since you told me about it, I've thought it sounded really strange that they didn't do a welfare check as soon as Rose realized she hadn't had any contact with Marie in over a day. That doesn't make any sense. I've never heard of a police department refusing to do a welfare check, even on an adult. It's not the same thing as reporting someone missing or starting a formal investigation into a disappearance."

"It really doesn't make sense," Sam agrees, spearing a potato wedge with his fork. "I didn't want to make waves and disrupt what investigation was going on, so I didn't argue with them. That's the way they said they did things around there, and I really had no place pushing back against them about it. Every department has the right to come up with its own policies and procedures. A welfare check isn't a law enforcement process. It's a courtesy. They don't have the right to kick down a door or anything, but I've never encountered a department that would refuse to go to the landlord or superintendent of a building to gain access to an apartment if the person who lives there hasn't been seen in a while."

"But you didn't want to shake things up and make them angry right off the bat," I say, understanding the situation.

"Exactly. I'm not really a part of the investigation. As much as I want to be, the reality is they are keeping me involved only out of professional courtesy and they could just as easily cut me off. Rose is so upset about the whole situation and already feels like they aren't doing enough. I haven't wanted to risk not being connected and her feeling like she's missing anything. It's just getting to the point where something needs to happen. They can't keep pretending Marie just wandered away or that there's nothing suspicious about her disappearance."

"Have they considered her disappearance has something to do with Rocky's death?" I ask.

"Not formally. Because there's still no clear answers as to what happened to him, they don't want to make what they consider a leap in connecting the two cases."

"I don't really think it's that much of a leap," I say.

"Neither do I. It feels like more of a stretch to say the two things aren't linked. But until they can construct some sort of explanation and timeline of his death, they're only thinking of it as an episode of prison violence. That's an easy thing to call it when they don't have any idea what happened and don't want to think they're missing something."

"Even though they don't have any idea what happened or how," I say. "Including how someone got near his cell undetected and then got out of the prison also undetected."

"Between this and Jonah, prison security really isn't looking too good these days," Sam mutters. He opens up his roll and shovels inside a mix of chicken and pasta salad, to make a miniature sandwich.

"Xavier offered to go undercover at Jonah's facility and try to figure out what happened," I tell him.

"Seriously?" Sam asks.

I nod and use my spoon to scoop up some of the thick, incredible-smelling loaded potato soup in front of me. The first bite warms me to my bones and I have to hold back an indulgent groan.

"Yeah," I say when I've gotten over the effect of the soup. "He thinks if we coordinate with the warden to have him processed in as a legitimate inmate and arrange for him to be put into the same area as Jonah, he could figure out the weaknesses of the prison and puzzle out what happened with Jonah."

"That's brilliant."

"Sam!" I admonish him. "It's ridiculous."

"Why?"

"You know what prison did to him. You think it's a good idea to put him back in that kind of environment?"

"I know what the warden did to him. Keep him away from sugar pills disguised as supplements and he'd probably be alright. According to Ava, he has a mean headbutt, so I figure he'd be pretty safe," Sam shrugs.

"I don't like the qualifier," I say.

He shrugs and starts to say something in response, but Marlowe walking up to us stops him.

"Emma?" she asks. Her voice sounds softer than it does when she's on set.

"Hi," I say, looking up at her, then look at Sam again and gesture toward Marlowe. "Oh. Sam, this is Marlowe Gray. I told you about her. She's playing Lakyn Monroe in the mini-series."

"That's right," Sam nods. "Nice to meet you, Marlowe."

"This is my husband, Sam," I tell Marlowe.

She nods at him in acknowledgment, then looks back at me. "Can you come to my place tonight to talk for a while?"

"Your place?" I ask.

She nods. "It's not too far from here."

I look over at Sam. "Sam just got back into town and…"

"No, it's fine," Sam insists. "You go. It will be better if it's just the two of you. I'll just go to the house and get some sleep. I'll see you when you get there."

"Are you sure?" I ask.

He nods again as he stands up. "Absolutely. I'm exhausted. I haven't been sleeping great while I've been in Michigan, so it will be nice to get some actual rest."

"When are you going back to Sherwood?"

"Day after tomorrow," he says.

"Alright. I'll see you later."

He leans down to kiss me. "I love you."

"Love you."

He leaves and I look over at Marlowe, wondering what she could want to talk about with me. She looks uneasy and I wonder who she's looking for as her eyes slide around the tent.

CHAPTER NINETEEN

"I JUST COULDN'T STAND THE IDEA OF SPENDING THE ENTIRE TIME we were on set living in a hotel or in my trailer," Marlowe says as we're on our way into the parking lot. "So, I rented an apartment. It's not too far from set, just in the next city over. It's a lot more comfortable. And I feel like I can actually get some privacy while I'm away from the set. When I'm at a hotel, there's always someone who's going to spill. Even though the directors or Frederic go ahead of my arrival and ask for discretion, it never actually works.

"Someone is always going to be the one who wants to feel special knowing I'm there and telling everybody. They want to be the one who gets to post it on social media or try to sell a picture of me to the paparazzi. I've actually been shuffled through the back and into freight elevators and stuff before just to avoid having to go through crowds, but there are still people who figure it out."

I can't say that I commiserate with her entirely. People know my name. They know who I am. But it's nothing like what Marlowe goes through. I can still walk around without having people rush up to me wanting an autograph. I can go to the grocery store in no makeup with my hair bundled up on top of my head wearing Sam's college sweatshirt and not worry I'm going to end up with a horrible headline over me on the front of a tabloid.

Marlowe's fame is still new in the greater scheme of things. It wasn't too long ago that she was just doing videos she posted online, just like Lakyn with her theme park review videos. But she caught traction. She's going somewhere. Just looking at her makes me worry she's going so fast she could lose her footing and the ground could get swept out from under her.

"This is me," I say when we get to my car. "I'll follow you."

She nods and I glance through the window into the back seat before climbing into the car. A quick look into the rearview mirror completes the ritual I've gotten down to a science in the years since my first undercover job. I sit behind the wheel and watch as Marlowe goes to the edge of the lot to where a car is waiting for her. I wonder if she gets tired of not driving herself.

I've heard so many times people talking about how nice it would be to have the kinds of service and attention as celebrities. A driver, a cook, a housekeeper. People to do all the things for them that they don't necessarily want to do for themselves. In a brief thought, it might seem like it would be great to have somebody doing all those things. But I couldn't imagine a life with that little control. It wasn't a luxury to give up everything, to not be able to go anywhere without asking someone else to be there for me. To always have someone else have a part in everything I did.

The car pulls out of the parking lot and I slide in behind it to follow. Just like Marlowe said, the drive isn't long. We're pulling into a driveway separated from an apartment building by a tall brick wall twenty minutes after we leave the parking lot and I notice the driver slow and lean out of the window to put a code into a keypad. My phone buzzes where I put it in the seat beside me and I pick it up. There's a text from a number I don't recognize with four numbers.

Ahead of me, Marlowe's car turns a corner and disappears. I pull into the place where it was and see a metal gate sliding closed around the corner. Leaning out of the window the way the driver had, I type the four numbers from the text into the keypad. The gate slides open and I drive through, thinking how strange it is for her to not only have my phone number, but to have given me the code to her building gate so easily.

The area behind the building is fairly small and I see the car parked at the very end of the lot. The driver is still behind the wheel, but I don't see Marlowe. I get out of the car and turn toward the building. Another wall similar to the one separating the drive from the building itself blocks the building from the lot, partitioning off what looks like a courtyard. A door sits off to the side of the wall, and I notice a pathway that leads around to the side of the building into the space between the building and the other wall.

Marlowe appears at the door and waves. I go to her, and she gives a hint of a smile.

"I hope you don't mind that I have your number," she says. "Delta gave it to me."

She doesn't offer any sort of explanation as to why the producer gave it to her, or if she asked for it. I nod, not really knowing what to say. She lets me through the door and as it's closing behind us, I hear the engine of the car start up behind me. I'm guessing the driver waits for her to go inside before leaving any time he drops her off if she doesn't have security with her. Even with a code required to enter the area, I can understand the compulsion to be sure she's safe before she's out of sight.

The door leads onto a square area that takes up the back of the building but is blocked off from the side by another brick wall. The strange honeycomb of brick walls feels like it's getting tighter, closing in around me as Marlowe leads me toward the building. Small flower beds are lining both sides, but the winter weather keeps them sleeping. This is the kind of area where I'd expect to see furniture, maybe a grill, but there's nothing. It's a temporary home, so she hasn't seen any point in settling all the way in.

I look up at the building as we walk across the concrete space, trying to judge how many apartments might be inside. It's not a huge building, but it does look like at least four stories. There are no windows for the first story and I notice the upper floor has a large balcony that stretches across the building.

She gets to the door and punches buttons on the keypad beside it. Opening the door, she stands back and gestures for me to go in first. I'm expecting to walk into a room in the apartment. Instead, I'm at the foot of a flight of steps. There are mirrors on either wall, reflecting the area beneath the steps, and bright lights lining the walls and hanging overhead on the landing above.

I climb up to the landing, then look down at Marlowe. She gives a slight nod like she's telling me to keep going, so I continue on. The steps wind up through the building and eventually reach a hallway with a door that looks like it leads into the apartment. I step back so Marlowe can unlock it and we go inside.

"How many apartments are in this building?" I ask.

"Hmm?" Marlowe asks, turning to look at me from where she's kicking off her shoes in the corner.

"I was just noticing the way the steps led up here from the back. I was wondering how many other apartments are in the building."

"Oh," she says, making her way down a hall that leads further into the apartment. "I think there are three others. Two on the bottom and another like this on the other side." She gestures vaguely toward that side of the building. "I haven't really gotten to know any of the neighbors."

The apartment is what I would expect from someone just temporarily taking up the space. It obviously came furnished and has an almost generic air to it, but there are a few touches Marlowe has added to make it more hers. I notice a couple of framed pictures and a messy stack of mail. Shoes sit in different corners and a couple of articles of clothing are draped on the backs of furniture in that way people do to be able to stand back and look at them when considering what to wear.

She doesn't make any moves to clean up or give the hollow apologies that are so frequent when walking into a vaguely messy space, which I appreciate. I think those sentiments are meant to make a visitor feel more at ease, but they've always just made me uncomfortable. It's like I'm being passively aggressively scolded for noticing something before I can make a comment about it.

I stay in the front of the apartment and a few moments later, Marlowe comes back in sweatpants and a long-sleeve t-shirt. She still has her makeup on, so I assume she'll go through the full process of showering and getting ready for bed when I leave, but she didn't want to stay in her clothes any longer. She's carrying a plastic tote like I saw people who lived in the dorms in college use when going to shower in the shared bathrooms. When she plops down on the couch, she sets the tote onto the table in front of her.

"Come sit," she says, gesturing toward the chair beside her with her eyes. I sit down and watch as she reaches into the tote for cotton balls and a container of nail polish remover. She props her foot on the edge of the table, then looks at me. "Do you mind?"

I shake my head. "Go for it."

Taking the top off the bottle, she sets a cotton ball on it and tips the bottle to the side to absorb the chemical inside. The sharp smell comes to my nostrils, bringing to mind a strangely vivid memory of sitting beside my mother while she took off fingernail polish she'd put on for a Christmas party. Red glitter. I thought it was amazing. She found bits of it in her cuticles for days.

"This is my nightly routine," she explains, going to work on the polish on one toe. "I know it's weird. I don't even remember how I got into it, but every night as soon as I get home, I take off my toenail polish. Then I just put it right back on in the morning. It makes no sense."

She lets out a small laugh and I shrug.

"My best friend eats cinnamon rolls right out of the pan by

unraveling them. Sam eats all types of cereal except for the cinnamon toast kind sitting at the table, but that he has to eat standing over the kitchen sink. Xavier bakes gingerbread men in the middle of the night immediately after Thanksgiving dinner. We all have a thing."

She nods as she continues along her toes. "You really do spend time with him."

It's somewhere between a statement and a question. Like she's acknowledging it, but also asking for one more confirmation.

"I do," I confirm. "I'm staying at his house while I'm consulting on the project."

She looks at me intensely. "Everything you said about him… it was true."

"Yes."

"He didn't sound real when I first heard about him."

"I can understand that."

She focuses on her toes for a few more seconds. "Why do you think she wanted to help him?"

"Lakyn?" I ask.

Marlowe nods. "She didn't know him. She didn't know the man they accused him of killing."

"Andrew," I say, remembering my promise to Xavier.

"Andrew," Marlowe says. "She probably didn't even pay attention to the news at her age when it all happened. So, why? Why would she go through all of that for him?"

"She wanted to help people," I shrug. "Innocent people are put in prison every year. Some spend many years there or are even executed for things they didn't do. It doesn't happen frequently, but it can. She wanted to prevent that."

Marlowe seems to think as she finishes one foot and moves onto the other.

"I wonder if she ever thought about anyone helping her," she says.

CHAPTER TWENTY

It's quiet, almost under her breath, and I think she might not have meant to say it out loud. I wait for her to elaborate, or to say something to cover it up, but she doesn't do either.

"Is there something you needed to talk to me about?" I ask. "Something about the case you want to know more about?"

Marlowe shakes her head. "I just thought it would be nice to get to know you better. I feel like I can trust you."

There's a lingering pause and I can almost hear what she isn't saying. She isn't saying that she doesn't feel like that about other people in her life. I think about the code she gave so freely. It could be something she changes frequently so it wouldn't really matter if I have it just for tonight. But it could also be a grab for that feeling, a way to connect us. She wants to trust me, so she threw something at me to seal it.

And at the same time, it almost feels like a test. Not to see if she can trust me, but to see if she can trust her own instincts. She feels like she can trust me, but she has no control over her life. She doesn't make her own choices. Now she wants to see if she can.

"You can," I tell her. I don't know if she actually needs to hear that from me, but I offer it up anyway.

"What did my mother tell you about me?" she asks.

That wasn't what I expected to come next in this conversation.

"Nothing really," I say. "I didn't get much of a chance to talk with her. Just briefly before I saw some footage with Delta. She seems to be really excited about this project."

Marlowe nods and puts her foot down, finished with her routine for the evening. She scoops up all the used cotton balls and brings them into the kitchen where she throws them away.

"She thinks this is going to be my big break," she calls over her shoulder.

There's no excitement in the statement. Instead, the edge is almost sarcastic.

"What about you?" I ask. "What do you think about this project?"

"If people like it, I think it could be good for my career," she shrugs.

"That's not what I asked," I point out.

"I know," she says. "But it never matters what I think about a role. That's not the point."

"What do you mean?"

She sits down again. "The first part of an actress's career is about getting noticed and holding people's attention. The next part is about doing roles that will build up her reputation and keep her in front of people so she'll be in demand and keep getting jobs. Once she's successful enough to sustain a career without constant work and her name is known across demographics, then she can start doing things she actually cares about."

Marlowe sounds like she's reading from a twisted, outdated book of acting advice. The distance she puts between herself and her career with every time she says "she" makes the words more uncomfortable. I wonder who has said those words to her and how many times it took to burrow them so deep under her skin.

"Maybe," I say. "I mean, this isn't my industry. Obviously, I don't know everything about it. Or even much about it, really. I guess that could be right if all you care about is commercial success. But if you chose this career because of a desire to create and for artistic expression, you should at least have thoughts about the projects you do. You don't have to be completely in love with everything and I'm sure the vast majority of actors would say they've done things just for the paycheck. But that doesn't mean you need to put aside any thoughts of caring about the roles you do just because you haven't been acting for a long time. Again, though, I could be talking totally out of turn. I hate when people try to tell me how to do my job, so I shouldn't be telling you how to do yours."

"It's alright," she says quickly. "I appreciate you saying that. Sometimes I forget why I got here at all."

"What do you mean?" I ask.

"It all happened so fast. Sometimes I feel like I've lived someone else's life this whole time. Not just when I'm on set. All the time. It's like I'm looking in and seeing myself doing all these things and it seems too good to really be my life. I've dreamed about being famous. About the money and the recognition. About being able to live the kind of life you see on magazine covers. Sometimes I wake up in the middle of the night and I wonder if I'm actually doing this. Like I think it's all been just a long, elaborate dream and I'm going to climb out of bed and be back in that cramped apartment, wondering what the hell I was going to do with my life."

"So, you didn't always want to act?" I ask.

"I always wanted to be successful," she says. "And I like to perform."

Yet again, that doesn't really feel like an answer to my question.

"Is it everything you hoped for?" I ask.

A slight veil goes over her eyes. She described her life as "too good", but it doesn't feel like she meant it in the way she hopes it would be heard.

"I didn't know what to expect, so I didn't really hope for anything except to make money and I'm doing that. Like I said, one day when I'm successful, I can think about what I really want and do projects that matter. For now, I need people to know who I am," she says. "And they do. I have more than a million followers. I can't keep up with the messages and emails and things I get in the mail. There are people out there who look forward to watching me. That's the beginning," Marlowe says.

I can tell she has more of a drive for acting than Lakyn did. But there's something behind her eyes I can't figure out. I can't imagine trusting the words she regurgitated out to me about her career. They made her sound like a puppet just waiting to one day be a real girl.

Then again, maybe she doesn't really trust those words. They're just what she knows and she's starting to understand there is more to them than the surface skimmed across by whoever said them to her. I can tell the conversation is getting to her, so I steer it in another direction but still skirt along the edge.

"I can't even begin to imagine having that many followers. I don't even do social media," I offer.

"Neither do I," she says, actually letting out a tiny laugh. "At least, not anymore. I used to have my own, but it was too easy for people to try to get close to me through the personal one I handled. Now Brittany takes care of all that. That's her place and she's good at it."

"What exactly does she do?" I ask.

"She posts things about me. Or for me. When I make a video for my virtual fan club, she posts it and does the engagement," she explains.

"Delta was talking about that, too," I say. "What is a virtual fan club? I have trouble wrapping my head around the idea of a fan club at all, so you're really going to have to break this down for me. I thought fan clubs were about like sending out signed photographs and doing special appearances. How do you do that virtually?"

"Well, it is that kind of stuff, but the appearances are online and are a lot more frequent. Fans subscribe and the amount of money they pay every month determines what level of the club they are in, and the kinds of perks they can get. So, Brittany handles things like sending out photographs or special merchandise, but then I also make videos and things that are posted only for the people in the club," she says.

"That sounds like a lot of work," I note.

"It's her job," Marlowe says. "She's not doing it as a favor. And those are the things she's good at. Behind the scenes. She hasn't had to want for a job since I started getting regular roles."

"It must be good to have your best friend with you all the time," I say. "My best friends work for the Bureau, too. But we don't live near each other or see each other nearly as often as we used to."

Marlowe nods. "It is." She looks over to the side, then back at me. This time, there's a bit of a smile on her lips. "Do you want to see my favorite part of this place?"

"Sure," I say.

She gets up and heads over to the huge window across the back of the room. It's the one I saw stretching across the building in front of the balcony. She uses a handle to open a door disguised to look like a segment of the window. She steps out and I follow her. I shudder in the sharp wind that whips up around us, but she barely seems to notice it.

"This was the selling point for this place. I had already looked at a couple of other apartments and hadn't found one that was what I wanted, but then I saw this." Her hands slide over the curved cement edge of the wall around the balcony. "It reminds me of a balance beam. Sometimes, I just have to..." she suddenly jumps up onto the edge.

"Marlowe!" I gasp. "Stop. Get down."

She spreads her arms open to the sides. "It feels so good up here. So free." She takes a few steps. "Nothing up here has any expectations of me. It doesn't want anything from me. It won't tell me what to do. Everything is perfect."

"Marlowe," I say again. "You need to get down."

She turns to me, the widest smile I've seen on her face. "Emma. Don't be afraid. I'm not going to fall."

CHAPTER TWENTY-ONE

THE IMAGE OF HER ON THAT LEDGE STAYS WITH ME EVEN AS SHE walks me back down the stairs toward the parking lot. The rest of our conversation had been unremarkable, and I wonder if she really had just asked me to come because she wanted to spend time with me away from the set and the rest of the cast and crew, or if there was something else she planned on saying, but couldn't bring herself to once I was there.

As we get to the door leading out into the parking lot, I half expect Marlowe to stop and say goodbye to me still within the walls of the courtyard. I realize how strange that thought is when she follows me out. There shouldn't be a reason for her to cloister herself. I understood her compulsion to have security, but she shouldn't have to hide away from everything, especially so close to her own home.

"Do you have any plans for the weekend off?" she asks as we walk toward my car.

"Well, it's not off for me," I tell her. "I have cases I'm investigating, so I'll be working on those. Dean is also working on a couple of cases that have been really complicated, so I might help him with those as well. I want to spend as much time with Sam as I can before he leaves town again, too."

"Sounds busy," she comments.

"That tends to be my life," I tell her. "What about you? What are you doing?"

"I guess I don't really have it off, either. I'll be studying the script and doing some extra rehearsing for the scenes coming up next week. It feels a little odd to still be preparing for scenes when my character is now dead, but that's how it goes," she shrugs. "I also have to meet with Frederic about some contract negotiations, and Brittany and I are getting some extra content done so it can be scheduled for the last push of the shooting schedule and the few days I want to take off over the holidays and my birthday."

"Sounds like you're busy, too," I say.

"I try to keep it that way. It makes it easier," she says.

I'm about to ask her what she means when her eyes move to the side of the parking lot like she hears something I didn't. I follow them and see a man coming down the pathway that leads around the side of the building. He's concentrating on his phone in his hand but looks up when he gets to the parking lot. There's a car parked in the shadows that I didn't notice when we first came back out and that I'm sure wasn't there when we got here, but he doesn't walk toward it. Instead, he strolls toward Marlowe.

His casual gait and focused look in his eye aren't matched by Marlowe's reaction to him. She doesn't smile or greet him. She doesn't move toward him. There's no emotion as she seems to wait passively beside me, like there's nothing she can do about his inevitable approach.

"Evening, Marlowe," he greets her.

"Hey, Branson," she says.

"How are you doing?"

"I'm fine."

"Good. Good."

He glances over at me and I extend my hand.

"Agent Emma Griffin."

He shifts a bright green dog leash from where it was wrapped around one hand into the other so he can shake my hand.

"Agent?"

"FBI," I clarify.

He nods, recognition flickering in his eyes. "That's right. You worked on the case Marlowe's new project is based on."

"I did," I confirm. "And you are?"

"My neighbor," Marlowe says. "He lives in the other upstairs apartment."

"I was just heading out for the night. Got to get myself into a little bit of trouble. Nobody's going to do it for me. Right?"

He laughs at his own uncomfortable joke while Marlowe and I stay silent. With a little wave that shows he didn't even notice we weren't in on him thinking how amusing he was, he backs off a few steps, turns, and heads for the other car.

"I thought you didn't know your neighbors," I say when he gets behind the wheel.

"I know of him," Marlowe says. "That's about the extent of our interaction. We run into each other in the parking lot sometimes, so we introduced ourselves."

"But I'm assuming he already knew who you are." She searches my face like she's trying to figure out why I would say that. "He mentioned the series, but the way you reacted to him didn't seem like the two of you are on the kind of terms that would involve a conversation about your career to that level. It just doesn't seem like you would stand around telling him about the series or the story that it's based on. Not enough for him to recognize my name, anyway. Which means he was likely already familiar with you and your career and had heard about the project through entertainment news."

Marlowe nods. "Wow."

"What?" I ask.

"I just feel like I've been FBI-ed," she says.

That makes me chuckle. "I don't know that I've ever heard someone use the acronym as a verb."

She smiles. "Well, it definitely is when it comes to what you just did. You're right. Branson already knew who I was the first time we spoke to each other. I'd seen him a couple of times, but he didn't say anything. I got the impression it was because I was always with security or my driver and he didn't want to deal with that. But I went out for a jog one day and when I came back he was getting out of his car and he introduced himself. He already knew who I was and told me he was a fan and was looking forward to the mini-series because he had followed the case."

She doesn't give off the impression that she's creeped out by the man, even though he looked a bit older than her. It's more like he's just a part of what she deals with. I can imagine it's far better to have just one person who she might run into who will see her as a public figure rather than a person, than it would be to have an entire hotel full of them.

"You go out jogging by yourself?" I raise an eyebrow. "You're not concerned people are going to recognize you?"

Marlowe leans toward me slightly. "I go incognito. It's amazing what a hat and some big glasses can do, especially when I don't wear makeup and put my hair up." She straightens. "It's just a little bit of freedom. I need that sometimes. My mother and Frederic don't know I do it."

She doesn't ask me not to say anything about it, but the implication pulls heavily on the words.

"I think everybody needs that," I reassure her. "Have a good weekend."

I get in my car and head back to Xavier's house. Meeting Branson has me thinking about the other people who live in the building. She described him as living in the other upstairs apartment and told me she thinks there are two on the bottom. From the way her balcony stretches across the back of the building like her courtyard does, but the stairwell only takes up a portion of it, I assume the downstairs apartments are smaller, taking up only the corners of the building and likely just the first two floors.

Her apartment was made into an L-shape, which is probably separated from Branson's by a stairwell leading into the center where the two L shapes would come together. That puts the four spaces at diagonals to each other, creating an arrangement that nestles the living spaces in with each other, but has none of them directly next to each other.

The way the path leads up the side of the building and her courtyard takes up the entire back tells me there is likely a balcony on the side of the building I didn't notice and that is positioned so it can't look down into Marlowe's courtyard, the same way hers is made so it wouldn't look down into the courtyard I'm assuming goes along with the other side. That configuration along with the brick walls establishing almost foreboding barriers creates a sense of isolation. If there are other people living in those apartments, it wouldn't surprise me if they had never encountered Marlowe and didn't even know she was living there.

I get back to Dean and Xavier's house fairly late, but there are still lights glowing in the windows. I'm not surprised. Sam wouldn't want to go to bed without me being home. And Xavier is likely making up for all the conversations he hasn't been able to have with Sam while he's been in Michigan.

When I get inside, I can hear the three of them talking. Their voices are animated and when I get into the living room, Dean gets up and comes toward me.

"Mark Webber is talking."

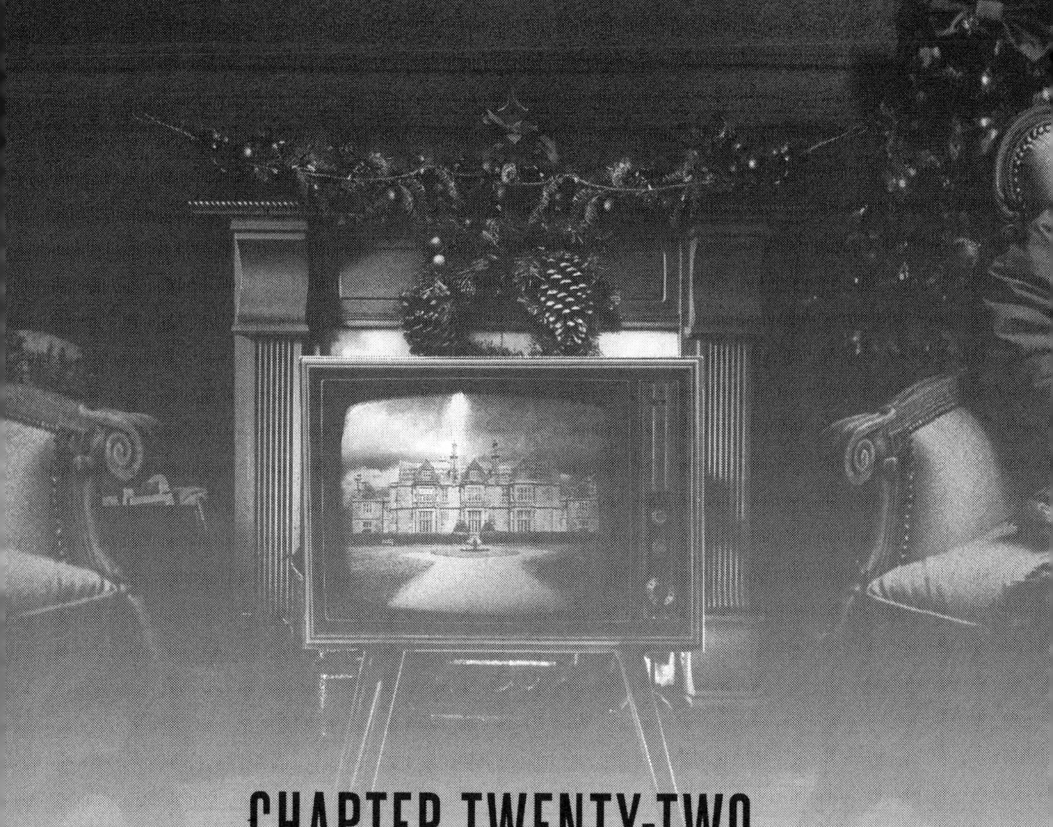

CHAPTER TWENTY-TWO

I SIT DOWN ON THE COUCH NEXT TO SAM AND LISTEN TO DEAN TELL me about the call he got just shortly before I made it back to the house. Noah called him to let him know that the hospital called him and told him Mark Webber was ready to talk. He'd finally recovered enough and was feeling strong enough to tell us about what happened to him.

It's something we've been waiting for since Eric nearly died using himself as bait to uncover the truth behind Dean's abduction. While him essentially handing himself over to the Emperor to be transformed into a gladiator and used for sport hadn't actually gotten us the details we need about what happened to Dean, they have helped us better understand Salvador Marini and his gruesome string of crimes.

But there's so much more to know. And now we have a chance of getting that information.

"He doesn't want to talk about all of it over the phone," Dean says. "He wants to meet with us to talk about it in person."

"I can understand that," I nod. "But he did give an indication that he remembers things? Enough to corroborate what we already know?"

"Noah said he mentioned fighting and that he wants to give us details," Dean says.

"It sounds promising," Sam notes.

I nod. "When does he want to talk?"

"As soon as possible."

"I don't have to be back on set for a couple of days. We can go tomorrow."

Curled into Sam's arms that night, I finally sleep. It doesn't last nearly as long as I would have wanted, but when I wake up just before the sun the next morning, I feel more rested than I have in a while.

We use an address Noah gave us to go to a small house in a town nearly an hour from Harlan. Noah is already waiting in the driveway, leaning back against his cruiser with his head tucked down toward his shoulders so the collar of his jacket covers as much of his neck and ears as possible. Steam from the cup of coffee in his hand rises up through the cold air. He's holding it close to his face, but I don't see him take a sip. It's like he has it just for its warmth.

"Good morning," he greets us as we all climb out of the car. "Got the whole crew, I see."

"Hey, Noah. Do you think having us all around will overwhelm him?" I ask.

"We'll see. He sounded pretty put together when he called last night. I'll admit, it was a shock and a half to hear from him. Especially so late. I left my direct number at the hospital so he could get in touch whenever he was ready, but that was a surprise," Noah says.

"You never know when someone is going to decide they're ready to talk about something," I say. "Maybe something happened yesterday that triggered more memories or made him just feel like he couldn't hold it all in anymore."

"Doesn't matter why he wants to talk," Dean says. "What matters is he wants to talk. So, let's get in there."

He's determined as he takes long strides up the walkway to the front door. He's ringing the bell before we even get all the way to the porch with him. The man who opens the door looks decidedly healthier and stronger than the version of him I saw in the hospital just after we rescued both Eric and him from the gladiator arena. He's confused to see Dean standing in front of him and I notice he keeps the door part of the way closed. If I don't miss my guess, he has one foot firmly planted behind it so he can close it quickly if he needs to.

"Mr. Webber," Noah says from behind me.

Mark Webber looks his way. "Detective Smith." He notices me. "Agent Griffin."

"Are you still up for talking?" Noah asks.

"This is Dean Steele," I say, gesturing to Dean as I step up beside him. "We think he went through the same thing you did. And this is Sam Johnson, my husband. And this is Xavier..."

My voice trails off as I think of a reason why he's here with us.

"I'm an unwitness to what happened to Dean," Xavier fills in for me.

Mark looks at me with the inevitable question in his eyes.

"We think Dean was abducted outside a house and Xavier was inside it at the time," I explain.

Mark nods. He looks at each of us again as if he's evaluating whether he's really ready for this, then steps back and lets us inside. We settle in the living room and he offers us coffee. None of us accept. We just want to get down to the conversation.

"Mr. Webber," Noah starts.

"Mark," he corrects him.

"Mark. When you called me, you said you are ready to talk about what happened to you before you were rescued from the arena. First,

I want you to tell us what you remember about what happened there. What you were doing in that place."

He's being as careful as he can not to lead Mark with the words he chooses to describe the arena. He doesn't want to influence the way he talks about his experiences or what he says happened there. I know where he was because I was there. Like the other one we found, it was an underground structure built with a large open space in the middle, surrounded by observation balconies overlooking the space, hallways encircling it, and rooms coming off the hallways. Some of those rooms appeared to be offices and storage, but most were cells.

"Trying to survive," Mark says without hesitation. "From the second I got there, I had to fight to stay alive."

"The fight against Agent Hernandez was not your first?" Noah asks.

We already know it wasn't. The doctors detailed a long list of injuries he had sustained and described many of them as being in various states of healing. He had been through a lot before we found him trying to rip Eric apart with his bare hands. The gunshot wound should have killed him. Instead, his body seemed to simply shut down when it happened, like that was the final thing that needed to happen for it to stop trying to keep going and instead change the meaning of fighting to live.

But we have to let him tell us in his own words.

"No," he says. "I fought many times before that."

"How long were you there?" I ask.

"At least two weeks. But I don't remember exactly how I got there. The day I was taken isn't very clear. I just remember waking up with my face in the dirt and a man running at me with a spear."

"You weren't even conscious when you were brought into the arena for the first time?" I ask.

He shakes his head. "No. I have a few flashes of someone picking me up under my arms and dragging me into a building. But I can't remember how I got there or what happened before."

"How many fights were you in?" Dean asks.

"I remember six," he says.

"You were there for two weeks," Noah says. "If you fought six times, where were you on the other days?"

"In a cell or a training yard. There was no light and almost no ventilation in the cell, but if I was in the training yard where there was more light and air, the man wearing the mask forced me to exercise and train the entire time. If I stopped for more than a few seconds, he used a cattle prod or a hot poker on me.

"There was light and air," Sam points out. "So, you were outside? The training yard wasn't underground?"

"I don't know," Mark tells us. "I couldn't see the sky or the sun. There was a roof above me and no windows. But it didn't feel as closed off as the cell."

"Could that be how you got out?" Noah asks Dean. "Maybe you didn't actually escape from an arena, but a training yard that got you outside?"

"Got out?" Mark asks, his eyes snapping back and forth between Dean and Noah. "What do you mean got out?"

"I was abducted from in front of my house and found by the side of the road, unconscious. I was beaten to hell but didn't have any idea what happened. I remembered a woman's voice, the sound of a gunshot, and a dirt floor. But I didn't know where I was or what I was doing," Dean tells him.

"That's one of the biggest reasons we wanted to talk to you," I explain. "We're hoping the information you can give us will help us figure out what happened to Dean, and if there are others."

"You got out?" Mark says again. "How many times did you fight?"

"Once," Dean says. "I think. I don't remember. But I was only missing a few hours."

The color drains from Mark's face and he looks like he might get sick. His face drops into his hands.

"Mark," I say as carefully as I can. "What happened to the men you fought?"

All he can do is sob.

CHAPTER TWENTY-THREE

"HE WAS REPORTED MISSING ABOUT TWO WEEKS BEFORE HE WAS found, just like he said," Noah states, coming into the room with a file. "But it wasn't filed by anyone in his life."

"What do you mean?" I ask.

He sits down across the table from me and turns the file so I can look at it. "His car was found abandoned by the side of the road. When the police ran the tag, they traced who it belonged to and tried to get in touch with him, but he didn't respond. They went to his house and it was empty, mail and newspapers built up for a few days."

"His work didn't report him not coming in?" I ask.

"Apparently, he worked from home most of the time and he wasn't exactly the most reliable of employees. He'd actually just been fired."

"So, he wouldn't have been reporting for work anyway," I say with a sigh. "There was no one to notice he was gone."

"Exactly."

"So, what happened after they found the car and realized he had disappeared?"

"They did a welfare check in the house and he wasn't there, but there weren't any signs of any foul play. Nothing broken or out of place. No blood. Just a basic house. It took a couple days, but they found out the last time he was seen was at a bar in the next town over. According to the bartender, he got angry when he was told he'd had enough and he stormed out."

"I think we need to have a conversation with that bartender," I say.

~

When Noah told me Mark Webber was last seen at a bar, I envisioned a seedy, rundown dive where someone would go drink themselves into oblivion. Instead, I find a far more modern version that looks like it's trying to resemble one of those places but still wants to be a bit glossy.

It's too early for there to be a lot of drinking going on, but the man behind the bar is preparing for the waves of patrons to come in later. He stands in the neon pink of a lighted sign advertising some new trendy liquor, drying glasses with a white cloth. Around him, music pulses but there's no one to dance and no voices to balance out the sound.

I drum on the bar with my knuckles to get his attention and he looks up at me, seemingly unconcerned with my presence. I gesture toward the speakers anchored above the bar and he uses a remote to turn the volume down to a point where I can hear myself think again. Maybe it's a sign of my age, but music that loud is no longer amusing to me. Instead, it makes me feel like my brain is going to liquefy.

"Sorry," the bartender says. "Just filling up the silence before the customers come in, you know."

"Sure. I'm looking for Bentley Joseph," I say.

"I'm Bentley," he says.

"I'm Agent Emma Griffin. I'm investigating a case and I think you might have some information that could help me," I say.

"A case?" he raises an eyebrow. "I don't know anything about a crime. Nothing has happened around here."

"Don't worry," I say. "No one thinks it has anything to do with the bar. It's just that one of the people involved was last seen here. Does the name Mark Webber mean anything to you?"

"Mark Webber," he echos, low under his breath like he's just trying the name out to see if he's said it before. He shakes his head. "It sounds familiar, but I can't place it. I see a lot of people in here every day. Unless they're a regular for a few months, I'm probably not going to remember them by name. I'm sorry."

"No problem. Here. Look at this picture and tell me if you recognize him."

I show him a picture of Mark from before the incident and the bartender immediately nods. "Yeah. I do remember that guy." He takes a few steps down the bar and reaches out for something. When he comes back to me, he's holding something he flattens on the bar in front of me. It's a picture of Mark. "He's on our do not serve list."

"Why's that?" I ask.

"Because he came in here one too many times causing shit and pissing me and my staff off," he says.

"So, you own this place as well as tend the bar?" I ask.

Bentley nods. "I do. I built it from the ground up and I hate it when people like this ass come in and cause issues. I threw him out and put him on the list. Police already came and talked to me about this. It didn't click when you first asked about him. That was a while ago. He's still missing?"

"No," I tell him. "But he looks like this now."

I take out a picture of Mark's injuries and Bentley recoils.

"Holy shit. What happened to him?" he asks.

"That's kind of what we're trying to figure out. What can you tell me about the last time he was in here?" I ask.

"He came in here wanting to talk. Which is fine. A lot of people want to think of me as their therapist. I guess it beats the price of a real one and comes with alcohol, so it's a pretty good deal. He was talking about losing his job and his girlfriend leaving him. Just life happening, but it was hitting him hard. He just kept drinking and kept drinking. Finally, I told him he'd had enough and I wasn't going to serve him anymore. He was furious and made a scene, screaming and yelling, knocking stuff over. I told him to cut it out, but he was riled up."

"If he was that drunk and causing that much trouble, why did you let him drive away?" I ask.

"I didn't," he says firmly. "I'd never do that. I do have some level of concern for other human life. Besides, if he got in a crash or something and the law found out I'd over-served him then let him drive away, I could lose my license and get sued. I made him give me his keys and called a cab. But it turned out he'd given me the wrong ones. He slipped out before the cab got here.

"So, I called the cops. They came and gave me all sorts of shit for losing him, but I hadn't done anything wrong. I went through the process exactly like I was supposed to. He just managed to get away."

"Did you make a police report?" I ask.

He nods. "Yes. He'd left without paying his tab, damaged the bar, and was driving with way too much alcohol in him. I wasn't going to just let that slide. If nothing else, I needed to cover my own ass. Making the report recorded that I had refused to serve him more and did go through the process of getting him a different ride home in good faith he would actually give me his keys when asked."

"Do you remember anything else about him or about the night he was here? Someone he was talking to, or someone who didn't seem familiar who was hanging out at the bar when he was here, but left around the same time Mark did?" I ask.

Bentley shakes his head. "Not that I can remember."

"How about any of the other nights he's come in?"

"No. Sorry. As I mentioned, we can get pretty busy. It's hard to notice people if they don't bring attention to themselves."

"Alright. Thank you," I say. "You were really helpful."

~

The next morning I'm sitting in the kitchen drinking coffee and eating part of a cinnamon roll when Dean comes in.

"You the only one up?" he asks.

"I think so," I say, not taking my eyes off my phone to answer or to pull off another piece of roll.

"What are you so invested in?" he asks after pouring his own coffee and coming around to stand beside me so he can look at the screen over my shoulder.

"A video Noah had sent to me from the police department near where Mark Webber lives. The bartender told me he made a police report about him. That made me wonder if they sent out a car to look for him, so I requested his information and got this. It's a dash cam video."

Dean takes the phone and resets the video. "Is that Webber being pulled over?"

"Yes. He was pulled over for speeding, but nowhere near where his car was found. Now, watch what he does when the officer gets him out of the car," I say.

We watch as a uniformed officer approaches the back of Mark's car. He lightly touches the car like police do to leave their fingerprints, then walks up to the driver's side door. He leans in and they talk for a few seconds before he steps back and Mark climbs out.

"He's doing field sobriety tests," Dean observes.

"Yes, he is," I nod. "But watch."

He gets through each of them perfectly fine.

"He's had that much to drink, was so drunk he got kicked out of the bar, and yet he's able to make it through the tests without any indication he's drunk?" Dean sputters. He watches a few more seconds and lets out a stunned scoff. "And he just drove away. He's that drunk, yet he completely gets away with it. How is that even possible?" he asks.

"I don't know."

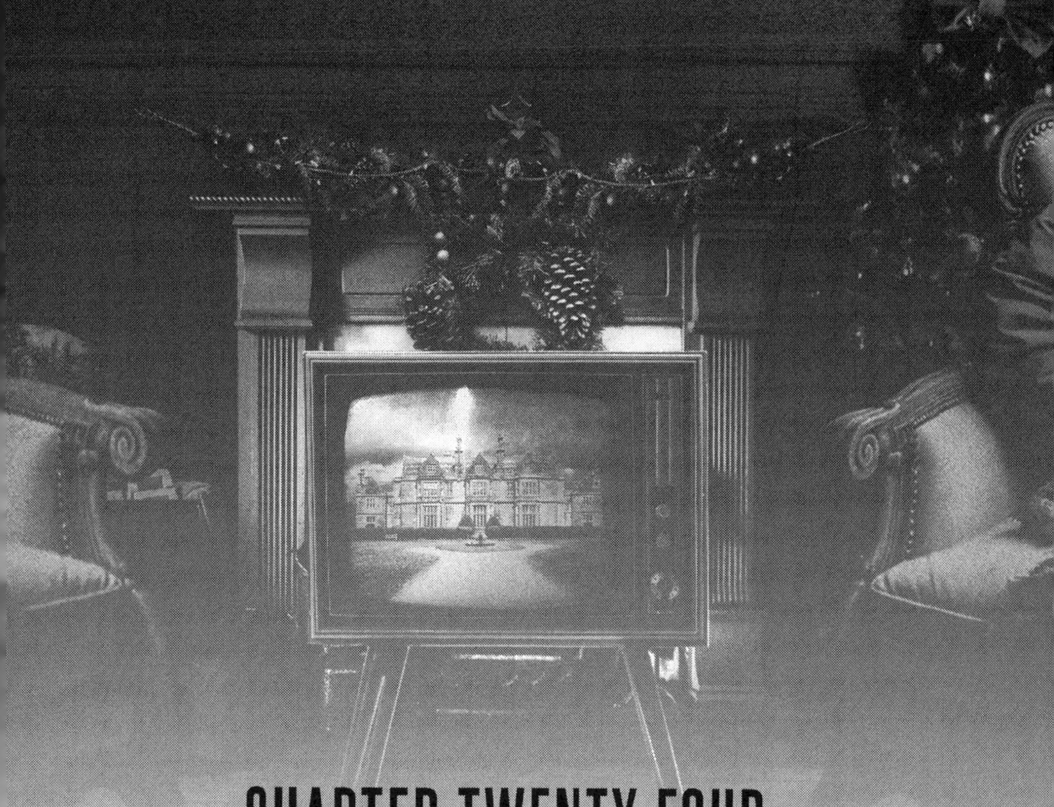

CHAPTER TWENTY-FOUR

Going back to the set after spending the weekend trying to unravel another shadowy layer of the Emperor and his bloody legacy feels surreal. It was already strange to begin with, traipsing through recreated versions of places I've been and things I've seen. To hear fictionalized versions of conversations I had and heard. But now I'm jumping from the depths of a very real tangled mess still being navigated to a cold, murky fantasy mixed with stark reality risen up to the surface from years ago.

An icy morning without any scenes I would be a part of means I don't have to be on set until early in the afternoon. I get there as everyone is breaking for lunch, but I've already eaten. Rather than going to the tent, I go to find Delta to talk to her about the rest of the filming schedule. I know it's been thrown off by some of the changes and I want to make sure she understands I still fully intend on not being here on my anniversary or over the Christmas break. It's not that

I want to be mean to her or make her feel like I don't want to be a part of this. It's just that I've now seen how fluid these shoots can be and know it's possible, if not probable, she'll make changes that would interfere with what I've already planned.

It's my first anniversary with Sam and I'm not going to put him aside. I haven't admitted it to anyone, including myself, but I know I've done that far too many times over the years. All too often, I've immersed myself so much in cases I've lost touch with my life beyond the Bureau. I've pushed aside the things that made me my own person and the people I love. There have been times where I had such blinders on that I didn't think about the fact that I could really lose them permanently, and when those thoughts did come into my mind, I convinced myself if that happened, it was the sacrifice I had to make to do what needed to be done.

That's not an option for me now. I can have both. I won't so easily lay down the things that give my life meaning beyond my badge.

"I told you the program must have glitched. We went over this the other night."

My thoughts are broken by the sound of Frederic's voice. The words are kept low enough I would almost describe them as being hissed. I look around for him but don't see him.

"The point of a program like that is to prevent mistakes, not make them. I don't understand how you could say something like this just happened."

This time it's Marlowe's voice. There's venom in it and I can't help but think about her manager being in her trailer the other night. She'd mentioned she was supposed to meet with him to talk about contract negotiations, but that isn't what this sounds like. It's none of my business, but I feel a tug to find her. Despite her intensity and her sometimes dismissive ways, I know there's a vulnerability in her that makes me feel protective of the young actress. Maybe it's just the role she's playing getting to me. But maybe it isn't.

"Just let me go over everything again. I'll start from the beginning and input the numbers again."

"Fine, but I want to see everything. I want to see where the mistake happened and why, and how it's been fixed."

As I walk toward where the voices seem to be coming from behind the trailers, I hear a phone ringing. Marlowe mutters something and answers it sharply. She suddenly darts out from behind the trailer, taking long, angry strides toward the parking area. She doesn't seem to notice me and I hear her chastising whoever is on the other end of the line, telling them 'she said not to do this'.

A few seconds later, Frederic appears. He looks flustered but pastes on a smile when he sees me.

"Emma," he says. "It's good to see you again. When you weren't here this morning I was wondering if you were done with your consulting."

"Not yet," I tell him. "There are a few more days Delta wants me on set, then I'll be around during editing."

He stretches the smile a little further. "That's great to hear. Are you enjoying yourself?"

As he speaks, he seems to be making his way around me, almost like he's herding me so I'll go toward the trailers rather than the parking area as if he knows I saw Marlowe and doesn't want me following her.

"It's definitely a different experience," I say. "Something I'll never forget."

"Good. Is there something I can help you with?" he asks.

"Yes, actually. I was wondering how Marlowe's contracts are handled. That whole process," I say.

His expression doesn't falter, but there's a tiny flash in his eyes I can't quite decipher.

"Her contracts?" he asks.

"Yes. I've been asked to do some cameo appearances in projects before, and I've never taken the opportunity, but being here and seeing all this has made me think that if I'm ever approached again, maybe I'll take them up on it. But clearly, I don't have a manager or anything, so I was hoping you might give me some insight into how that process works. I mean, do people approach her directly with projects? Or do they have to go through you? Does she get a contract to review before she signs on for the project? Or does she make the commitment and then go through negotiations? It seems like a complicated situation."

He nods slightly. "Well, there's some variation depending on the situation, but for the most part, she only sees a select few of the projects people want her for. She has gotten to a point where she's getting more offers than she could possibly take on and it's critical she only participates in those that are good for her and her career. So, she's given vetted ones to review."

"So, she doesn't get to make the decisions about what's right for her," I comment. "She isn't even given the option."

"Professionals in the performance industry aren't solitary beings, Agent Griffin. You might see the most famous ones out and about, seeming like they are making all their own decisions, totally in control of everything on their own, but that's not the case. Behind them is a team dedicated to helping them make the most of their careers. Marlowe is at a very important juncture in her career right now. The decisions that are made regarding what roles she takes, her appearances, her public image, they will all shape her level of success going forward."

"So, she will never have control over what she does. You'll choose the projects you think she should do without ever letting her know what else is available. I assume that means you also go over the contracts and make decisions about the specifics within them before ever letting her see them. And you make negotiations. If you're doing all that for her now, she'll never learn how to do it for herself."

Frederic stares at me for a few moments, searching my eyes like he's trying to understand what I'm really asking.

"I thought you wanted to discuss how the situation would work for your future opportunities, Agent Griffin," he says.

His voice has changed. It's lost its professional, cheerful sheen and has taken on something drier.

"Frederic, there you are!"

I turn to see Meredith scurrying up behind us. She has something clutched in her hand and looks like she doesn't even notice I'm standing here until she's just a few steps away.

"Oh, hello, Emma," she says.

"Hi, Meredith," I say.

"Frederic, have you spoken with Marlowe today?"

"I have," he confirms. "But our conversation was interrupted by a phone call. She walked away just a few minutes ago."

Meredith's eyes narrow. "A phone call? From who?"

"She didn't say."

"Where did she go?" she asks.

"Toward the parking lot," he points.

Meredith doesn't say anything else, but turns on her heel and hurries in that direction. Before I can decide if I'm going to follow her, Delta comes out of her trailer.

"Hey, Emma," she says. "Everything alright?"

"Everything's fine," I say. "I was just coming to talk with you about the schedule."

"No problem. I just need to find Marlowe really fast. There's a change in the script for this afternoon's shoot and I want to go over it with her," Delta says.

"It seems like you're joining a pretty popular hunt," I say. "She got a phone call a few minutes ago and headed for the parking lot, and Meredith just went after her."

A hint of frustration briefly veils her expression and I remember how aggravated she was with Marlowe's mother the other night on set. It's obvious that Meredith interjects herself far more than is welcome and Delta is rapidly reaching her limit.

She glances at her watch. "Alright. We need to get going on this, so I'm going to find her."

"Mind if I walk and talk?" I ask. I figure it's a way to find out what's going on with Marlowe without seeming like another intruder.

"Sure," she says.

She's already walking toward the parking lot and I catch up with her, falling into step beside her. She's distracted as I talk about the upcoming filming dates and my schedule. Even though she's making acknowledging sounds and occasionally throwing out a response, her focus is on her phone and the papers she's carrying on her clipboard. By the end of the conversation, I know I'll be in Sherwood with Sam for our anniversary and then there will be a break in filming for the Christmas holidays. It's all I needed to hear.

As we're approaching the lot, I notice several cars stopped at odd angles close to the security booth. Marlowe and Brittany stand off the side, obviously engaged in a tense conversation. I can't hear what they're saying, but Marlowe seems upset about something and Brittany looks somewhere in between trying to comfort and reassure her, and trying to defend herself.

"What in the hell is happening here?" Delta demands, looking at the cars. Meredith steps into view from the security booth, her arms flailing overhead. "Meredith!"

Delta stalks over to her and Meredith comes to meet her.

"Who are these people?" she demands.

"Excuse me?" Delta asks.

"They say they're here for a tour of the set. I want to know why something like that would be authorized without going through me."

"I didn't authorize any such thing, but more importantly, it would be my prerogative if I did. I can do whatever the hell I want with my own production, Meredith. I've been very clear with you about that, and I don't understand why you can't seem to understand it," Delta snaps.

"Having strangers wandering around a set compromises the

integrity of the work and also Marlowe's safety. Do you have any idea what kind of people are out there?"

"Marlowe is an adult. She is adequately protected, but she also has the ability to walk away from a situation that is not safe for her. But that is not what's happening right now. She is not being put in that situation because this was not something I allowed. As for the integrity of the work, that is not any of your concern."

"Of course, it's my concern," Meredith fires back, her voice getting louder.

"Mom, what's going on?" Marlowe asks, coming over to us as people start getting out of the cars in the lot, cell phones in hand.

"Shit," Delta mutters. She picks up her radio. "We need extra security in the lot, please."

"This is my daughter we're talking about," Meredith says angrily. "My daughter and the future of her career."

"Are you more concerned about your daughter or the money she'll make?" Delta counters.

Meredith gasps. "How dare you?"

"Mom, seriously, what's happening here?" Marlowe demands.

"I want to know the same thing, but Delta won't give me any information."

The people in the lot are getting closer, taking pictures and recording. Some of them have gotten serious, attaching sticks to their phones so they can hold them out and record themselves talking about what's going on. Two security guards are holding them back from getting closer, but it looks like some of them are looking for ways to get around them unnoticed.

"Why don't we move this somewhere else," I suggest.

"You again?" Meredith asks angrily. "What is it with you and sticking yourself in where you don't belong? Do you get off on being nosy, or do you really just think you're so important you should be a part of anything that happens in your general vicinity?"

"Mom," Marlowe gasps, sounding shocked at her mother. "What is wrong with you?"

"Don't start with me, Marlowe," Meredith says. Her expression suddenly softens. "I'm sorry, honey. I didn't mean to snap at you. I'm just so worried with everything going on."

"Not another word," Delta says through gritted teeth. "Meredith, I've given you far more leeway and leniency than you deserve. At this point, I've run out of patience. You've pushed too far, too many times and I'm done. You need to leave the set and security will have instructions that you are no longer permitted during filming."

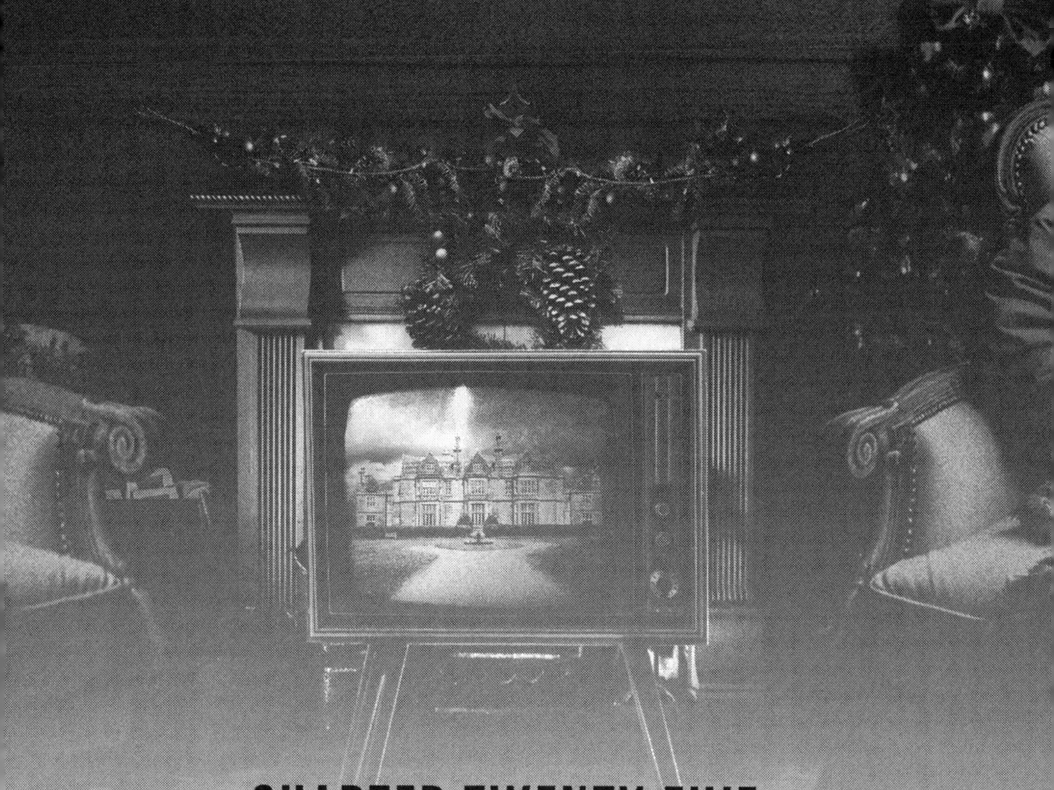

CHAPTER TWENTY-FIVE

MEREDITH LOOKS LIKE SHE'S GOING TO EXPLODE. THE PEOPLE IN the lot are loving what's happening and I try to move myself into a position to block as much of the recording happening as possible.

"All of you need to move, right now," I call out. "Unless you want every word of this conversation to be plastered all over the internet in the next ten minutes, I suggest you get your asses in motion and go down to the craft tent."

Meredith looks at me with fury in her eyes, but Marlowe doesn't hesitate. She walks away with Delta's arm around her, muttering under her breath. I don't quite catch what she's saying, but I definitely hear the word 'pills' in there somewhere. Brittany scurries to catch up, appearing from where she'd stayed at a distance from the rest of us after her conversation with Marlowe. She gets close to Marlowe, but Marlowe tightens, curling away from her. Brittany drops off a little, but continues to hurry along beside them.

I turn to the parking lot where security vehicles have shown up and are working on corralling the people. Meredith starts toward them.

"Don't interfere," I say firmly. "You've done enough. Let security do their job."

She stops and turns around to look at me. "You aren't in control here."

"And you aren't authorized to be on set."

She draws in a breath, her spine straightening. "We'll see."

She stalks toward the tent and I walk over to the lot, coming up behind the guards pushing back against the people continuing to try to record and take photos.

"Be advised that every one of you is currently trespassing. Any and all photos or video on your devices is evidence of this crime and will be used against you during prosecution to the fullest extent of the law. Any proprietary information distributed through this material could also subject you to copyright infringement charges. This is not public property and you are not protected by any laws regarding recording in public. I suggest you delete everything you have on your devices right now, get in your vehicles, and leave. You've already been recorded entering the property and are currently being recorded, including your license plate information. Don't make this situation any worse for yourself."

"Who are you?" a guy shouts from the back of the crowd.

"FBI," I say.

Most of the crowd hurries to delete what they have on their phones and tablets, but I know not all of them will. Some will keep it just for the sake of being able to say they went against the orders of a federal law enforcement agent. Others don't realize they don't understand the law the way they think they do and will keep the pictures and recordings because they believe if they are not inside a private residence there is no such thing as expectation of privacy. And still others are probably assuming I'm lying, just some crew member trying to scare them. But some have been deleted and that will at least lessen the impact.

"Everyone move out," one of the security guards demands. "Police will be called in thirty seconds and all those still here will be detained."

I turn and walk away, wondering if they could tell my bluff about the security cameras. I hope there are recordings being made to monitor everyone who enters the area, but I don't know for sure. What matters is they believe they can be traced so they are more likely to comply with orders. I only hope whatever guard is in the booth right now has been writing down as much information as he can.

The group is even tenser when I get to the tent. Delta stands between Meredith and Marlowe, and Brittany is off to the side, watching. Frederic is coming up from the other side as I walk toward them.

"What is going on here?" he asks.

"Meredith's authorization to be on set during filming is revoked," Delta tells him. "I don't want her anywhere near filming and she isn't to be given any proprietary information. That includes filming schedules, script details, appearances, anything."

"You can't do that," Meredith protests.

"Yes, I can," Delta replies. "This is my production. I can do whatever the hell I want, and I want you out of my way."

"If I have to leave, Marlowe won't stay," Meredith says. "You lose me, you lose her. Right, Marlowe?"

"Mom, maybe it's better if you just leave," Marlowe whispers.

"What?"

Meredith sounds genuinely shocked and I can't help but notice Marlowe won't look directly at her.

"We're already running late with the schedule for today and this is taking up more time."

"I'm here making sure that you are being treated the way you deserve to be. I'm your advocate, Marlowe. And now you're turning on me?" Meredith asks.

"I'm not turning on you," Marlowe says. Her voice is starting to sound unsteady. "I just want to be able to move the production forward, and you being here is interfering with that. Just go back to the hotel. I'll call you when we're done tonight."

"If Delta gives you permission, I suppose. Or maybe Emma," Meredith snipes, venom coloring her tone.

"That's enough, Mom," Marlowe says. "Emma didn't do anything to you. She's helping me."

"She's sticking her nose in where it doesn't belong," Meredith says. "She's here to make sure the details of the case are correct. Not to tell people on set what to do."

"No, that's my job," Delta says. "And I told you to leave. I'm trying to give you the respect and dignity of going on your own, but if you don't, I'm not above calling for security to escort you."

Meredith looks at each of us, then backs away a few steps before turning and stomping out of sight. Marlowe sags down onto a seat at one of the tables. Her head falls into her hands and she lets out a breath.

"It's going to be fine," Delta says. "Security is handling everybody at the front, and you know your mother. She'll be fine when you call her tonight. It's better for you if she's not here anyway. You don't need the stress."

"Maybe we should take a break for today," Frederic offers. "She's obviously having a rough time."

"I'm fine," Marlowe says.

"The production needs to continue," Delta says. "There have already been too many delays and with the holidays coming up, we need to stay on track as much as possible."

"I'm fine," Marlowe says again.

"And what are you going to do about the effect of the people who just swarmed the set? She should have the expectation of feeling safe and not being broadcast by wannabe vloggers all over the internet. I think we need to discuss compensation for the time lost and the extra work she's going to have to do to make up for it," Frederic replies to Delta as if Marlowe hadn't said anything.

Marlowe slams her hands on the table in front of her and stands up sharply.

"I'm fine. Stop speaking for me. Both of you."

She storms out of the tent toward the set and Delta and Frederic exchange glances.

"I'm going to try to salvage this day. I suggest you start figuring out how you're going to fix that mess," Delta says, eyeing Brittany.

They both walk away. Once the dust settles, I head over to Brittany.

"What happened?" I ask. "Marlowe looked pretty upset when the two of you were talking up near the parking lot."

"I accidentally made a post with the location information still on," she says. "Everyone who looked at it was able to track us down."

"Us?" I ask.

"The production," Brittany says. I can't help but notice the speed of the words, like she's trying to shove them over the ones she's already said. "It was a mistake, but Marlowe is pissed. Not that I'm not used to that."

"What do you mean by that?" I ask.

Brittany shakes her head. "Nothing."

"You obviously meant something."

"Marlowe is my best friend," she says. "And the reason I have this job. I don't ever want to talk badly about her. If you'll excuse me, I have to go do some damage control."

She leaves and I take out my phone. It doesn't take much searching to pull up Marlowe's social media. The most recent post has the location turned off now, but there are already thousands of interactions. I stare down at the photo. It was obviously taken early this morning with the sun coming up over the set making the cornstalks mostly silhouettes against the glow at the edge of the sky. I'd think it was a beautiful picture if I wasn't so distracted by the caption.

Come take a tour through the corn with me. I'll be waiting by the path.

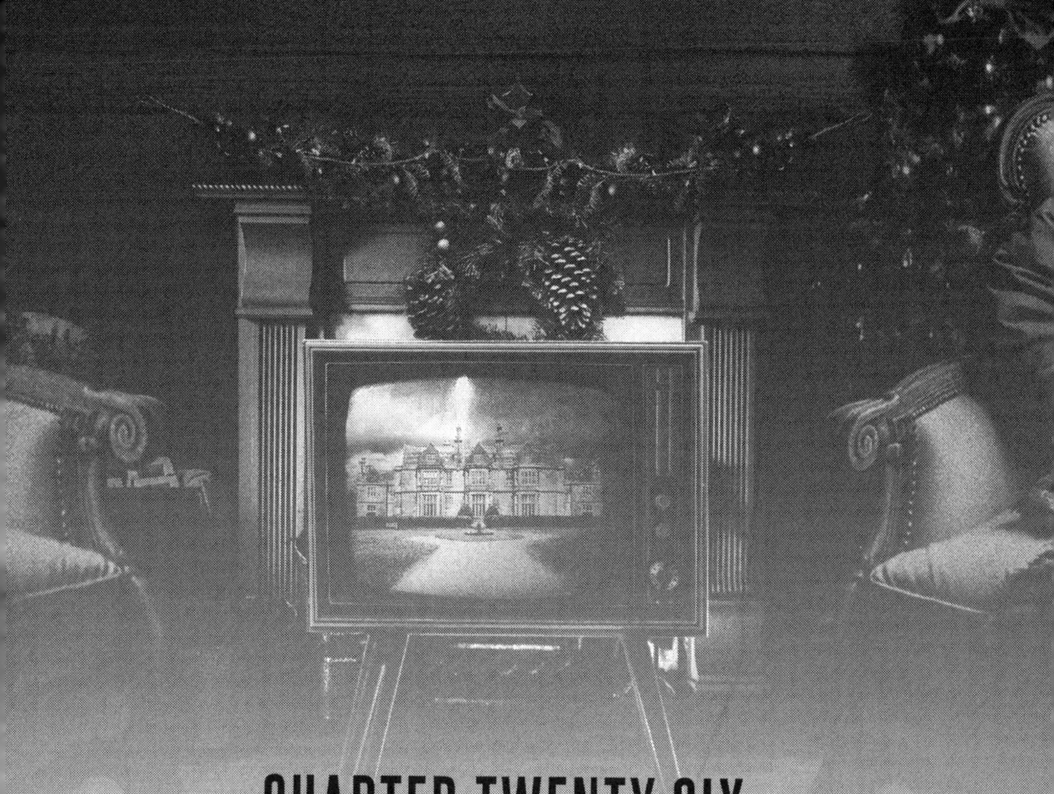

CHAPTER TWENTY-SIX

"I'M SURE IT WAS JUST MEANT TO BE CUTE," SAM SAYS. "LIKE when celebrities take pictures of themselves holding cocktails on the beach and caption it 'drinks anyone?'. It's not supposed to be taken seriously."

"Those pictures don't usually have the location activated," I point out. "That's something that doesn't just happen. She had to do that on purpose. And the entire post was gone when I went to talk to Marlowe about it later."

"You think Brittany wanted all those people to show up?" Sam asks. "Like she did it on purpose as some sort of publicity stunt?"

"I don't know," I shrug. "She is in charge of Marlowe's social media and she admitted she left the location on, but I don't see what benefit it would be to have all those people show up like that. All it did was cause a lot of chaos and get some really unflattering videos and photos posted. It wasn't as much as I would have expected, but what did get out there didn't make Marlowe, her mother, Delta, or the production look great, so I don't know why she would want that to happen. Her job is to make Marlowe look as good as possible."

"She's young, babe. She makes mistakes. She probably thought she was being artsy and didn't realize people would actually take her seriously."

"Well, she has her work cut out for her fixing the damage. Marlowe was a mess for the rest of the day. She got through it, but I have a feeling we didn't do as much as Delta was hoping."

"Did you get a chance to talk to Marlowe about what happened?" Sam asks.

"No. She went right from set to her trailer at every break. I think she just needs some time to herself. I'm just worried about her. She was really worked up about it," I say.

"It'll blow over. By the time you're back, everything will be back to normal. It's just part of the industry drama everybody in it thrives on," he says. "It's like manure making plants grow better."

That makes me laugh. Leave it to Sam to be able to boil everything down to something that simple and be able to make me feel better with it.

"I love you," I say. "I'll be home soon."

"I'll be waiting."

The few hours left of the drive feel like they take forever, and when I finally pull into the driveway in front of our house, I just want to sit and look at it. This isn't the longest I've been away from it, but for some reason, this time feels harder. I've missed being at home, and though I've had a good time with my cousin and Xavier, I'm looking forward to a few days of hunkering down in my own home, surrounded by the smells of Christmas and Sam, and not thinking about much of anything else.

I'm reaching for my seatbelt when my phone alerts me to a new message. Thinking it might be Sam asking why I'm sitting out in the cold in my car and telling me to come inside, I pick it up. It's not Sam.

Instead, it's Marlowe. Apparently, my chance to just be home hasn't started yet.

Marlowe: *I'm sorry for everything today. I hope my mother didn't offend you.*

Me: *It's not your fault. And don't worry about it, a lot worse has been said to me.*

I sit there for a moment reflecting on today's events before keying out another message.

Me: *Are you doing alright? I didn't get a chance to talk to you before I left.*

Marlowe: *You left?*

The message comes back so fast it's almost like she'd already typed it and was just waiting for me to say something so she could send it.

Me: *Just for a few days. I'm home to celebrate my anniversary with my husband. I'll be back on set after.*

There's no response. I wait for a few minutes, but nothing comes. Finally, Sam appears at the door and I can't resist the darkened outline of him against the inviting glow of light coming from inside the house. I grab my bags and head in, stopping for a long hug and kiss before stepping inside.

~

Two days later I go grocery shopping to pick up a few things I need to make Sam a special anniversary breakfast the next morning. He's at home getting the pile of laundry he brought back from Michigan clean since apparently, he doesn't think there are laundry facilities in other states. I call him from the store and ask if there's anything else he wants.

"You know that fudge ripple ice cream with the raspberry jam?" he asks.

"The one from that fancy specialty organic ice cream shop?"

"Yeah. I've been craving that for days."

It seems like an odd request in December, but he's been through a really stressful time, so I'm not going to question it. If my husband wants fudge ripple raspberry ice cream, that's what I'll get him. I finish shopping for the groceries and head for the ice cream shop. They are closing up for the evening, but I get to the door just in time to catch the owner.

He opens the door and gives me a quizzical look. "Emergency ice cream run?"

"Sam," I say, and he nods. That's all the explanation he needs.

With a couple of pints of ice cream in hand, I make my way back to the house. When I arrive, I notice new lights have been added to the front walkway. We've had the Christmas lights up since the day after Thanksgiving per the agreements of the Xavier Convention from a couple of years ago, but now extra ones are glowing up to the porch, then off to the side. I leave the groceries in the car and get out to look at the lights.

I follow them and find a note tucked into the wreath on the front door.

We may have only been married for one year, but you've been mine forever.

I try the door, but it's locked. I search for my keys, but when I unlock the door, I find the slide bolt is in place. Going back down onto the walkway, I notice the lights leading around the side of the house, so I follow them, looking for the blue among the white. They bring me to the backyard, where he's done so many projects for me. Another wreath hangs from the hammock he put up for me and that has become one of our favorite places to spend a summer evening.

Another envelope tucked there contains a second note.

And I'll be yours always.

I notice the hammock is hanging low like something's in it. I pull it open to find a wrapped package tucked inside. I take it out and see a tag that says not to open it until I'm inside. Bringing the package with me, I walk across the yard and up to the back door.

This door is locked, too, and the key to it is missing from my keychain. A thought occurs to me and I check behind the loose piece of rock on the side of the porch where I always kept an extra key up until it was used by someone else to get inside my house. The rock moves to the side, and I see the key at the end of a piece of ribbon.

What is Sam up to?

I take out the key and a small box comes along with it. This one has a tag that instructs me to open it now. Inside, another key is nestled onto a bed of white velvet. I open the back door and go into the house. The lights lead me through the kitchen to the table where they form a bright, glowing heart around an assortment of my favorite takeout food and a pizza box that's still hot.

It's all I can do not to burst out in laughter. I've never seen anything so romantic.

Remembering the package under my arm, I unwrap it and find a brand-new sweatsuit. It's perfect. My laughter spills over, and I can't help a teary guffaw as I think about the ridiculous lengths this man has always gone—and will always go—for me.

A tag pinned to the neckline says "wear me" and I quickly change into them. There are more lights leading out into the living room and I think I know what's waiting for me. Grabbing the pizza and one of the takeout bags, I follow them and find Sam sitting on the couch in his own new sweatsuit.

"Happy anniversary," he grins.

"It's not until tomorrow," I say.

"I know," he says. "But tomorrow starts at midnight, and we have a lot of food and TV ahead of us."

I set the food down on the coffee table, then climb into his lap and he gathers me close for a kiss.

"All the groceries are in the car," I tell him.

"I figured."

"Including the ice cream," I add.

He shrugs. "I needed some extra time."

"What is the extra key to?" I ask.

"A new lock on the front door," he says. "Another for your collection."

Shaking my head, I grab his face in my hands and give him another hard kiss. He's ridiculous, but I never want anything else.

CHAPTER TWENTY-SEVEN

I'M SO USED TO STRUGGLING TO SLEEP IT FEELS STRANGE TO suddenly be jostled out of it. The movement in the bed next to me isn't gradual like Sam is getting up to use the bathroom or go scavenging in the kitchen for some of our anniversary leftovers. Instead, it's sudden and rough, like the only thing on his mind is getting out of bed.

Opening my eyes, I watch him put on his bathrobe and walk out of the bedroom. He is answering his phone and the tense look on his face tells me the conversation coming through the line isn't a happy one. That wakes me up the rest of the way and I climb out of bed. The floor is cold enough to make the bottoms of my feet sting and I'm thankful for my own thick robe hanging nearby.

The rest of the house is quiet in the early morning hour. We spent from the time I got home all through the day yesterday eating our way through the takeout he already ordered and ordering more, watching TV, and hiding from the world exactly the way we planned our anniversary.

It was perfect, but now it feels like we've been yanked back into the real world.

"How sure are they?" Sam asks. He pauses. "And they actually think he can be trusted?"

I go into the kitchen and find him sitting at the table, one elbow propped up as he rubs his forehead with his fingers. One leg bounces anxiously under the table. Without saying anything, I go to the cabinet to start a pot of coffee. Once it's brewing, I make my way into the laundry room to make sure everything of his has been washed and dried. I have a feeling his bags are going to be packed before long.

"Alright. Tell them I'll call them as soon as I can," he says as I walk back into the kitchen, confirming my suspicion. When he stands, he looks startled to see me, like he hadn't even noticed me moving around him. "Did I wake you?"

"What's going on?" I ask. "Was that Rose?"

He nods. "The detectives working Marie's case think they have a new lead. One of the guys Rocky told me about showed up at the station to answer questions. They think Rocky was telling the truth about not knowing Marie, but some of the information he gave is interesting. Apparently, someone of her description was seen in certain areas leading up to her disappearance, and this guy thinks he might have seen her. They want to look into it and see if they might be getting closer."

"You need to go," I say without hesitation.

"Emma, it's our anniversary," he protests. "I don't want to leave you like that."

"Yesterday was our anniversary," I tell him. "And we celebrated early, too. It was exactly what I wanted it to be. Your family needs you right now."

"Are you sure?" he asks.

"Of course I am. Go on and get ready. I'll book you the next flight."

"Thank you," he says, hugging me. "You're amazing."

I don't necessarily feel like that's true. He's been understanding for me far more than I have for him. But I'm not telling him to go as some sort of reciprocation. He really does need to be with his aunt right now. The longer that goes since his cousin went missing, the harsher the reality becomes. There's always a chance she's still alive. I've seen for myself people who have re-emerged after many years of being missing. After people had given up on them and simply figured they were dead.

But being hopeful and being prepared for the probable outcome are two different things. We can continue to hope we will find Marie and she'll be able to tell us what happened. But we also have to acknowledge that with every day that passes, the chances of her actually being alive get smaller. He doesn't want to think about that. He doesn't want to feel like he's giving up on her.

He also doesn't want to let resisting reality keep him from following the truth. Above all, he wants to be the one to bring her home. No matter what that means.

The rest of the morning is a whirlwind. I manage to find him a flight that leaves in a few hours, so we rush to get him packed again and off to the airport. When the door closes behind him after one final kiss, the silence descends on me again. I'll go back to Dean and Xavier's house tomorrow. But for now, I don't want to be in the car again.

Instead, I take a long shower and settle on the couch with my laptop as a pot of peppermint hot cocoa warms on the stove. I pull up Marlowe's social media again. There are a few new posts, including a video of her that seems to be addressing the incident that happened on set.

She's sitting on one of the tables at the craft services tent, wrapped in a blanket and holding a cup of something hot.

"Hey, guys. I just wanted to take a second to talk to you guys about my new project and some things that have been going on. I don't want to get into too many details because I don't want to bring more attention to it. But here's the thing. I appreciate the love you show me and how much some of you feel like you know me and want to be a part of my life. That's amazing. And I know my real fans would never disrespect or hurt me, and they would never make problems for a project that means as much to me as this one does.

"The work I do might just look like fun all the time, but it is hard. Especially with something this heavy. It's so important for me to stay focused and for us to do the best work we can. Trust me, it will be worth it when you get to see what we've been working on. Remember, just because you see it, doesn't mean it's real. Just because it's on the internet, doesn't make it true. And just because someone says they saw it doesn't mean they know what they're talking about. Keep that in mind." She lifts her cup toward the camera. "Thanks for having a cup of coffee with me. Time to get back to work. Bye."

The video fades on an image of her waving and smiling. Her words sit heavily with me. I can understand why she is avoiding talking about the specifics of the situation. It would only rile people up more and make them want to find out what happened. She's doing the right thing trying to minimize it while also addressing the situation. But I don't feel like she's only talking about the people coming to set. There was more to that statement and I wonder what she's trying to say.

I think back on her inviting me to her apartment for us to get to know each other and realize I know little about her. We talked some while I was at her apartment. But it didn't get any deeper than her talking about her apartment and discussing the project. I still feel like there was more she wanted to talk about, but stopped herself before she could.

I decide to explore through the internet. I find articles about her, trying to gather details about who she is and where she came from. It's hard when it comes to a celebrity like her. We might be living in a world where people talk about being honest and living unapologetically authentic lives, but talk and action don't always align.

That's especially true when it comes to the entertainment industry. Audiences get a strange mix of information from these people. There's the image they create of themselves, the details they want to share, and what they want people to see when they look at them. Then there are the details that are ripped away from them and tossed to the masses like bits of meat and bone thrown to beasts. These are the pieces of a person's life they don't mean to have shared, but end up being found and used to taint the version of themselves they wanted to share.

I want to find out both about Marlowe.

The articles I find about her paint the image of a smart, talented girl raised working on her family's farm but finding fulfillment in the arts. She discovered her love of acting, dancing, and music when she was very young. Her mother recalled her frequently singing to the animals or dancing through the fields when she was doing her chores. It was like a musical. I keep finding that sentiment in these articles. Any time her mother talks about what it was like raising Marlowe, she talks about watching her like she was living in a musical.

She was always telling stories. Always singing and dancing. But she was hardworking and never let her mother down.

She worked hard to honor the father she never knew. Nearly every article I read and interview I watched had her mother tearing up when she talked about that. Marlowe's father, the love of Meredith's life, died before he even got to meet his little girl. He gave his life in the service and she was as proud of him as Meredith knew he would be of Marlowe.

Marlowe dedicated everything to the memory of her father, from her gymnastics performances when she was young to her career now. Meredith didn't have an artistic bone in her body. All of it came from him. She was such a reminder of him. Such a gift.

I finish the last article with an uncomfortable feeling shivering down my spine. Something is off. I can't place exactly what it is, but there's something not sitting well with me.

CHAPTER TWENTY-EIGHT

I'M SURPRISED TO SEE MEREDITH STANDING JUST OUTSIDE THE security booth in the parking lot when I arrive at the set a couple days later. Well, that's not entirely true. More accurately, what I'm surprised about is that she's just standing there patiently and calmly rather than trying to force her way past.

"Good morning, Agent Griffin," Lewis nods as I show my credentials.

I wave and make my way past him without acknowledging her. I've only made it a few steps when I hear her behind me.

"Agent Griffin?"

Her voice is soft, almost contrite. I want to just keep going like I don't hear her, but I make myself stop and turn around.

"Yes?"

She walks up to me cautiously. "Can I speak with you?"

It's one of those questions that doesn't make any sense to ask.

Clearly, she can speak with me or she wouldn't have already. What would she say if I told her no, she couldn't? Would she be able to just take all the words we had already said back and put them back in her brain?

As quickly as those thoughts go through my mind, I can almost hear Sam's voice chastising me, telling me I'm being petty. To be nice. One thing I can always rely on my husband for is to reflect my flaws back to me in a way that ensures I know I'm doing it but I don't feel judged.

I'll be the first to admit I formed a hard shell during my years in the Bureau before I found my way back to Sam. I got an edge, a hardness around me. It protected me, but also kept me isolated. I'm not the most patient person and I react sharply and quickly before thinking most of the time. With a gun strapped to my hip and my focus on ruthless murderers, that impulse can be dangerous. I've learned over time to not always follow the first compulsion to roll through me, to not always go out on my own.

Not that I will ever do everything exactly according to the rules. My impulse to go against standard protocol and do things my own way has gotten me into trouble many times before. It's what landed me behind a desk for six months, got handcuffs slapped around my wrists more than once, and nearly claimed my life more times than I care to sketch out.

But it's that same impulse that has solved cases and taken down criminals. It has saved my life, the lives of people I love, and the lives of intended victims.

Sometimes I am forced into a corner and have to do what I'm told rather than what I know I should. But at my core, I am what I am. When I have the option and the need is there, I will do what has to be done.

Instinct will always come before protocol. Skill before training. Truth before procedure.

Impulse before acceptance. I'm working on that one.

"What can I do for you?" I ask.

"I just want to apologize for the way I behaved the last time we spoke," she says.

"I don't really remember us speaking," I reply. "I remember you screaming at and insulting me."

Meredith cringes slightly and nods. "Yes. That. I am so sorry for saying those things. I had just gotten some difficult news and everything that was happening with Marlowe and those people who showed up really got to me. I shouldn't have taken it out on you."

"I appreciate you saying that," I say. "I want you to understand that I'm not here for any reason but to make sure that this project is done respectfully and accurately."

"I know that. And I'm sure it hasn't been easy for you. I should have been more compassionate. But can you understand how hard it is for me to watch Marlowe do this?"

"She's an actor," I say. "This is what she has chosen to do. And she's an adult."

Meredith nods. "She is. She's also my daughter. And after all that she's gone through trying to get to this point, I want to make sure she's safe."

That perks up my attention. "What do you mean? Why wouldn't she be safe?"

"She's a beautiful girl, Agent Griffin. And her career puts her in the public eye. It makes people feel like they have ownership over her. Just watching her videos or seeing her on TV makes men think they have some sort of relationship with her. Then they pursue her. There are always going to be people obsessed with beautiful, successful women. I don't want her to be another tragic headline."

I feel the slither down my spine again. The sound of her voice doesn't match the words. There's something vaguely exploitive about it. Almost like she's saying what she wants people to hear, hoping it will be picked up and make its way into other ears, onto pages and websites. In one way or another, she is always on.

Out of the corner of my eye, I notice Delta coming toward us. She doesn't look happy to see Meredith, and as she gets closer, she eyes me apprehensively like she's waiting for another blowup to happen.

"Meredith," she starts when she gets to us.

Marlowe's mother holds up her hands like she's demonstrating her innocence. "Before you say anything, I know you don't want me on set. That's why I'm waiting here. I want to apologize for the way I acted. I've already spoken with Emma and apologized to her for the things I said about her."

Delta looks over at me and I nod.

"She did," I acknowledge.

"You know how important it is to me to be a part of this with Marlowe," Meredith says. "This could be such a major turning point for her career. You know as well as I do that her name is going to be a big part of the appeal of the series."

"I believe the series stands for itself," Delta says. "Marlowe is talented. She's lovely. But the appeal of this story is the story itself. People are going to watch it because they want to know what happened, not just because of the name of the actress in the role."

Meredith wants to argue. I can see the way her shoulders tighten and her chin lifts just slightly. The change in her is subtle, but it speaks to the emotions going through her and how hard she's fighting right now to keep swallowing down the reaction she really wants to have. But she knows if she does, her feet are never going to get past the gravel and onto the fields again.

"Absolutely," she says. "And it will do amazing things for her career. This could get her the attention she needs to really launch her into the lifestyle we want."

I can't help but notice the word "we" appearing in that sentence.

"I don't understand what that has to do with you being on set," Delta tells her. "When this project first began, I agreed to have you on set with her because of the sensitivity of the project and your feelings regarding her father's death. That didn't have anything to do with making sure she is getting the attention she wants. Or that you do."

Meredith looks like she's trying to find the right words.

"That's not what I'm saying. It's not about the attention. It's about making sure she takes this seriously. She's young, Delta. She hasn't been around this industry her whole life. She's just really getting started and I don't know if she understands just how important it is for her to take every single step seriously. To put all of herself into it and go above and beyond so she can make the most of this opportunity and everything that comes next. I want to be here to be sure she's performing and behaving in her best interest."

I hate the way she talks about her like a child and also like a commodity. I can see in Delta's face that she feels the same way, but she is trying to avoid more drama.

"You will not have full access. Moving forward, sets will be closed during filming and you will not be permitted to watch. You can stay in the tent. You can stay in Marlowe's trailer if she gives you permission. But that's the extent of your access," she says.

"Thank you," Meredith says.

"I need you to understand I am not asking for your collaboration. Your input is not needed or requested. I don't want to hear any more suggestions about the script, commentary on directing. Anything. If you're here, it's only for Marlowe's moral support and that's it. If she doesn't want you here, you'll be asked to leave."

"What do you mean if she doesn't want me here? Of course, my child would want me here," she bristles, the aggravation starting to leak through into her words.

"I'm not arguing with you. I'm making a statement, Meredith. When Marlowe returns to set, it will be up to her whether she wants you to be here from day to day."

Meredith's head tilts to the side in a silent question. "When she returns to set? What do you mean when she returns to set? She's on schedule for today."

"Yes," Delta says, nodding. "She was on schedule for today. But she called me last night to let me know she's sick and won't be able to film. I've had to rearrange the shoot yet again. Fortunately, Paisley was able to come in and do her scenes early and we shouldn't lose any time. But

I'm hoping Marlowe is better soon or we're going to lose far too much ground."

She sounds like she's getting wound tightly inside and sooner or later, it's going to snap.

A smile suddenly pops onto Meredith's face. She swipes her hand through the air in a dismissive gesture.

"You know what? She did text me last night. She said she wasn't feeling great and was getting to bed early. I think she's just having a rough month, if you know what I mean. I'm sure she'll be fine tomorrow. Well, I guess I'll see everybody then."

I do my best not to shudder. She turns and leaves and Delta and I exchange glances.

"Can I ask you something about her?" I ask.

Delta nods, starting back toward set with the expectation I'll follow her. "Sure."

"The night you filmed Lakyn's death scene, Meredith and Marlowe seemed to have an argument about something when she got out of the car. Do you have any idea what that was all about?"

Delta shook her head. "No. It's not all that unusual to see the two of them arguing."

"Why is that?"

Delta shrugs. "Mothers and daughters argue, I suppose. I get the feeling Meredith has put a tremendous amount of stock into Marlowe's career and wants to be able to control it."

"I agree with you on that. What about the pills?"

She glances at me. "What pills?"

"When Marlowe was upset she said something about needing her pills."

Delta shakes her head. "I don't know. I don't remember that."

She does. She knows exactly what I'm talking about. She just doesn't want to tell me.

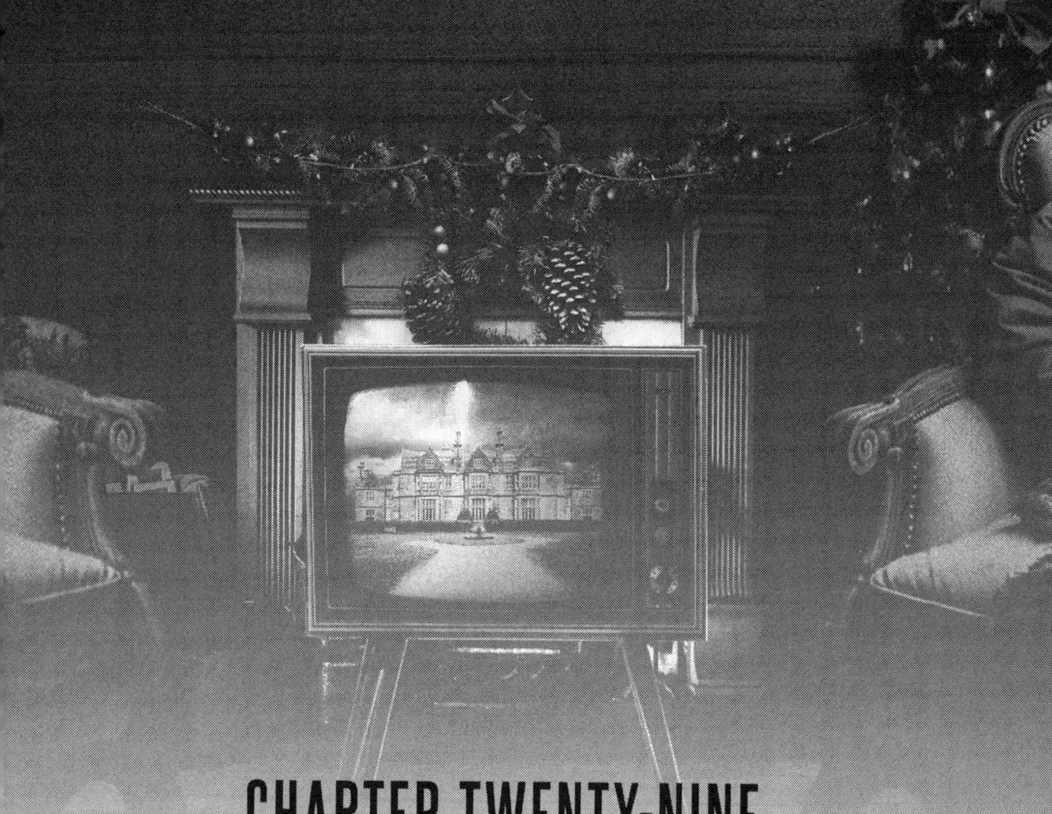

CHAPTER TWENTY-NINE

The day on set is shorter than I anticipated it being. Paisley got through her scenes quickly and I was happy to see bringing everyone to the field of bones and tearing everything down to the raw reality had an effect on her. She's more restrained and controlled now. I wouldn't go so far as to say she is embodying me exactly correctly, but there's a line between parody and fictionalization that she was dancing along and has now jumped off in the right direction.

She isn't me. She can't really understand what I've seen or what happened. No one who wasn't there can. But the way she's presenting it now is close enough to the truth to offer structure to the story rather than reshaping it. I'll take it.

As I'm leaving, my car seems to automatically pull in the direction of Marlowe's apartment rather than Dean and Xavier's house. I pick up my phone and send her a quick text, asking if she's feeling better and saying I was thinking of coming to check on her. She immediately responds, eagerly accepting the offer. When I get to the apartment building, I use the code she sent me, wondering if it will still be active.

The gate opens without hesitation and I pull into the parking lot. I look around, taking note of the car parked in the corner, the same place it had been the last time I was here.

I let myself into the courtyard and then the building. Marlowe meets me halfway down the flight of steps. She's in yoga pants and a sweatshirt, her hair wound in a knot on the top of her head. I notice her bare toes are polished, but her clean face looks softer, younger than she does when she's fully made up.

"I'm glad to see you," she smiles. "Thank you for coming."

"Delta mentioned you weren't feeling well, so I wanted to make sure you're alright and don't need anything," I tell her.

I'm sure if she did need something there are countless people a press of a button away who would happily fulfill it for her. But I still want to offer, for her to know there's someone willing to do something for her without a title or a paycheck attached.

"I'm alright," she tells me. We walk slowly toward her apartment. "I'm feeling better."

"Did your mother get in touch with you?" I ask.

She rolls her eyes as she closes the door behind us. "Yes. She was pissed when she got here. I didn't even know she was coming and suddenly she's blowing up my phone asking why I wasn't working."

"She said you messaged her last night and told her you weren't feeling well. She didn't check on you then?"

"I didn't message her," she says.

She walks into the kitchen and reaches into the refrigerator for a bottle of soda. She holds it up to offer one to me and I shake my head.

"When Delta mentioned you weren't on set, your mom seemed surprised, then suddenly said you told her you were sick," I said.

Marlowe goes into the living room and curls into the corner of the couch where she sat taking off her toe nail polish the first night I visited her. She shakes her head as she twists the cap of her bottle back and forth.

"I didn't tell her," she says. "But she's never going to admit that to anyone. She wouldn't want anyone to think she and I are anything but attached at the hip. If I'm sick, I'm obviously going to want my mommy. She was furious when she got here." Her eyes close as she lets out a sigh and runs her hand back over her head. "I just needed a day. Just one day and she couldn't even give that to me."

"A day for what?"

"To breathe," she says, letting out a mirthless laugh. "Just to breathe."

"This is going to sound really strange, but I was looking on your social media today," I say.

"Why does that sound strange?" she asks, taking a sip of her drink. "That's why it's there."

"Doesn't that ever feel intrusive?" I ask. "Your mother was saying she worries about you because there are all these people who get obsessed with celebrities and men who think they have relationships with you when they don't even know you, but every day you put up pictures and videos of yourself. Or Brittany puts them up."

"I put those up because it's part of my job. There's nothing lascivious. I'm fully dressed. I don't get drunk. I never show my home. The only thing my mother worries about is that I'm not going to get the next role or the next paid appearance. You heard her the other day. She wasn't really concerned about my safety when those fans showed up at the set. She loved all the uproar and attention. She didn't want spoilers about the project to get leaked because she thought it might get fewer viewers, or that if there was trouble, other directors wouldn't want to work with me. That's her actual concern," she says bitterly.

"And what about you?"

"What about me?" she asks.

"Do you ever worry about the people out there?"

She lets out a breath and takes a sip of her drink like she's using the gesture to fill the silence.

"There's enough to worry about right here." I don't have a chance to respond to that before she glances behind her toward the hallway and then back at me. "Can I show you something?"

"Sure," I say.

She puts her drink down and hurries down the hall. A few seconds later, she comes back with what looks like a thick sheaf of paper in her hands. She sits down and holds it close, eyeing me.

"Keep a secret?"

"In my line of work, people saying things like that usually isn't good," I joke, but she doesn't seem to get it, so I just nod. "Of course." She hands the papers out to me and I look down at them as I take them from her. "A script?"

Marlowe nods. "Mom and Frederic don't know I have it. The director wants me specifically, so the director got in touch with me without going through Frederic. That's not what they're supposed to do, technically."

"I know. I talked to him about that," I tell her.

She gives me a quizzical look. "You did?"

"I was curious about how it all works. You'd mentioned contract negotiations and I was just curious about how that all comes together. How you find out about projects and choose the ones you're going to do. How much you have to do with the contracts themselves. That kind of thing."

"Nothing," she shrugs. "That's how much I have to do with the contracts. At least, that's how it feels. He's the one who goes over them and does negotiations. I only see what he feels should be the final agreement. Sometimes I have changes I want to make and he might go negotiate them again, but most of the time what he comes up with is what goes. He says it's to protect my best interests and keep my stress down, but a lot of times I feel like I'd have less stress if I was more involved."

"Then get more involved," I tell her. "Be the one who does the negotiations. Be the one who makes your own needs known."

"It's not that easy," she says. "In this industry, your representation is essential. You're nothing if you don't have someone gatekeeping for you. If people deal directly with you, they can take advantage of you much more easily. Frederic is pretty well-connected. He's been around a long time in the industry. He knows how to talk to all the different kinds of people and to advocate for better payment terms and scheduling. All those things. People know I don't know those things so without terms being reviewed by someone else, it would be really easy to screw me over."

"That doesn't mean you shouldn't have more of a say. And you said you were doing negotiations with him the other day."

"Not my own," she explains. "His. He wants to change the terms of his own contract and I wanted to discuss with him that I think he's been trying out those terms already."

"So, what about this?" I ask, holding up the script.

"It's a project I really want to do," Marlowe says. "They contacted Frederic about it months ago when it was just in development. They wanted me to be a part of it from the beginning, but he wouldn't even talk to me about it. He cut them off immediately. So, they went around him and came to me. It's definitely not the kind of thing he, or my mom, would want me to do. They'd say it isn't commercial enough and that it wouldn't be good for my career."

"Because you're not successful enough yet to choose things that matter to you," I say, remembering what she told me about the hierarchy of projects according to her manager.

"Exactly. And I'm used to just going along with what they say. I figure just like with the contract negotiations, Frederic knows better. Even if I want to do other things, it's more important that I make a name for myself and build up a reputation so I can make money and be sought out for as many projects as possible. Only this one really speaks to me. From the second I heard about the project, I wanted to do it. I can't stop thinking about it."

I scan through the script and notice the name of the main character has been crossed out and replaced.

"Did you change the name?" I ask.

Marlowe shakes her head. "No. Originally, the character was named Amber, but then as the project developed, they didn't feel like that was the right name. When I spoke to the producer about it and said I'd think about taking it, he said if there was a chance for me to play the character, he wanted to make sure the character had a name that fit me better. It was Sylvia, but it was changed in my script to Vera. Only a few people have scripts at this phase, just people who are auditioning for the roles, but mine is the only one they changed."

"What are you going to do?" I ask.

She reaches for the script and holds it in her lap. "I don't know. There are other girls lined up to audition for the role. A few names. A few unknowns. Brittany said there's a lot of chatter about the project and I know a decision is going to have to be made soon."

"You told Brittany about it?" I ask.

"Not that I was in contact with them. She'd heard about the project through some other personal assistants and was talking about it. I just told her it sounded interesting and I might consider doing it. I didn't want a chance for it to get back to anyone, though. Not until I really decide what I'm going to do."

"You think she would tell them? Even though she's your best friend?" I ask.

"She is my best friend," Marlowe says. "But you know how people who have gotten famous say their best friends never lost sight of who they were before they were famous? Mine hasn't lost sight of who I am now."

A sharp knock on the door makes her jump and she looks in the direction of it like she's trying to decide if she's going to acknowledge it. There's another knock and she gets up, telling me she'll be right back. I hear her open the door, but she doesn't let anyone inside. She's gone for a few minutes, then comes back into the room with a darker look in her eyes, brushing something from her arms.

"Is everything okay?" I ask.

"It's fine," she says. "Just business."

She walks out of the room and comes back tipping something out of her palm into her mouth. She chases it with her drink and closes her eyes, letting out a breath as she swallows it down.

CHAPTER THIRTY

Then

You were an inspiration, Lakyn. Lives are better because of you.

Your work will carry on. We won't forget what you were trying to do.

I've started studying criminal justice because of what you were working toward. I hope I can do something as amazing as you have one day.

No one will ever forget you.

"All these people," Lakyn's mother whispered, running her hand along the names and messages written on the huge pieces of paper hung up at the memorial to her slain daughter. "None of them ever even had a conversation with Lakyn. But they had so much of a connection to her through what she was doing. I hope what they're saying is true. I hope she'll never be forgotten."

Soon

You were a bright star, Marlowe. Now you'll shine on forever. Your absence will always be felt. —Frederic

I love you, Mars. You'll be my best friend for the rest of my life. You have no idea how much you inspired me. I've always wanted to be just like you.—Brittany

You were only in my life for a short time, but it has meant more to me than I could ever say. I won't remember your face on a screen. I'll remember who you really are.—Branson

"She touched so many people," Meredith whispered, slowly turning the pages of the guest book just outside the viewing room. "I just wish we could have kept the casket open. They would have loved to see her one more time." She picked up the pen beside the book.

You will always be my pride and joy. My greatest achievement. I'll carry you always. I love you.—Mom

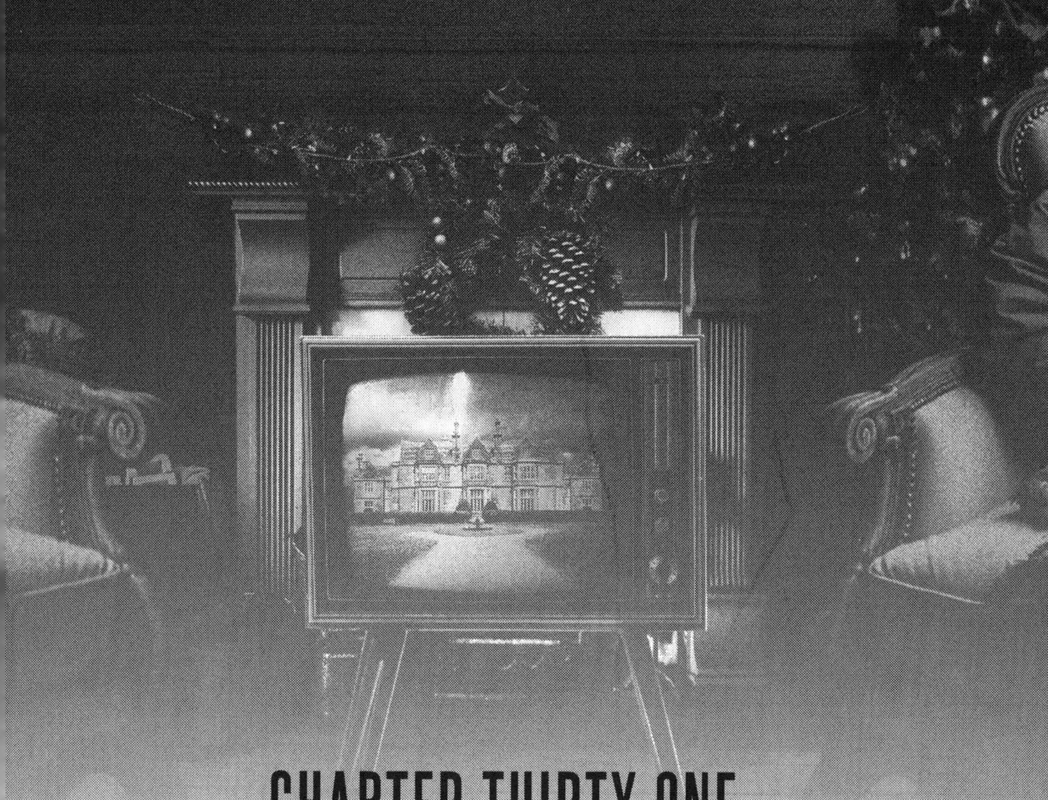

CHAPTER THIRTY-ONE

Now

My house is so quiet when I get back. I don't feel like I'll ever really be prepared for that. Which seems strange considering how many years I lived on my own. From the time I was eighteen years old, I lived alone. From the house my father signed over to me before he disappeared, to the one I live in now, where my grandparents lived and I still have memories of my childhood, I've been by myself.

I was used to coming home to an empty house. I got accustomed to the ritual of checking to make sure the lights I'd left on were still on, and the ones I'd left off hadn't been turned on. I had a whole routine of glancing at each of the windows to make sure they looked secure and running my fingers over the locks to check for scratches and ridges possibly left behind by someone trying to get inside.

It wasn't fear that drove me to do those things. I don't really know how to explain the motivation. Acknowledgment. Recognition of the truth I lived every day. Knowing that my Boogeymen were very real and had different faces.

But as soon as Sam became a fixture in my life again, I got used to the life he brought into the house. The bigger our chosen family grows, the more I expect sound when I walk into the house. My ears search for familiar voices and the sounds of daily life. I expect to walk into a day already in progress rather than one that is waiting for me.

Getting home to Sherwood for the Christmas break in filming reminds me that the people I love are scattered right now. Eric, Bellamy, and Bebe are back home near DC. He's healed enough to go back to work as the interim supervisor. Dean and Xavier are in their house in the suburbs outside of Harlan. Sam is in Michigan.

They will all be here soon. I look forward to the house coming to life for Christmas. I feel like this year I need it more than before. My phone rings as I'm putting my clothes away.

"Hey, babe," I answer when I see that it's Sam.

"Are you home?"

"I just got here. It feels so weird for it to be so empty. Especially being used to staying at Dean and Xavier's house recently, it's so quiet."

"I would think it would be a relief to know you could walk from room to room without potentially getting gravely wounded," he offers.

"That is definitely a plus. I heard from Ava today."

"How is she doing?" he asks.

"It sounds like she's busy. The case she's working on is really complicated and she wanted to go over it with me," I tell him.

"That's sweet," he says. "She still thinks of you as her mentor."

I groan and roll my eyes even though I know he can't see me. I hear him laughing.

"How is everything going with you?"

"The private investigator I contacted is putting together a map of places to search. The detectives got a lot of information from that informant, but they don't know everything he was talking about. Of course, he isn't just going to lead them to drug houses and places where people go to buy and sell or party. But the PI has some more details, so we're hopefully going to get boots to the pavement in the next few days."

"I miss you," I tell him.

"I miss you, too. I wish you were here. You're my favorite investigation partner."

I smile even as my heart aches. But the words stay with me through the rest of our conversation and as soon as I hang up, I'm searching airlines for the next flight. It's still several days until Christmas and I don't have any intention of spending them alone.

~

The next night Sam meets me at the airport and I stand in his arms for a long time, not caring who around us is watching. When we finally step apart, he takes my carry-on and we walk to the luggage carousel holding hands. Soon we're at Rose's house where he's been staying. The sweet older woman looks like she's aged many years since the last time I saw her. Her makeup is fully done and her hair is perfect. To some people that might seem like she doesn't care as much about her daughter being missing. That no mother worried about her child, even an adult child, would be able to go through all that effort just for themselves.

I know differently. To me, that's a sign of her struggle. I see the way the makeup is caked in the wrinkles at the corners of her eyes and the smears on her lips from tears. I see the tightness in the curls in her hair that tell me she stared into the mirror as she styled it, lost in her thoughts until she nearly burned the piece off. She's going through the motions, doing what she has control of so she doesn't come completely undone.

That night, Sam fills me in on everything about the investigation so far. I'm here to be with him, but also to do my part. This is my family, too, now. I want to help in any way I can.

The private investigator came through with the map and as I look at it, my stomach feels slightly sick. All the places marked on it are places where lives are thrown away. People offer them up to drugs and sex, to brief moments that feel like power but are nothing but oppression.

The image of the map stays in my head as we start the process of dismantling each of the marked spots the next morning. It doesn't surprise me when the first several we visit give us nothing. These places are as transient and tenuous as the people who frequent them. One moment it can seem like they are pulsing with toxicity and constant threat, and the next they're empty. Those who survived have moved on.

The next day it's more of the same. All I can do is watch as my husband slowly comes unraveled. This has shaken him. Not just as Marie's cousin, but also a man of the law. He believes strongly in himself as a sheriff, but he hasn't had much experience with cases like this. Sherwood doesn't see murders and disappearances frequently. The horrific serial killings that brought me back still hang heavily over the town. It's scarred and will never really be the same.

Neither will Sam. And this is changing him more. He hates that he can't find the key, the turning point that will make everything come together. He knows it's there. She's out there somewhere. People don't vaporize. But he's on the outside. He's not in charge, but even if he was, he doesn't have all the information and details he would need. We're searching on assumption, hoping we'll eventually find ourselves on the right path.

But we both know that isn't a guarantee. The evidence from her apartment has pointed us in this direction, but it was vague. It was didn't give us everything. He's pored over it trying to think of every angle possible and this is where it has led him. All I can do is give him fresh eyes to see it and be by his side as we walk through stained, dank houses on the brink of collapse, kick through piles of refuse deep in the woods, and wade into trash-filled water teetering on the dual hope of finding her and not finding her.

On the third day, the hope topples.

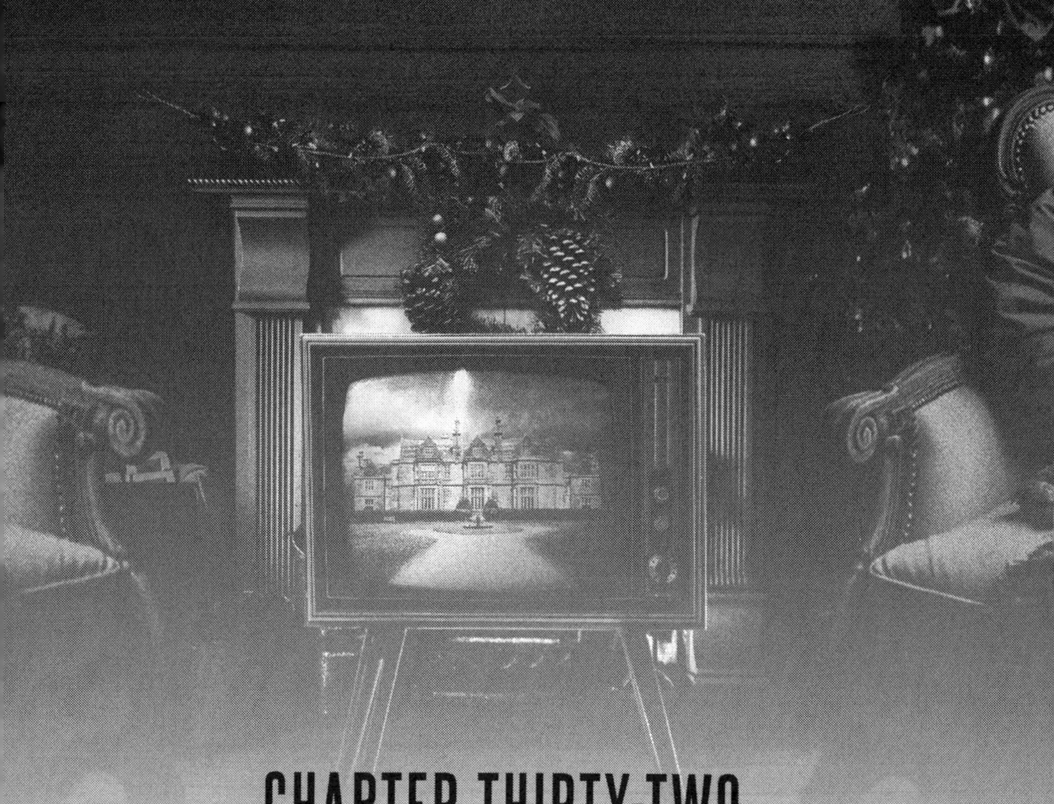

CHAPTER THIRTY-TWO

"I CAN'T TAKE THIS ANYMORE."

"Marlowe?"

"I just can't. I've tried. I've been doing everything I can, but it's too hard. I can't do it."

"Marlowe, what's going on?"

I'm not sure what time it is. The ringing of my phone brought me out of sleep, and I can't tell if the darkness in front of my eyes is the depth of midnight or that slice of ink just before the sun breaks.

"Emma? What's wrong?" Sam groans from beside me, pulling his head out from under the pillow and rubbing his eyes.

I rest my hand on his back to try to calm him. "It's Marlowe."

She's crying on the other end as I climb out of bed and throw a blanket from the end of the bed around me.

"It's not working anymore. Nobody understands."

"Nobody understands what?" I ask. "Marlowe talk to me. Tell me what's going on."

Her voice keeps sounding farther away, then closer, then farther, almost like the phone is sitting still and she is moving around it. I slip out of the bedroom and make my way down the stairs so I won't wake up Rose. Turning on the light makes my eyes sting, but it helps to burn through the sleep that's still making it hard to follow what she's saying.

"Just let me go. I just want to go."

"Marlowe, stop."

It's another voice, but I can't place it over the sound of her crying. There's a shuffling sound and the call ends. I look down at my phone. It's late rather than early. It's only been a couple of hours since I went to bed, which means Marlowe is likely still up. The time difference is messing with me, but it's earlier here than it is there, which means she's up even later than I thought. Not so late that it's out of the ordinary for someone young and enjoying the spoils of success.

Only Marlowe doesn't sound like that's what she's doing. That voice wasn't the voice of someone enjoying anything. There was desperation like I've never heard from her. It was pain ripped from deep down where she's been hiding it away from anyone. A kind of pain she never intended anyone else to know about. But someone knows now.

I call her back, but it rings until the voicemail takes over. Another call does the same. Another does the same.

The fourth goes straight to voicemail and after three messages, Sam comes around the corner into the kitchen where I'm standing.

"Hey," he says. "There you are. What's going on?"

"Marlowe," I say. "She just called, and she sounded really frantic. I tried to get her attention so she would talk to me, but she wouldn't. Then there was another voice that told her to stop and the call ended. She's not answering."

"What was she saying?" he asks.

"That she couldn't do it anymore. That she wanted to go."

"Do you have any idea who the other person was?" he asks.

I shake my head. "No." I scroll through the contacts on my phone and find Delta. She answers on the third ring, sounding exhausted. "I'm sorry for calling so late. Have you heard from Marlowe?"

"Marlowe? No. Not since we went on break. Why?" she asks.

"She just called me and sounded really upset about something. I'm not in the area or I would go check on her. I called her several times and it's going straight to voicemail."

"Alright. I'll get in touch with her. Thank you for calling."

"Have her call me when you hear from her," I say.

"I will."

I look down at the phone in my hand, wishing there was someone else I could call. It doesn't feel like enough to just call Delta. There has to be someone else. I don't know her mother's number or Brittany's. That thought brings me to another screen.

"What are you doing?" he asks.

"Checking her social media," I say.

The most recent posts show her smiling or looking artistically dramatic on set. Nothing matches the tone of her voice or the desperation in her words. I look through the comments, waiting for something to stand out.

"RIP," Sam says.

"What?" I ask.

He points at the screen, at the hashtags at the end of one of the comments. "RIP."

"What the hell?" I read the comment. "'Carlsbad Hotel. Never forget, today or ever.'"

"What does that mean?" he asks.

I shake my head. "I don't know." Pulling up a browser, I search the key terms of the comment, adding Marlowe's name at the end. It doesn't take long for the information to come up. "It's where her father died." I read through some of the article. "She did an interview a few months ago talking about it. Apparently, there was a hostage situation and a shoot-out, then a massive fire. Several officers died."

"Officers? I thought he was in the military," Sam frowns.

"So did I. Her mother said he died in service. But this says he didn't survive the fire and when they found his remains he had two bullet wounds, but there were signs that he was trying to open a window. He was trying to rescue the other people involved."

Sam shivers. "Damn. That's a horrible way to die. I can't even imagine being trapped in a burning building."

"I don't have to imagine it," I say.

I can still feel the heat of the flames in the house in Feathered Nest when Jake Logan was holding me in his childhood bedroom.

"Is it the anniversary of the fire?" Sam asks.

"Close. It was a couple of days ago."

"Maybe that's what she's upset about."

"Maybe. I don't know, though. She never met him. Not that I'm minimizing her father being dead, but it wasn't like they had a relationship and she can remember what it was like when he died. I don't see her getting that worked up about being close to the anniversary of his death. And the things she was saying—it didn't sound like she was sad. She was broken. When she said 'let me go'..."

I don't want to finish the thought. I've heard that kind of blackness in someone's voice before. I know how it ends.

"You have someone checking on her. There really isn't anything else you can do," Sam says. "Come on. Let's go back to bed and get some sleep. We have an early start tomorrow."

"Wait," I say, taking hold of his arm when I notice something else in Marlowe's feed. "Look at this picture."

"Who is that?" Sam asks, looking at the picture of Brittany laughing as she comes out of a bar.

"Marlowe's best friend. She handles her social media. But look." I scroll back through the images and stop on one I remember seeing the first time I went through. "Those clothes. They're Marlowe's."

"That's strange," Sam says. "Is she an actress, too?"

"Not that I know of. Marlowe called her a personal assistant."

"So, why is she wearing Marlowe's clothes and going out to a place like that?"

"And why did she post the picture on Marlowe's account?" I ask.

~

I stay up for another hour waiting to hear from Delta, but eventually, Sam urges me back to bed so I can try to get some rest before we meet up with the search party in the morning. I still haven't heard from her the next morning when I bundle up in thick layers and guzzle a few cups of coffee to fuel me through the search.

I call Marlowe again, but her voicemail inbox is full. Another check of her social media shows a new video posted, but it looks like one of the ones she'd created ahead of time to post on a scheduled date. She's talking about Christmas coming up and her favorite traditions from when she was younger. Getting a tree and decorating it. Drinking mulled cider. The luminaries around her neighborhood. She looks hopeful, but after hearing that phone call, I'm more attuned to how she's speaking. She's trying to come off as candid, but there's an almost rehearsed quality to the video, like she's saying what she planned to rather than just talking.

Not that there's anything wrong with that. I'm sure lots of celebrities try to come up with ways to fake being relatable. But it stands out to me. The contrast between the persona of "real Marlowe" on this video and the real Marlowe I've actually met in her own apartment couldn't be broader.

I'm still waiting for the call from Delta when we're walking through what remains of a factory later, early that afternoon. The carcass of the building was ravaged by drug users and anyone wanting to find a place to block themselves away from society. A floor once used to create useful goods is now scattered with trash, needles, and abandoned remnants of the temporary lives that have passed through here. Clothes caked in the blood and sweat of who knows how many people. Mattresses that have seen things I don't even want to think about.

It's sunny outside, but the cold beams of light aren't enough to get through the corners of the factory floor. Our flashlights get through the layers of grime, overlapping and crossing to fill up as much of the space as possible with illumination so we can see what's around us.

The smell is overwhelming. It's one I've encountered countless times before, but it never fails to make me take a step back. This is the smell decay and loss. It's years of disuse and misuse. It's death.

"We'll need to take apart that pile of wood piece by piece," Sam instructs the people with us. "Be careful and aware of everything around you. Look at everything you pick up and move. Even some really small things can be important."

"I'm going to go into the next room," I tell him. "It looks small, so I want to clear it."

"Be careful."

As I'm making my way toward the room, my phone rings. I take it out as quickly as I can.

"Hello?"

"Emma?"

"Marlowe," I say, letting out a relieved breath. "Thank god. I was really worried about you."

"I'm sorry. Delta told me what happened. I'm sorry about the call last night."

"You don't have to apologize for that. Are you alright?" I ask.

"Emma," Sam calls from the other room.

"I was just having a bad night. I didn't mean to upset you."

"Marlowe, it doesn't matter if I'm upset. I want to know that you are okay. What was going on?"

"Emma," Sam calls again, more intensely.

Marlowe hesitates. "It's nothing."

"I don't believe that."

"Can we talk? I mean, in person?"

"Emma, I need you in here!" Sam shouts, his voice frantic.

"I'm not in town," I say. "I'm in Michigan handling an investigation."

"Oh. I didn't mean to interrupt. I'm sorry."

"You're not interrupting. We can have a video chat later. Would that work?"

"Emma."

His voice is close now and I turn to see Sam standing in the doorway a few feet from me. His face is drawn and his eyes are round with emotion.

"Marlowe, I'm going to call you back."

I lower the phone.

"We found her."

CHAPTER THIRTY-THREE

Monroe, Lakyn

- Severe decomposition, exposure to the elements for several months
- Identification through dental records
- Skeletal remains with some mummification
- Clothing degraded but thought to be intact upon death
- Hair matted, sections appear to be torn from scalp
- Broken bones consistent with beating
- The body is too decomposed to identify a specific cause of death, though the extent of the injuries suggests a very violent assault more than sufficient to kill

Long after death

"She wants to remain anonymous," Emma said, holding the sheets of paper filled with tight, precise handwriting. "She does not want the media to know her name or her involvement. She's willing to talk to the police. For now, this is her statement. She witnessed Lakyn's death. This will answer all the questions from the autopsy. It will tell you the story of how she died."

Gray, Marlowe

- Very early signs of decomposition
- Extensive head trauma consistent with a fall onto a hard surface
- No signs of struggle or other notable injuries

Just after death

"Aren't there any security cameras around here?" Sam asked. "In a place like this, there have to be cameras."

"No. Not at the back of the building, anyway," Emma said. "The point of this building is to provide privacy. Her entrance was secluded and only accessible with a code. There's no need for a security camera."

"Unless you need to know how someone died," he pointed out.

Emma looked down at the bloodstain still on the patio. If she closed her eyes, she could still see Marlowe lying there, her bloodied face and fingertips.

"Marlowe will have to tell us herself."

CHAPTER THIRTY-FOUR

Now

I WALK THROUGH THE REST OF THE DAY IN A DAZE.

The cold of the hospital hallway amplifies Rose's scream and the squeal of her shoes against the floor as Sam pulls her back, keeping her from running into the room where Marie's body lies in a black bag on a gurney.

I close my eyes and rest my forehead on the wall. The sides of me are battling.

Sam's wife wants to be with him, to hold him and comfort him as he tries to hold his aunt up and get her through these horrific first hours. I want to be there beside him while he explains to her that the identification is only preliminary based on her clothing and some personal articles found around her, along with a metal piece in her leg that is likely the one implanted after she broke it when she was a little girl. That she can't see her body. That it won't be released until after positive identification and preliminary investigation.

The FBI agent wants to pull myself out of the emotions of the moment so I can break it down into its parts. I want to dissect the scene, the evidence, and every detail so I can figure out what happened to Marie. Everything around her at the factory suggests she was a victim of exactly what was expected. A drug overdose. Her body was heavily decomposed, but drug paraphernalia around it looks like so many of the overdoses I've seen in my career.

Toxicology of the tissues that will be harvested from her during her autopsy will give a better idea of what happened in her final hours. The extent of her decomposition tells us she was likely already gone by the time her mother even considered that she was missing.

It can't be that simple. I don't want it to be that simple. Sam feels betrayed by the thought that his cousin was struggling with this side of her life and he didn't know anything about it. He feels like he should have known. If he did, he could have done something about it.

No matter how many times I tell him that isn't true, he won't listen. He can't make himself believe this isn't somehow his fault.

It's late by the time we get back to Rose's house. It feels completely different now. The air that filled it when there was still at least a little bit of hope is gone, and I watch as Rose moves around, trying to learn to live without it. She doesn't want to talk. She doesn't want us to sit with her.

She goes into the kitchen and puts on a pot of water for tea, then goes into her room to change. It screams on the stove as her door stays closed. I finally take it off when the bottom is nearly dry. Sam is in the shower and I use the silence to call Marlowe.

When she answers, the flashing lights and blaring music around her nearly obliterate her face and the sound of her voice. She's out partying.

"I'm going to do it," she says before anything else.

"What?"

"I haven't told anybody. I'm celebrating."

"The part?" I ask.

She spins around, swirling the colors of the lights across the screen. Her voice sounds different. It's not the same person I talked to last night. The switch has flipped again.

"Frederic won't take this from me, too," she says. "Not this time."

"Marlowe, are you alone? Is Brittany there with you?"

"No. It's just me."

"Go home, Marlowe."

"I don't want to go home. I don't want to think. I just want to dance."

"Marlowe, I can't do this right now. I need to know you're going to be alright," I tell her.

"I'm fine," she insists. "I just want to dance."

"I need you to go home," I say. "Should I call someone to come get you?"

"No," she says. "I'll go soon. I promise."

I have to tell myself she is an adult. She's an adult with a famous face. By now, she's been recognized. I need to focus on where I am, on being here for Sam. I have to trust that she's recognizable enough that she will get home safely. She said she's alone, but I imagine that means her driver is waiting outside. I can't be responsible for her. I don't know why she's chosen me, but right now, I can't take that on.

Sitting on the couch with Sam's head in my lap an hour later, I get a text from Marlowe.

Marlowe: *If someone has a secret but it's about me, is it mine or theirs?*

I consider for a moment before typing out an answer.

Me: *It depends on the secret.*

Marlowe: *Can you keep another secret, Emma?*

Me: *If you want to tell me.*

Marlowe: *I do. I want to tell everyone.*

I hesitate, trying to figure out what to say to that when she sends another message.

Marlowe: *But I don't know if it's worth it.*

"Did she message again?" Sam asks the next afternoon.

Our schedule feels completely thrown off. We sat up until almost sunrise before falling asleep. Now we are treating the early afternoon like morning. He's making coffee while I stand in front of the pantry, looking for something that might bring our appetite back.

It takes him asking that question for me to realize I'm gripping my phone and looking down at it every few seconds. I shake my head.

"No. But she posted earlier and seems fine. I'm sorry. I shouldn't be so fixated on her."

"You're not fixated. You care. It's different," he shrugs.

"There's something going on with her. I'm worried. But I'm here with you and that's what I should be focused on. I'm sorry. It just doesn't feel real yet," I say.

"No, it doesn't," he agrees. "But at least it's over. I hate to say that. It makes me sound horrible."

"It makes you sound relieved to know. No one can blame you for that."

"She's really gone," he says, like the protective shell that has kept that information from really getting all the way to him is gradually dissolving away and the painful acidic drip of what is really happening is sinking in.

"She is," I nod. I reach a hand over to his shoulder. I wish there was something better I could say to him. I wish I could make this easier. But there's nothing that's going to change it.

"I should have found her sooner," he says.

"You can't do that to yourself. You had no way of knowing where she could have been. How could you possibly know that?"

"They should have gone into the apartment," he replies, suddenly sounding angry. "If they'd gone into her apartment when Rose first noticed she was missing, this wouldn't be this way. We would have found her. She wouldn't have just laid there like that."

"Yes, they should have," I nod.

"And I'm going to fucking find out why," he adds. "I'm going to rip them to shreds."

"Stop." Both of us turn to look at Rose where she's appeared at the doorway. "I can't stand to see you like this. It's not going to make anything better."

"Aunt Rose," he starts.

"No, Sam," she shakes her head. "I can't watch this eat away at you. Marie is gone. It won't do any good for you to torment yourself about something you had no control over. You told me yourself she was probably gone before I ever called the police. It wouldn't have mattered if they walked into that apartment the very first day. It wouldn't make a difference. Please don't do this to yourself."

"It might not have saved her, but we would have known more earlier. We could have found her sooner and have more information about what happened," Sam protests.

"She's coming home, Sam. That's what matters to me. I can't have her back. And I have to live with the way she died. I have to live with knowing that she didn't tell me what she was going through. I don't want this to become about the police. It's about Marie," Rose says. "I don't want them hanging over me while I make plans to lay my daughter to rest and spend Christmas without her."

"You'll have us," I say. "We'll spend Christmas here with you."

She gives me a soft, tearful smile. "No. It's time for you to go on home."

"We don't have to stay in the house," Sam offers. "We can get a hotel. We just don't want you to be alone."

"I need to be," she says. "And you need to be at home. I need this time and I can't bear the thought of this being your holiday. Please. I have others here. If I need someone, I won't be alone. But for now, I just need the space to figure out life again."

"Are you sure?" I ask.

Rose nods. "You've already done so much. Especially you, Sam. I love you and I appreciate you. That's why I want you to go. Go home. Enjoy Christmas. Be happy and be together."

"If you change your mind, we can be on the next flight," I tell her, and mean it. "Or we can bring you to our house."

"I know," Rose says. She kisses his cheek and hugs him close. "I have to make some calls. As soon as her body is released, I want to be ready."

She walks out of the room and Sam looks at me, his eyes both sad and shocked.

"How can she be reacting like that? How can she want to be alone?" he asks.

"No one really knows how they are going to react to something tragic until it happens," I say. "There isn't one way to react. For Rose, she wants to be alone because that's what her life is now. With Marie gone, she needs to figure out how to live a different life. And she doesn't want to delay it."

"I'm not going to let this go," he says. "None of this makes sense. An overdose fits everything found in that apartment, but too neatly. It's supposedly linked to Gerard Collins, but he couldn't have had anything to do with it. Not with the timing of her death. So why was his information in that phone? And why did he die? And why was no one allowed in the apartment for so long? There's something else going on, and I'm not giving up."

Part of me—the part that's his wife—wants me to tell him not to get too wrapped up in it. Not to let himself drive himself crazy with theories and connections that may well prove nothing, and would never bring her back.

But the other part of me—the FBI agent—agrees with him.

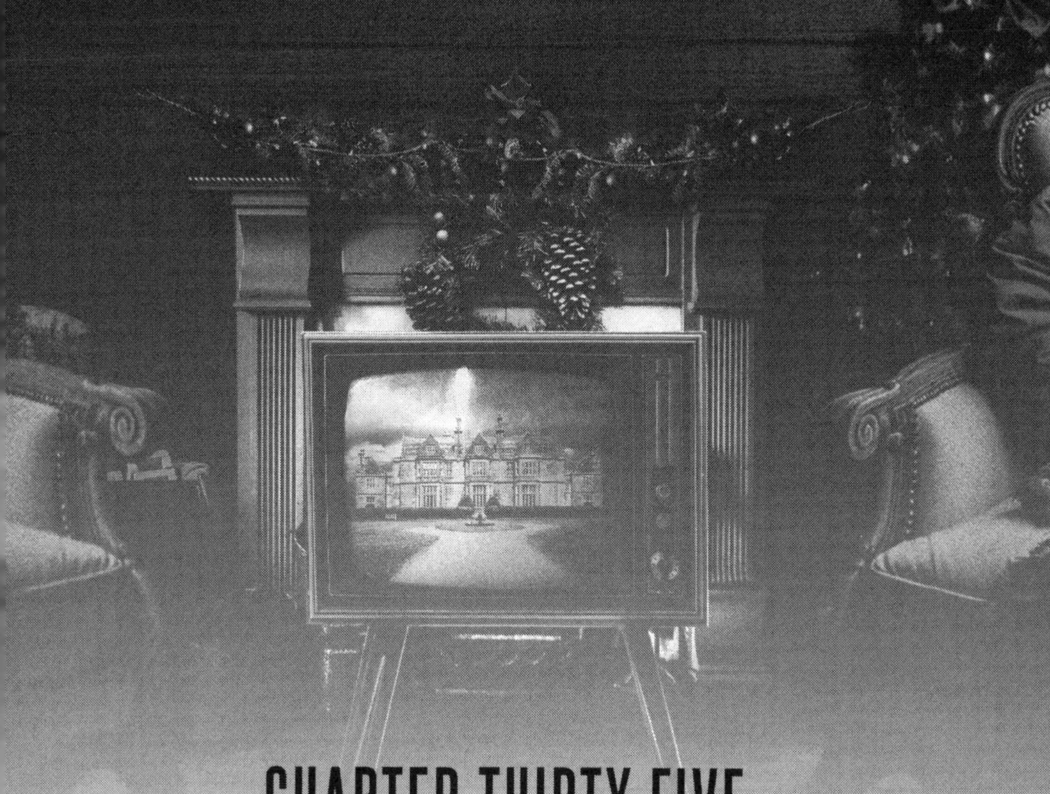

CHAPTER THIRTY-FIVE

It doesn't feel much like Christmas. I hope it will when everyone arrives, and we can try to enjoy the traditions we've built together.

Sam and I got back from Michigan last night and have been trying to get our feet back under us and carry on. He's brought down the special decorations I like to put up only in the days leading up to Christmas because they're old and fragile. There's a Christmas movie playing in the background and I try to follow it, but it just flows over me.

Now that I'm home, my conversations with Marlowe repeat through my mind. The way she was acting when I called her while she was out dancing was unsettling. I can't help but wonder about some of the things she said. I've taken to checking her social media throughout the day, questioning the image that's being presented and wondering what's actually going on beyond the veneer of what Brittany is showing.

When I called her earlier today, she sounded calm. When I asked about the secret she said she wanted to tell, she hesitates, then laughs, saying she doesn't even remember what she was saying. She must have had a couple too many.

I don't believe it.

"You'll come to my birthday, right?" she asks. "New Year's Eve. I'll send the information."

I wanted to turn her down, especially since I have a feeling it's not going to be the type of party Sam and I would describe as our scene, but I couldn't bring myself to. So, I told her we'd be there.

Now I'm trying not to think about it too much as I simultaneously string popcorn and continue digging through everything we have about Salvador Marini and the attack on Dean. My eyes are blurring from reading through the same report over and over. The night of Mark's disappearance doesn't make any sense. He was pulled over far away from where his car was found. He was drunk enough for the bartender to refuse to serve him anything else, but got through the sobriety tests without a problem.

There has to be something else that I'm missing.

"What are you working on?" Sam asks when he gets home from a grocery run.

I tell him and let out a sigh as I stretch my neck. "Mark Webber. What is it that I'm not thinking about? Why was his car stopped where it was?"

"Do you know how long it was between him getting stopped by the police and his car being found?" Sam asks.

"His car wasn't found for a couple of days," I say.

"Alright, so you don't know what happened between him getting pulled over and him stopping there. Let me make a phone call really fast." He comes back a few minutes later. "I had a hunch and I don't know if this is actually going to give you any real information, but it's something. There was another emergency call later that night asking for police to respond to a car stopped by the side of the road with the door open. An officer responded to the area around where the car was found."

"Did he speak with Mark Webber?" I ask.

"There's no report of contact with a driver," Sam shakes his head. "Another emergency call came in and the officer was rerouted to that call. He made the statement that he didn't see any cars in the area so he felt comfortable leaving."

"But the car must have been there," I muse. "Which means he was covering it up."

"That doesn't mean he was involved. It just means he was protecting himself," Sam says.

"But why didn't someone else respond?" I ask.

He doesn't say anything, and when I look up, I realize he's focused on the TV. The movie's over and I didn't notice a celebrity gossip show has taken its place.

"Have you seen this?" he asks, gesturing at the screen with the remote.

As he turns up the volume, I realize the thumbnail image at the top of the screen looks like it's of Marlowe. She's wearing sunglasses and there's a hat held in her hand, reminding me of how she described her outfit from when she went jogging. She's holding something in her hand, a flash of bright green is visible against the gray of her jacket sleeve, but she's close to a building that blocks everything around her from view.

"It looks like famously single Marlowe Gray may have someone to kiss under the mistletoe this Christmas after all. Reports are coming in of Marlowe getting cozy with an unidentified man on a few different occasions over the last couple of weeks. The two seem to be determined to keep things under wraps, but we're hoping to learn the identity of the mystery suitor soon. Maybe by her New Year's Eve birthday. We hear she's planning a blowout celebration at a nightclub near the set of her new mini-series based on the life and death of Lakyn Monroe.

"These pictures come on the heels of others taken by fans who noticed Marlowe out dancing this week, though it didn't seem her male companion was with her."

"Just when people were saying she seemed like a more mature

version of a young Hollywood star because she hasn't been the focus of scandals, it looks like Marlowe might be starting to look for more attention," another reporter adds.

"Could be," the first says. "It makes you wonder about that post that brought a surge of followers to the set for what they thought would be a personal tour with her. She hasn't addressed that situation directly or explained why the now-deleted post had the location activated, but could we be seeing her leaning into her role as starlet? What do they say? No publicity is bad publicity?"

The reporters laugh and move on to another innocuous picture of a different celebrity, managing to take it and twist it into something far more than it actually is. I suppose that's the point of celebrity gossip, but it gives me a slimy feeling.

Sam and I look at each other.

"Do you know who that guy is?" he asks.

"I didn't see a guy in those pictures," I say. "It was just her standing there. She looks like she's talking to someone, but I couldn't see who."

"But she never mentioned anybody to you? She's not seeing someone or talking to someone?"

"No. At least, she didn't say anything to me, and I think that's something that would have come up. She's getting upset about not having more control over her contracts and the projects that she chooses. I think if she was seeing someone, there's no way she would hide it. That would feel like she was just giving them more power over her. She'd have told me something about it," I say.

That evening I find myself back on the path of trying to find out who Marlowe really is. Not the person in the pictures or the one up on the screen. The one with no makeup who takes off her nail polish at night and likes that her balcony reminds her of a balance beam. Her words trail through the back of my mind, whispering into my thoughts as I read old blog posts and articles, sending me sliding down a slope that brings up more questions than answers. Soon I'm not just wondering who Marlowe is.

Who are the people around her?

My phone rings as I read a screen grab of a post that had been deleted but questioned the timeline of Marlowe's birth. I pick it up without looking.

"Hello?"

"Hello, Emma," Jonah says. "It's been a while since we spoke."

My jaw tightens, my teeth grinding together.

"What do you want, Jonah?" I ask.

"To give you my condolences about Sam's cousin," he says. "It's too bad, someone that young."

"How did you know about that?" I ask. "It hasn't even been on the news."

"I hear about things, Emma. I hope you and your husband are handling it as well as you can be expected to," he replies. "It's so sad when something like that happens."

He hangs up without another word, leaving my hand so tight around the phone I feel like it might snap.

CHAPTER THIRTY-SIX

On the twenty-third of December, my true love said to me…

"Babe, have we finished our Christmas shopping yet?"

Oh, damn.

With everything that's been going on, it seems some of the preparations for Christmas have slipped my mind. The house is decorated to the nines and the tree looks particularly glorious this year, if I do say so myself. The refrigerator and freezer are filled to bursting with all the ingredients for the mountains of food I prepare for the days surrounding Christmas.

I just forgot the little detail of making sure I have presents for everyone.

Not that gifts are what Christmas is all about. The joy of the season. Charlie Brown and his tiny tree that miraculously sprouts new branches because of ornaments. The Grinch and his cardiac symptoms and all that. But getting together at Christmas feels like a way to relive the joy and traditions of our childhoods. And in some instances, make up for ones we would rather forget. Or, in my case, try to replace years I don't remember at all.

And a big part of having a fun family Christmas is exchanging gifts. When you're married to Sheriff Samuel Johnson, that's brought to a new level. My husband turns into a big kid when it comes to Christmas and I love every second of it. One thing he loves the most is stockings. In his mind, everyone should have a stocking stuffed to overflowing on Christmas morning, and it's the first thing we all rip into.

Despite the tremendous and valiant efforts of various marketing companies to convince us that adults no longer need such frivolous things as fun or delight, and would rather open a stocking filled with toothbrushes, razors, and plain socks, that's never going to fly at our house. With the exception of a few things I smuggle in because their size makes putting them under the tree seem like I'm just asking for them to go missing and not be discovered until spring, stockings in our house overflow with candy, silly novelties, and the occasional toy.

I am not ashamed.

My name is Emma Griffin Johnson and I buy grown-ass adults toys for Christmas.

Unfortunately, I haven't this year. Which is why I'm throwing clothes on without a particular amount of care into what they look like and if they have any kind of seasonal flair to them. I debate strapping my gun to my hip, but that doesn't exude the holiday spirit, so I bring it with me in my bag instead. I've learned over the years that it's best if I have my service weapon with me, even if there is no indication I will need it, but I definitely don't always need to have it on full display.

Nothing zaps the sparkle out of last-minute Christmas shopping cheer like an FBI agent storming the aisles with her gun in view.

"If you have any particular ideas for what you want to get for anybody, text me," I call to Sam. "I love you."

"I love you. How long do you think you'll be gone?"

"I'm Christmas shopping for a house full of people on December twenty-third," I deadpan him. "And one of those people is Xavier."

"I'll see you tomorrow," he chuckles.

"Oh, everybody should be getting here tonight. All joking aside, I hope I am here and alive by the time they get here. But if they don't, there is macaroni and cheese, roast chicken, and greens in the refrigerator. Tell Xavier his ornaments are at the top of the attic stairs, and if he won't go up, get them for him."

"I still don't understand why he has to put more on the tree. He was here the day after Thanksgiving when he insisted the tree go up. He put ornaments on then. Why didn't he finish?" Sam asks.

"They are Christmas Eve ornaments. They are only there for that short time," I explain. "Much like people who only put out jack o' lanterns on Halloween night."

"I don't agree with those people, either," he says.

I kiss him. "I know you don't, babe. Bye. I'll see you when I get back."

I have a choice here. I could go to Main Street and explore what the fine small businesses of Sherwood have to offer, or I could jump ship, head a few towns over, and hit the big box store and the mall. Sherwood has my heart, but necessity has my gut, so I send a promise to the little boutiques and shops that I'll stop by later if I have a chance and hit the road.

The parking lot at the sprawling outdoor mall is reaching critical mass, but I brave it anyway. This is an adventure, I tell myself, and to be honest, I do have a little flutter of excitement in my belly as I weave through the floors of the parking deck to find that elusive spot I know is waiting for me. I find it and zip in pretending I don't see the other car that was approaching from the other side. I saw it first. And was closer.

There are a few packages and bags tucked in corners and hidden in closets and under beds at the house, but I still have plenty to get, so I take a breath and fling myself out into the chill.

Three hours later, I walk back out waddling under the weight of as many shopping bags as I can manage. It might be more than I would be able to manage on a normal day. We could have a Christmas miracle working here.

Tossing everything into the trunk and the backseat, I get into the car and get the heater pumping. While I wait for the frustratingly cold air that is coming out of the vents to warm up, I call Sam.

"Hey, babe," he answers. "How is everything going with Operation North Pole?"

"I like it," I grin. "That's a good title."

"I've been working on it," he says.

"What were the other options?" I ask.

"Code How Jingle Got His Bells Back," he offers. "Rudolph the Red-Nosed Christmas Shopper. How the Bit—"

"I'm going to have to ask you to stop," I cut him off with a laugh. "Is anyone there yet?"

"Gang's all here. Bebe's teaching your father all the different shapes and colors of her blocks."

"Very important."

"Eric and Bellamy are taking a well-deserved afternoon nap."

"Rough drive?"

"I heard there were a couple of diaper incidents on the side of the road."

I cringe.

"And last but certainly not least, Xavier is currently trying to help Dean get into the Christmas spirit."

I take a breath, worried about the question I'm about to ask.

"How is he doing that?"

"I'd tell you, but you really ought to see it for yourself," he replies.

I groan.

"Oh, thank god you're home, Emma," calls Dean as I bustle into the house. His voice sounds odd and a bit echoey, and I glance left and right to realize I can't see him anywhere.

"What have you two gotten yourselves into?" I groan. Sam plants a quick kiss on my cheek as he takes the overflowing plethora of packages, boxes, and bags from my hands.

"Explorations into the metaphysical conceptualization of Santa Claus and the magic of Christmas as a function of existence and perception," Xavier explains, as if it's the most obvious thing in the world.

I nod. "And how did that turn into Dean being stuck in the chimney?"

Christmas Eve

'Twas the night before Christmas and in my house, Dean has recovered from his foray into the chimney and I stopped Xavier from going to the pet store to purchase a mouse.

It took a little doing, but I did manage to convince Xavier he didn't need to continue on with the full list of experiments he had designed in order to push Dean into the spirit. There was no need to ponder if Santa and Mary Poppins share a form of magic that creates endless bag capacity. We didn't need to find out what wassail was and make it so that they could go a-wassailing. The mystery of sugar plums can remain a mystery for another year.

We laugh our way through dinner and I feel relaxed and at peace, happy to be surrounded by the people I love and not having to worry about anything or anyone else. I just want to savor this moment.

After we're all in our pajamas, Xavier adds the final ornaments to the tree and the rest of us fill in the gaps with candy canes. Bebe is still a baby, but we can't resist putting out a plate of cookies and a cup of milk, then curling up under blankets and listening to my father read The Night Before Christmas. It still makes my heart beat a little faster in my chest. This is one of the memories from my childhood I hang onto, something I love that I can actually, tangibly recall.

It used to be my grandfather who read the poem. We'd sit around together and listen to his deep, smooth voice go through the verses by heart. He didn't need anything to remind him and he never missed a single word. The year my father took over was hard, but I was happy to still hear the words. If I closed my eyes, I could still hear them in my grandfather's voice.

The baby is asleep by the time the poem ends and I give hugs and kisses all around as everyone heads to their own rooms for the night. It's late and I know the morning will start very early, but there's no rest yet for me. I have presents to wrap and stockings to stuff.

This is not entirely the fault of not shopping until yesterday. To be completely honest, the vast majority of the gifts I bought at the beginning of the season stayed unwrapped in their bags until I dug them out to hide in my room. I know all the experts say you should have everything in their perfect paper and glistening bows sometimes pre-candy corn, but I'm a devotee of wrapping on Christmas Eve. Like the rush that comes from finding that perfect stocking stuffer for Sam or the ridiculous massively huge amusement park building block set I can't wait to give to Xavier at the last minute on the twenty-third, wrapping through the night on Christmas Eve gives me a special holiday tingle.

I'll be exhausted in the morning. But that's what cinnamon rolls and coffee are for. I'm looking forward to the wrapping paper flying everywhere, the laughter as we dig into stockings, and then eating for hours on end.

Sam brings me a cup of cocoa and the plate of cookies for Santa as I sit on the floor wrapping presents. I know he'll look away when it comes to the stockings. That's why a Christmas movie during wrapping is essential. Background sound and distraction for Sam so he gets surprises. It makes me smile as I drop tangerines and handfuls of walnuts in their shell into the toes of each of the stockings. That's in honor of Xavier, who says the traditional gifts are a requirement. I don't fully remember why, but he appreciates them and acts like they are a surprise every year, so I'll keep doing it.

It's deep into the night when I snuggle the final present into place under the tree and hang the heavy stockings back in their place. Bebe's is too full and now sits on one of the chairs, surrounded by the overflow. This is the first year I think she'll be big enough to really get into tearing into the gifts. She might not really understand what's going on yet, but these memories are for us. She'll have plenty in the years to come. For now, I'm happy to etch the sound of her giggle and the look of that bright smile into my mind.

Sam has already gotten into bed by the time I take my shower and climb in beside him. His body heat surrounds me and I slide into sleep for the couple of hours I'll get.

Christmas

"What's that?" Sam asks the next morning when I step back inside with an envelope in my hand.

"It was on the front porch," I tell him. "I went out to bring Janet and Paul some cinnamon rolls and I found it when I got back."

I'm not sure I want to open it. The last time there was something waiting on my porch at Christmas, a severed hand sent me on a horrifying spiral into my past that forced me back into investigating a crime I had never been able to solve.

"Was it there when you left?" he asks.

"I think so. It was frozen to the porch." I open the envelope as Xavier rushes into the room and jumps into his corner on the couch.

It's a beautiful, if generic card with "Merry Christmas" written across the front in gold gilding.

"What's it say?" Sam asks.

"Your gift will be late, but it's on its way. Merry Christmas, Emma," I read.

"Who is it from?"

"There's no signature," I say.

I toss it down onto the table beside the door, not wanting to think about it anymore. There's no signature, but there doesn't need to be. I know who it's from.

Bebe lets out a squeal from across the room and I see that everyone has come together. Eric is looking every bit the proud father as he snaps pictures of her standing in front of the chair, clapping her chubby little baby hands as she looks over the sparkling pile of gifts. Bellamy is sitting on the floor next to her, pointing out the different objects and cooing to her. Dean and my father are beaming as they start to pass around the first round of gifts. I get Xavier's stocking and bring it to him, then nestle Sam's into his lap.

"Merry Christmas, babe," I whisper, leaning down for a kiss.

"There better be a slinky in here," he whispers back.

Santa, you did me right.

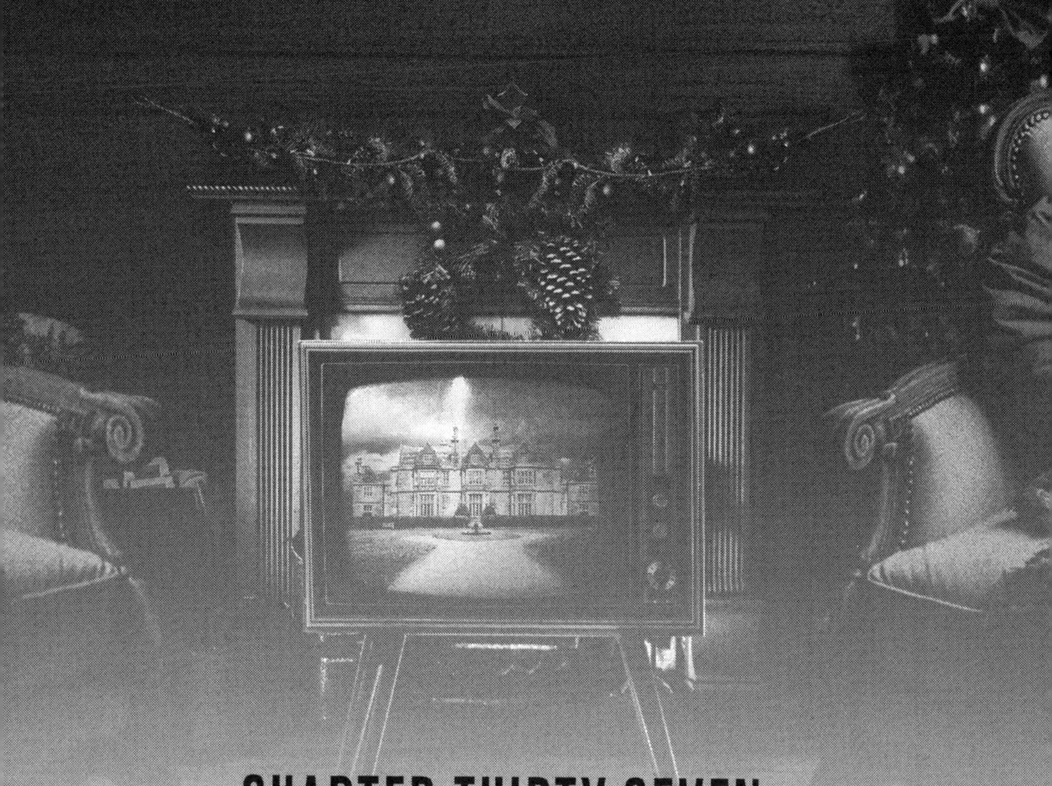

CHAPTER THIRTY-SEVEN

Christmas ends exactly the way it should, with my house smelling like peppermint and pine, sparkling bits of wrapping paper balled up in corners, and the warm tug of a day of laughter in my stomach muscles. Curled on the couch with one last cup of eggnog in my hand and the homemade cookbook Xavier gave me for Christmas in my lap, I'm ready to relax for a while before crawling into bed.

With everyone I usually spend the holidays with already tucked away in their various spaces in the house, I'm not expecting to see the wash of headlights across the wall or hear a door slam closed right in front. It could be a neighbor getting home from a celebration, or family visiting and just arriving late, but it sounds too close, and a few moments later, I hear steps on the front porch.

A soft knock makes me grab my phone and log into the stream of the security camera covering the door. The person is bundled up so much at first I can't tell who it is, but a shift in her posture and an accidental glance up toward the camera shows it's Marlowe. Confused and concerned, I open the door.

"I don't suppose there's room at this inn," she says.

It sounds like she's trying to make a joke, but there are tears in her voice and she's shaking.

"Marlowe? What are you doing here?" I ask.

The question takes the smile from her face and she steps back slightly.

"I'm sorry. I shouldn't have come here," she whispers.

She turns and heads back down the steps.

"No, wait," I say, stepping out after her. "No, that's not what I meant. Come inside."

She looks up at me. "Are you sure?"

"Come inside," I insist, my tone sincere.

She comes in and I look behind her at the unfamiliar car parked at the curb behind my father's.

"Is your driver in the car?" I ask.

She shakes her head. "No. I drove myself. I don't usually use my car. It stays at my mom's house most of the time."

I close the door behind us and lock the various locks, including the new one Sam installed for our anniversary.

"Let me take your coat," I tell her.

Marlowe shrugs out of her heavy coat and takes off her gloves, scarf, and hat, stuffing them into the pockets. She shivers more and I guide her over to the sofa where I drape a blanket around her.

"You probably think I'm some kind of stalker," she remarks, holding the blanket close. "Showing up like this."

"You're more polite," I say, hoping for at least a hint of a smile. She rewards me with it, but it lasts only a fraction of a second. "Can I get you something to help you warm up? Coffee? Cider?"

Her eyes tear up slightly at the mention of cider, and she nods. I go into the kitchen and fill a mug with the cider that has cooled on the stove. I put it in the microwave and fill a platter with some of the sweet and savory snacks we had throughout the day while it heats. When I get back to the living room with both in hand, Marlowe has the cookbook in her lap and is reading through it.

"Did Xavier really make this?" she asks as I set the food and drink down in front of her.

"Yeah," I nod. "He gave it to me for Christmas."

"I like that it includes your own cinnamon roll recipe," she says. "It's so surreal to hold this knowing he made it. I'm sure that sounds strange to you, but I've been hearing about him through this whole project and I guess this is what you meant by us thinking about everybody in the story as a character rather than a person. I didn't think I was doing that. I thought I was being more serious about it. And I know you've talked about him and told me about him being in your life, but I guess he was still kind of a character in my head.

"But I'm holding a book he made. With words he wrote. Including a disclaimer about it being unauthorized, but getting permission from somebody named Pearl."

"She owns the diner in town," I explain. "She makes my favorite biscuits and gravy."

Marlowe lowers the book back to the coffee table. "It just makes him very real."

"He is definitely real. He's also sleeping upstairs," I tell her.

Her eyes lift toward the ceiling like she's going to be able to see him. "I'm so sorry. I'm intruding. I found your address and I just drove here and I shouldn't have. I'll leave."

She stands up, but I take her by her shoulder and sit her back down.

"Marlowe, you're already here. Obviously, you came for a reason. Tell me," I say. "We'll talk about where you found my address later because that brings up some concerns, but however you did, you're welcome here if you want to be here."

"Thank you," she says, her head drooping. "I just didn't know what else to do or where else to go. I didn't want to be in my apartment tonight."

"What about your mother? Weren't you with her for Christmas?" I ask.

Marlowe nods. "For part of it. Then she told me she booked herself a cruise to help her manage the stress of the last couple of months and would see me in a few days. I guess we'll just consider that an extra Christmas gift from me to her."

"You support her?" I ask.

It feels like a really invasive question, but it feels like she's trying to reach and I need to grab on.

"From the first dollar I made," she says. "I know I make it sound like I hate doing it, but that's not it. She always took care of me the best she could, so I'm glad to be able to do the same for her. I just feel like over time she's seeing me less as her daughter and more as a..."

"Product?" I ask, filling in the space she leaves. She nods. "Did you tell her that you're taking that role?"

"Not yet," Marlowe says. "I don't know if I am."

"You don't know if you're going to tell her? Or you don't know if you're going to do it?"

"Both. I don't know if it's going to be an option anymore," she clarifies. "Not after the New Year."

"What do you mean?" I ask. "Was that the deadline they gave you?"

"It's the one I gave myself," she says. "I can't keep secrets anymore. And by the New Year, I won't anymore. But it's going to change everything."

"Marlowe, the other day you called me and you sounded really upset," I say.

"I don't remember that," she says.

"That's what you said before. But I don't understand how you can't remember. You called and said you couldn't do it anymore. What did you mean?"

She shakes her head. "Maybe I was just having a really hard workout."

"I think we both know that's not the truth. Someone else was with you. Who was it?"

"I told you. I don't remember calling you. I don't know why I would say that," she insists.

"It was just a couple days after the anniversary of your father's death," I say.

She gives me a questioning look, then something like realization crosses her face. "Oh. Right."

"I don't know much about him. Can you tell me about him?" I ask.

She looks down into her cup of cider. "He died before I was born."

"I know," I nod. "But your mother told me how much of a connection you've always felt toward him and that you got your talents from him. She must have told you about him."

"She says his name was Charles Gray and they met when she was in high school. He was the love of her life and she was always drawn to his singing and dancing. She says he was funny and everybody loved him. He didn't pursue his dreams of going into the performance industry because they decided they wanted to get married and start a family. They'd just found out I was a girl and he named me right before the fire."

"That's a beautiful inspiration," I say.

"Most fairy tales are."

She rubs her eyes and lets out a long exhale.

"You should get some rest," I tell her. "That's a long drive. You're not going to make it all the way back there tonight."

"I can't find a hotel," she says. "I'm sure you have a full house."

"There's room," I insist. "You're staying here."

A sudden hug startles me, but I hug her back. I show her the bathroom and my office, unfolding the couch for her to turn it into a bed. I go upstairs to get her extra blankets and on the way back through, I notice the bag she'd had over her shoulder sagging on the floor in front of the couch. I scoop it up to bring it to her and something falls out. Reaching under the couch, I pull it out and see that it's a pill bottle with her name on the label. The name of the medication sounds familiar, but it takes me a few seconds to place it. It's an anti-anxiety medication.

Stuffing the bottle back in the bag, I bring it to the room and leave it on the folded-out bed. I say goodnight to her through the bathroom door and head upstairs to bed, feeling even more like I'm on that slippery slope.

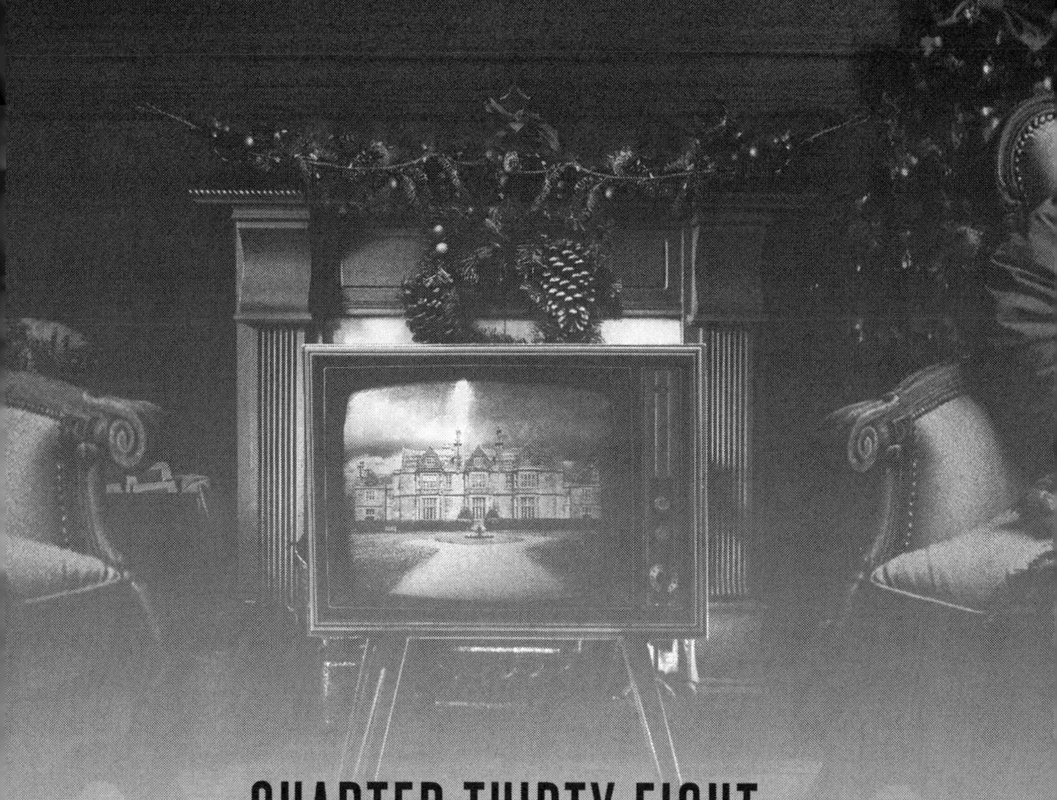

CHAPTER THIRTY-EIGHT

"SHE'S GONE?" SAM ASKS.

I'm leaning against the counter in the kitchen holding a note written on a piece of paper from the pad on the desk in my office. It's brief, just Marlowe thanking me again for having her and apologizing for intruding.

"She says she'll see us at her birthday party. Just like that. Like she was visiting from across the neighborhood, not a multi-hour drive away."

"Which I still don't understand. Why did she come here? Just because her mother left on Christmas?" Sam frowns.

I shake my head. "I don't think so. There's more to it. You should have heard her. It was like it was an impulse to come out here, then once she was here, she didn't know exactly why she was here. And that medicine bottle…" I shake my head again, pushing against the counter to turn so I can get a cup of coffee. "It's an anti-anxiety pill, but I was reading about some of the side effects, and they can be a little scary, especially if the person taking the medication isn't careful to handle it properly."

"What's bothering you?" Sam asks a few seconds later and I realize I've just been staring into the middle distance, tossing the encounter with Marlowe around in my head.

"When she was talking to me, it was a little scattered. Not like Xavier scattered, but like her brain couldn't focus down on one thing and was avoiding what she really wanted to say. She was talking about giving herself a New Year's deadline to stop living with her secrets and that changing everything. I asked her about the phone call, about her saying she couldn't do it anymore, and she says she doesn't remember."

"Maybe she's just embarrassed."

"Or maybe she really doesn't remember. This medication, especially if combined with alcohol or with certain other medications, can cause periods of memory loss. I remembered the comment on her social media from that day and the anniversary of her father's death, so I asked her about it. Just to see how she would react," I say.

"And? How did she react?"

"Like a puppet," I tell him. "There was no emotion. And when I prompted her, pointing out how much her mother talks about her connection to her father and how she shares his talents, she rattled off this description of him that sounded like it came straight off of one of those magazine pages. Everything started with 'my mother says'. She says his name was Charles Gray. She says they were high school sweethearts. She says they had just found out she was a girl and he named her. Like she's recounting a story."

"Well, it did happen before she was born," Sam points out.

"But that doesn't make her father's name subjective," I say. "I never met my mother's mother, but I would never say that 'she says her name was Evangeline'. That was her name." Something suddenly occurs to me. "Meredith says they just found out she was a girl and Charles named her Marlowe right before the fire that killed him."

"Right," Sam nods. "That was part of why it was so emotional. He was so looking forward to having a little girl and being a father, but he only got to experience knowing her daughter by name for a few days."

"The first interview I read about her, Marlowe describes her mother talking about how hard it was to get through the months of her pregnancy without him. That didn't click until right now. She doesn't mention the location of the fire, or even that it was a fire that killed him. Just that he died in the service."

"Which is kind of weird," Sam mentions. "A hostage situation with officers isn't quite what I'd call 'dying in the service'. Just a weird way to phrase it."

"Yeah, I agree. But our timeline lines up with him just finding out that she was a girl and naming her, which would usually happen right around four or five months into her pregnancy. But the fire at the Carlsbad Hotel was less than a month before Marlowe was born."

I put down the note from Marlowe and take out my phone.

"What are you looking up?" Sam asks.

"Something she said about her favorite Christmas memories," I say. It takes me a few seconds to find it, and when I do, I turn my phone to him. "One of her favorite things about Christmas was the luminaries."

"That's a pretty common tradition. The neighborhood used to do those when we were kids, don't you remember? The sheriff's department would sponsor the actual luminaries themselves and would hand them out to the neighbors a couple of days beforehand. Then on the chosen night, everyone would light them and we'd walk up and down the streets with cocoa looking at them and singing carols. I distinctly remember doing that with you at least once."

"I do, too," I nod. "It was beautiful and I can completely understand why she would have that memory. Except that she didn't grow up in a neighborhood."

"What do you mean?"

"The descriptions of her childhood all have her growing up on a farm. It never specifies exactly where, but her mother talks about her working so hard and helping so much even while she was singing and dancing around in the fields," I explain. "But then in this one interview, Marlowe says the luminaries around their neighborhood. I don't know of any people working a farm who consider it their neighborhood."

"Who else talked about where she grew up?" Sam asks. "You said she and Brittany have been best friends since they were really young. Has she ever shared any memories about the two of them climbing around in the barn or collecting eggs or whatever she'd be doing on a farm?"

"We'll come back to your understanding of agriculture, but no. She never talks about it because she never went there. They did an interview together once where she talked about wanting to go over to Marlowe's house for a slumber party but never being able to because Meredith said it was too far away. She had to get a waiver for her to go to the high school that she did and no one was ever allowed to go to her house. She spent time at other people's houses."

"Did she grow up near the Carlsbad Hotel?" Sam asks.

"The high school she went to was about an hour from there." I make a cup of coffee and take a sip of it as I make my way toward my office. "I need my computer for this."

Sam loves to tease me for still wanting to get out my laptop when I'm looking something up rather than just using my phone. But I prefer the larger screen and having it sitting in front of me rather than in my hand. It frees me up to take notes or drink coffee, and I don't have to constantly scroll around to look for what I want.

My computer is sitting on my desk right where I left it. Earlier when I went to check on Marlowe, I found the note from her on top of it, the blankets she used folded up and sitting at the end of the couch she had folded back up. It was almost like she'd tried to erase herself being there as much as possible.

I open the computer and pull up my search engine. I type in the name of her high school and get a map of the area. Scrolling it back so I'm looking at the entire surrounding area, I try to piece together the description of her youth.

"These are farms," Sam notes, pointing out plots of land. "But they look commercial."

"There are privately held ones further out," I say. "These are more than an hour and a half from the school, though. That's a long way to go just to avoid a rural school district. I wonder if the district has policies regarding how far a student can live from the school and still get a waiver."

Opening another search bar, I start to type in the name of the school district. It only takes a few letters before I see a recommended search term populate. The symbol beside it indicates it's in my search history.

"Marlowe used my computer," I say. I point at the recommended term. It's for a store with several of the same letters as the school district. "I've never searched for that."

"You don't have a password on it?"

"Our anniversary," I admit.

"Emma!"

"I know," I say. "We've talked about it. I know. But this computer rarely leaves the house and doesn't have any sensitive information on it. This is the one I have for personal use, not work research, so I didn't feel like it needed major security. And apparently she didn't have a problem guessing the password, because she definitely used it during the time she was here."

"Why would she use your computer?" he asks. "She would use her phone."

"Not if the battery was dead. Or she didn't bring it inside. I didn't see her touch her phone the entire time she was here." I click on the search history tab. "I wonder what else she was looking up."

The history reads like the night of an insomniac. She filled her time exploring different online stores and visiting news sources and blogs. In the middle of the list, I notice her name.

"Never read the comments," Sam mutters.

"She was reading more than the comments," I tell him, clicking on the link to bring up her virtual fan club page. "She was seeing what she posted."

"What do you mean?" Sam asks.

"I told you Brittany handles her social media. This is one of the things she does. It's a subscription-based fan club that lets people have access to additional content. Videos. Postcards. Signed photos. Special appearances. That kind of thing," I explain.

"People pay for it?" he asks.

"Monthly," I tell him.

"That seems like a kind of shady way to make a few extra dollars."

"A few extra hundred thousand dollars," I point out. "Every month. But they choose to be a part of it. They want to feel like they are in a closer fan circle to her and get more access to her. Besides, she doesn't keep all the money. Look."

I point out on the subscription signup page where a note tells prospective members proceeds from the club go to a fund that supports a variety of charities through regular donations.

"The donations are made anonymously," Sam reads out. "She wants to bring attention to the organizations rather than to herself."

"Maybe she's more like Lakyn than anyone thought," I offer.

I quickly type in my personal information and my credit card details.

"What are you doing?" Sam asks.

"Making a charitable contribution," I shrug. I finish signing up and go to the posts. "You can't see what she was looking at unless you're a subscriber."

"There's a post about her father," Sam says. "And a video from the set. A lot of what's here shows up on her other platforms later. The subscribers just get early access to it."

"An offer for fans to get a New Year's greeting from her," I murmur as I read through the newest thing posted to the platform. I stop on one with a timestamp indicating it was posted in the middle of the night. "Christmas memories."

I start the video expecting to see Marlowe as a little girl or spending time with her mother. Instead, it's images of Brittany and Marlowe from when they were younger. The slow-motion video plays against the sound of a woman singing and progresses through the years until what looks like footage that could have been taken last year.

"Are you noticing something about these memories?" Sam asks.

"That it seems to be a whole lot more of Brittany's memories than Marlowe's?" I ask, nodding. "Yeah. I did notice that."

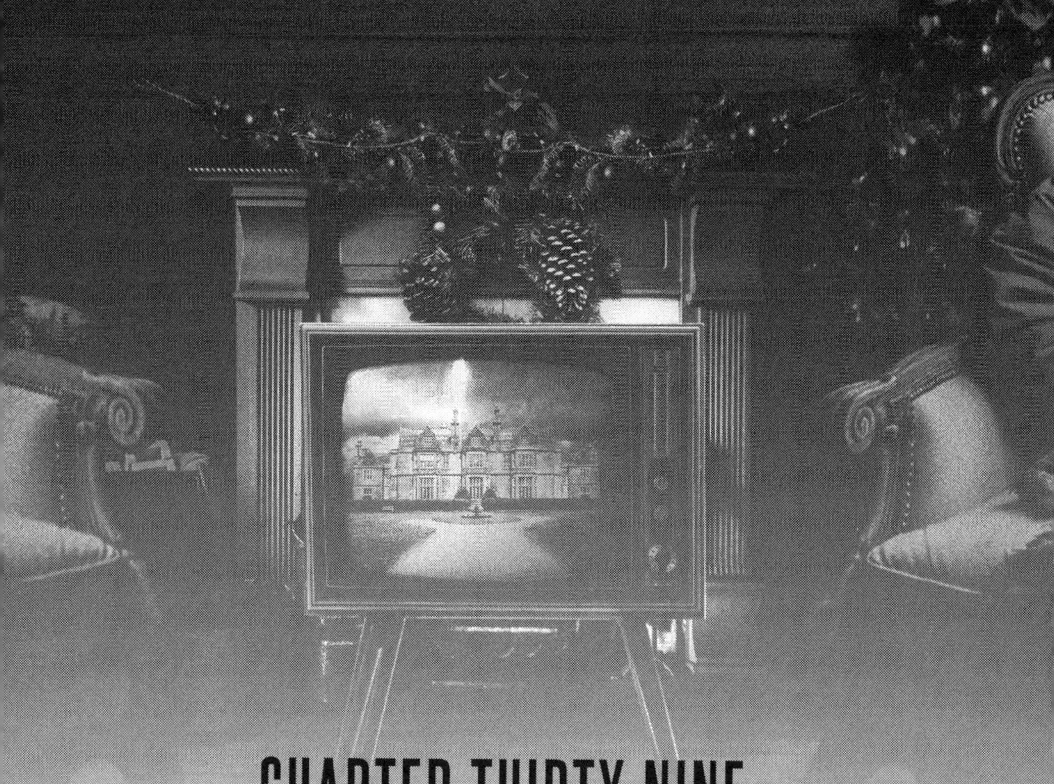

CHAPTER THIRTY-NINE

MARLOWE ANSWERS THE DOOR WITH A QUIZZICAL LOOK ON HER face.

"Hey, Emma. I didn't know you were back in town."

"I just wanted to come by and give you this," I say, holding a package out to her.

"What is it?" she asks.

"I told Xavier how much you liked my cookbook, so he sent you a copy."

She smiles. "Thank you. I wish I'd gotten a chance to meet him."

"You could have," I say. "But you left before anyone was up."

She nods, stepping back into her apartment so I can follow her. The smile has faded from her face when she closes the door behind us.

"I know. I'm sorry for ducking out like that. I just realized how insane it was that I showed up at your house on Christmas and felt like I should get back here."

We walk into the living room and she sets the book down on the coffee table. I notice some papers spread out across it and take a glance.

"Wow. Two days after Christmas and you're already dwelling on how much you spent over the holidays," I comment. "You're ahead of the game."

She looks down at the bank statements and other financial records strewn across the table.

"I like to get a jump on it," she replies. "You know, because I feel like I don't have a healthy enough amount of stress pushing me through my adult years."

"That's the big part of my nutritional triangle," I tell her. "Stress, coffee, and pasta. Right there at the foundation."

"And cinnamon rolls," Marlowe adds. "According to Xavier."

She glances at the cookbook and I nod.

"Some of those, too."

"Can I get you a drink?" she asks.

"Sure," I say.

She goes into the kitchen and I fight with the curiosity that wants to look at the papers. She comes back looking like she expected to find me speed-reading them, and hands me a mug of cider. It seems we've developed an exchange system.

"I was actually just going over my expenses for the last few months," she says. "It's another one of those things I haven't been handling on my own and recently I started looking into them more. I asked Frederic about building my investments and he didn't exactly give me the kind of answer I wanted."

"Frederic handles your finances, too?" I ask.

She nods, tucking her legs up under her. "He's a jack of all trades. Or an adulting solution in a box. Whichever you prefer."

I hate that the word 'adult' has become a verb. I'm usually busy enough. I don't particularly need a trendy word reminding me that just the act of being my age is also considered a task in and of itself.

"What did he tell you about your investments?" I ask. "I'm sorry if I'm being nosy."

She shakes her head. "No, it's fine. Essentially he wasn't able to give me clear details about my investments. What they are, how much they make, any kinds of plans for scaling up. He talked around it, kind of half-answering and telling me the reason people have professionals to handle their finances is so they don't have to worry about it."

"That sounds familiar," I note, thinking of how he talked about her contracts and negotiations.

"It definitely does," she agrees. "So I decided to check my bank account and credit card statements. Things I do have access to even if I don't use that access very often. That's how I realized how much my mother was spending. I confronted her about it, but she said she was only using the money I put in her account each month. Which is why I requested my full financial records."

"And why you said you wanted to take the role because you aren't going to let Frederic take anything else from you," I say.

"I said that?" she asks.

I nod. "During our video call the other night. You said you decided to take the role but hadn't said anything to anyone yet, and you weren't going to let him take anything else from you."

She shakes her head, rubbing her forehead with her fingertips. "I don't remember that at all. I know I went out dancing, but I don't remember our call."

"You seemed like you were having a good time and were excited about taking the role. But that you weren't going to say anything about it until New Year's. It's the same thing you said about getting rid of your secrets."

"It's a fresh beginning," she says. "But it also gives me time to think."

"You said not carrying around the secrets anymore was going to change everything. What were you talking about?" I ask.

Marlowe shakes her head. "I can't. Not yet."

"Does it have anything to do with where you grew up?"

She looks at me questioningly. "Why would you ask that?"

"Some of the things I've heard about your childhood haven't made sense. Your mother talks about you growing up working so hard on the farm, but the area around the high school where you went only has commercial farms. The private farms are too far out to have even allowed you to get a waiver. And you said you loved the luminaries around your neighborhood when you were younger. But a farm..."

"Isn't in a neighborhood," she finishes my statement, her voice sounding powdery as she gives in. "I know. I hoped no one would notice that."

"I don't understand. Why lie about something like that?"

"It wasn't my idea," she tells me. "When I first started posting videos, I didn't want to give a lot of details about where I grew up or my childhood. It just wasn't something I wanted to talk about. So I just mentioned little things like being able to see trees from my window or spending a lot of time outside. My mother never let me have anyone over, so it didn't feel like anyone would notice I wasn't giving all the details. Then when I started getting work and people wanted to know more about me, Mom made up the whole thing about the farm. I didn't even know she was going to do it until I heard her in an interview."

"Why would she do that?"

"She said a good life story was going to get me more attention. People want to hear about someone interesting and different, someone who is hardworking. Not just another rich girl who got the world handed to her. She told me it wasn't really lying. She was building an image for me. It was a backstory, just like for a character."

"But you aren't a character," I point out.

She gives a puff of bitter laughter. "No. I'm not. Ironic, right?" She sighs. "I leaned into it because I figured if I said that wasn't true, it would look terrible for my mother and would humiliate both of us. And then it turned into something. People really did seem to notice me or follow me because of this story. I wanted to act so much. I wanted to be somebody. So I went with it."

"And if you tell the truth, it would change the way people see you," I say.

"*When* I tell the truth," she corrects me. "I have to. I can't carry it around with me anymore. Any of it. I'm afraid of not being this person, but I also can't keep doing it."

"I understand," I nod. "Being honest is always going to be the best choice. Just know that your talent doesn't have anything to do with the story your mother told. Or the fact that you went along with it. People might like that story, but it doesn't matter when they are watching you. They appreciate what you bring to what you do, and you never know. Maybe telling the truth could open up new things for you."

Tears have started down Marlowe's cheeks.

"Emma, promise me you won't say anything to anyone about this. Please let me tell people my own way."

"I promise."

CHAPTER FORTY

The lights sparkle on Marlowe's dress as she dances. The shimmer seems to reflect in her smile. There's new energy about her as she celebrates her birthday. I wonder what she's feeling.

"Alright, everyone," Brittany says into a microphone, calling all of our attention to her. "You know why we're all here. To celebrate my best friend, the girl the whole damn world is falling in love with, Marlowe Gray!"

A cheer rises up through the entire nightclub as people from down on the main floor swarm around the roped-off private area where we're sitting. "And I have a little surprise for her, and for all of you. I've gotten really good at making videos about her recently, so I decided to use those skills to put together a birthday tribute. I love you, Mars."

There's an uncomfortable edge to the words, like she thinks she's being funny but it's falling flat. My eyes slide over to Meredith. It's taken everything I have not to confront her about what I know. But I promised

Marlowe and I'm not going to break that promise. At least now I have an explanation for the way that woman sets me on edge. She's a liar and a manipulator. She doesn't know it will all come to light soon.

January 1

Happy New Year, everyone! Thank you for celebrating my birthday with me last night. I had a blast! This is the beginning of a brand-new year. Make the most of it! Love, Marlowe

Happy New Year, Marlowe. I hope it's your best yet.

Happy belated birthday! I saw the pictures. You looked gorgeous! I can't wait to see what you'll do this year.

I can't believe you're going back to work tomorrow. How do you do it? I'm going to be worthless for about a week.

Where are you, Mars? I thought you were going to come say goodbye before I headed to my grandparents' house this morning.

Emma watched the comments populate under Marlowe's post. She kept coming back, waiting for another post. It never came.

Now

I watch Brittany move around getting the video queued up as a screen glides down from the ceiling. The tribute video is as sappy as I expect, with music behind pictures and video clips of Marlowe along with the two of them together. The voice singing sounds familiar, but I know it's not the original artist of the song.

The screen fills with pictures of Marlowe doing gymnastics and Meredith suddenly gets up and goes over to the laptop. She turns off the video and takes the microphone.

"Let's go ahead and turn that off. I think we've embarrassed the birthday girl enough." There's some laughter and a couple of protests. Brittany keeps a harsh, almost pained grin across her face, but nods. "Or maybe it's just time for some different embarrassment. Who's ready for gifts?"

Marlowe sits down and starts unwrapping the packages handed to her. Finally, Frederic steps up beside her and offers a small box. She looks at him briefly, then opens it. An uncomfortable look crosses her face and she sets the box aside.

"Thank you, everybody. I appreciate all of you coming out to celebrate with me tonight and I don't want to just sit around anymore. Let's dance!"

She moves quickly toward the center of the roped-off area before anyone can say anything. Her eyes close as she lifts her arms up over her head and sways to the music.

January 2

"Have you heard from Marlowe?" Delta asked when Emma walked out of the kraft tent with a cup of coffee wrapped in both hands.

"No. Not since the text message yesterday."

The same message that was posted on her social media came to Emma as a text later in the morning. She assumed everyone Marlowe knew well enough to message directly had gotten it. She'd waited to see more from her, but no other post ever came. No secrets ever came to light. Emma figured Marlowe had just gotten cold feet. She was looking forward to opening up, but once the day came, maybe it was too hard to face.

Delta sighed but didn't look concerned. It wasn't unlike Marlowe to be late, especially this close to a holiday.

"Alright. Thanks."

"She's not here."

"Has anyone heard from her? A text? Call? Anything?"

"She probably spent yesterday sleeping it off and still feels like crap so she's running late."

"She needs to get here. We already lost one day with her."

It was late in the afternoon and everything that could be done without her had already been shot. Everyone was waiting around for Marlowe to show up, but no one had even heard from her. Nothing had shown up on her social media and her phone was going straight to voicemail.

"She's not answering her phone. She hasn't gotten in touch with anyone."

Night had fallen and with it came the real worry. Marlowe might be difficult sometimes, but she wasn't like this.

"Has anyone checked her apartment?" Emma asked.

"Does anyone have a key? Where's Brittany?" Delta asked.

"She's out of town, remember? She went to see her grandparents because she wasn't able to see them over the holidays," Frederic said.

"That's right. Get in touch with her. Find out if there are any spare keys anywhere. Someone call the building manager for Marlowe's building. We need to get into her apartment."

"I know how to get inside," Emma said. There was no reason to wait. Calling the manager would take up too much time and the twisting in her stomach wouldn't let Emma hesitate anymore.

Delta looked at Emma in surprise. "You do?"

"There's a back entrance. Marlowe showed it to me. It's hidden and accessible only by keypad entry, but I know how to get in. Come on."

Now

I remember a time when waiting up for midnight on New Year's Eve seemed thrilling. But tonight, I'm just tired. The nightclub isn't my scene and I can tell Sam isn't having fun. At least he's here with me. Maybe that's selfish of me, but I'm going to call the marriage card on this one. If I'm here supporting Marlowe, he can be here supporting me.

She's still dancing. I don't know which is fueling her more, being newly twenty-one or wanting to stop herself from thinking.

I notice her eyes dart to the side. Some of the fun has drained from her face. She moves around more erratically, no longer focused on the people right there with her, but looking out over the crowd. She stumbles over to a table and downs a drink, her eyes still moving into the people surrounding her.

"She doesn't look good," I mention to Sam. "I think something's wrong."

I look back and find she's gone. Somehow in the two seconds I glanced at him, she slipped away. I search until I see her walking quickly toward the exit with her security guards. I get up to follow, but Sam stops me.

"Let her be," he says. "She's probably just tired and not feeling well. Everything's fine. Besides, this means we can get out of here."

I nod but take out my phone to message her.

Me: *Are you alright?*

Marlowe: *Just done with the party. Want to go home.*

Me: *Okay. Have a good night.*

Marlowe: *I'll talk to you tomorrow.*

Me: *Happy New Year.*

January 2

"Marlowe?"

The apartment was still. There were a couple of papers on the floor and the TV was on, but other than that, nothing was out of place. They called out to her first, not wanting to disrupt her if she was just at home sleeping off the party and avoiding the world.

They hadn't used the back entrance. Emma didn't want that many cars streaming through the back of the building, so she had them park out front with the plan of letting herself in and then coming for them through the front. Branson saw them gathering on the sidewalk and let them in through the front entrance using his key. Emma didn't think about them needing a regular key to the apartment until they got to the door. But it turned out they didn't need one. It had the same style of keypad entrance as the back door. Emma put in the code and called out for her.

But Marlowe didn't answer. They spread out, searching the rooms.

"This door is open," Sam announced, running his fingers along the edge of the sliding glass door leading to the balcony. "It looks like someone tried to shut it, but it didn't latch."

Emma could feel the tiny bit of cold air streaming in from outside. She pushed the door open and stepped out onto the balcony.

It reminds me of a balance beam.

She touched her hands to the stone edge around the balcony. Even from the high vantage point, she couldn't see the courtyard on the other side of the building, or the balcony that went with it. She felt hidden, yet still out in the open. Just like she imagined Marlowe wanted to feel.

She started to step away from the wall but noticed something on the stone. Dark spots that stood out from the lighter color of the textured stone. Her heart pounded in her chest as she cautiously leaned forward to look down into the courtyard.

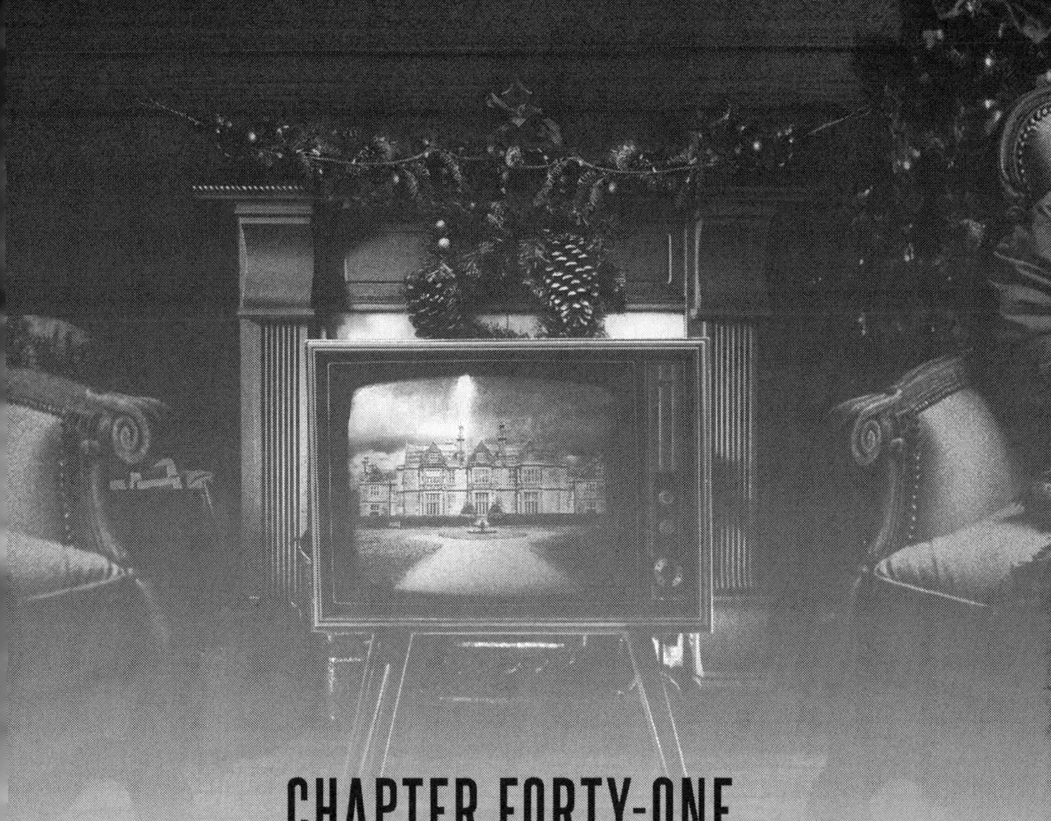

CHAPTER FORTY-ONE

Now

I CAN'T SEE ANYTHING AROUND ME AS I RUN THROUGH THE apartment and down the steps.

Why didn't I go to the back? If I'd gone through the back, I would have found her immediately.

My feet nearly skid out from under me on the ice as I run toward her. I don't need to hurry. I already know that. I can see the blood. I can see how she's not moving.

Marlowe is dead.

Branson appears behind me a few seconds later and I try to push him back into the building, but he won't move. He's staring at Marlowe's body broken on the patio ground. His mouth falls open and he looks like he's struggling to breathe.

"What happened? What happened to her?"

"Back up. You need to go back inside. Nobody needs to come out here."

But I can already hear everyone else coming. They saw me go down the steps and have discovered the back entrance. In an instant, the patio is chaos. I do my best to block Marlowe's body with my own, trying to keep everybody as far back away from her as possible.

We need to preserve this scene exactly as it is. No one can touch her. No one can move anything.

Sam steps in to help me get everybody back inside while I call the police. I'm trembling, but as I look down at her, the calm takes over. It has to. I have no choice now. I have to be in control for her.

It takes a lot longer than I would want it to for the police to arrive. In reality, it's probably no more than a few minutes. But standing there in the bitter cold, wanting so much to cover Marlowe, every second stretches on.

She still has her makeup on and the style of her hair is exactly the way it was on her birthday. But she's wearing pajamas. As the medical examiner's office zips her into a body bag to bring her away, I catch a glimpse of her feet and the nail polish still on several of her toes.

"I'm so sorry, Emma," Sam says as they leave, wrapping his arm around me.

"Looks like a suicide," the responding officer says, looking down at the blood on the ground. He looks up toward the balcony. "Or maybe an accident. Got drunk partying for New Year's Eve, tumbled down. It happens."

"It happens?" I ask incredulously. "That's your response?"

"Until we find out for sure, yes," he says.

He walks away to start collecting statements from everyone who was here when I found Marlowe's body.

"Then we find out for sure," I say, watching him.

"She wasn't on antidepressants. I would know if my daughter was on antidepressants."

Meredith looks defiant through the tears in her eyes. She refuses to listen to me. In the two days since Marlowe's body was found, Meredith has done everything she can to push back. Rather than being open to what was found in her daughter's apartment as the investigation began, she's closed herself off. She wants to keep up the image. She's convinced herself if she tells a different story, that will become the reality.

Not this time. She can't just make up what she wants to have happened or be happening and have that come true for her. This time, she has to face what's real.

And what's real is Marlowe's body in the morgue. Notebooks filled with brutal, dark poetry and gut-wrenching letters addressed to the people in her life. She had them hidden away in the back of a closet, tucked inside a satchel that looks like she should have carried it onto a college campus. Maybe if that was the path she chose, things would have turned out different.

I wish I could sit down and read those letters and know every detail of what was happening in her life. But she didn't make it easy. The writings are stream-of-consciousness, not fully explaining anything she says. These are words intended for her and for the person she's writing about.

She doesn't need to explain because she knows what they mean. And the subject would, too. But I'm starting to piece it together. I can take her words: the ones that she said, the ones that she wrote, the ones said for her, and put her broken life back together.

"Meredith, I need you to listen to me. Marlowe was going through a lot. And she was taking medication for it. Anti-anxiety and antidepressants. Both bottles were found in her apartment. And both had her name. We're going to speak with the doctor who prescribed them to her, but you can make this easier by telling the truth. When did she get them? When did she start taking them?"

"I'm telling you, Marlowe was not on drugs."

"I'm not talking about recreational narcotics, Meredith. These are prescription medications meant to help her handle issues that she was dealing with in her life."

"My daughter was not. She wasn't one of these people who can't handle life and need a pill for every little thing. She was happy. She was successful. She had everything in life you would want. Why would she go to some doctor and start popping pills?"

"Depression and anxiety are not weaknesses. They're nothing to be ashamed of. But they are dangerous, and unfortunately, if they're not managed properly, they can be even more dangerous. You were there on set that night when she asked for her pills. This is what she was talking about."

"No," Meredith insists, shaking her head. "No. She had a headache. She wanted a painkiller."

"She wanted the anti-anxiety medication that helped her deal with the tremendous amount of stress and pressure she was facing. I need to know when she started taking these medications," I say.

"I have nothing to do with it," she says through gritted teeth. "If she had those medications, it was because someone was stuffing them down her throat. She would never choose to take them. That wasn't Marlowe."

"And neither was the girl you talk about," I counter.

Her eyes flash, but she doesn't acknowledge the comment. "My daughter is dead and all you care about is a couple of pill bottles."

"Your daughter may be dead for the same reasons she has those pill bottles," I say. "For one second, stop pretending you are in a fucking musical that never happened and remember that Marlowe Gray was a real person. One you brought into this world. And now isn't a part of it anymore. It's game over now, Meredith. There was no farm. There were no animals. There was no version of Marlowe who sang in the fields, the version of her you seem to be clinging to instead of the reality that your daughter is dead."

Her mouth falls open and her arms drop from where they were crossed over her chest. Color comes to her cheeks and I can hear her trying to form words through the shock that's closed her throat. I stalk away from her. It's a little bit of vindication for Marlowe, a step toward the world knowing the truth. There's a picture on my phone that I was going to send to her when she was ready. The luminaries winding along the paths of the trailer park where she actually grew up. I wanted her to remember it that way. Not as a secret, but as a reminder of being true to herself.

Now I'll never be able to send it to her. But I can carry it with me. I can be the one to tell all her secrets.

I started investigating her death before it happened.

She helped me.

She gave me everything I needed.

CHAPTER FORTY-TWO

"I ENCOURAGED HER TO GET THEM. I COULD TELL SHE WAS DEALING with a lot of stress and seemed to be depressed. Not that I could blame her. Everybody thinks being famous is so wonderful. Like it's some fantasy world. But I can tell you more celebrities than not suffer from anxiety and depression. It's not an easy life to live, especially for somebody so young who is just getting started."

"Did she confide in you?" I ask.

"Not exactly," Delta admits. "But I approached her. I told her that I could see she was going through something and if she needed, I could get her to a doctor who could help."

"Did you know the medications she was prescribed are known to cause increased anxiety and impulsivity?" I ask.

She shakes her head. "No. I didn't even know what they put her on. What do you think that means? Do you really think she killed herself?"

"I can't say anything for sure right now. I'm still looking at all the angles. Thank you for your help."

I start out of the trailer, but she stops me.

"Emma?"

"Yes?"

"Do you think I should shut down the production?"

"No," I tell her. "Finish it. Marlowe deserves it." She nods and I start to leave again, then hesitate. "Can you let me into her trailer? It's going to need to be searched for the investigation anyway. It would be easier if you just gave us access."

"Of course.

"Emma."

I'm leaving Marlowe's trailer with my bag over my shoulder and my next stop already fixed in my mind when I hear Brittany's voice behind me. I stop and turn to face her. She's wearing black and streaks of makeup mark her cheeks.

"I didn't know you'd come back," I say.

"Of course I did. I couldn't stay away. My best friend killed herself. How could I possibly not get back here as fast as I could?"

"We don't know that she killed herself," I say.

"What do you mean? What else could have happened to her?"

"An accident. She could have slipped and fallen. Or someone could have pushed her. Right now, all the options are still on the table."

"How would you know? How could you tell the difference?"

"It's my job. There are some details that show up in investigations that people don't expect. Things you would have to be familiar with crime scenes and the human body to know. Fortunately, I do know those things. And what I don't know, the people around me do. I'll find out what happened."

"I hope you do. I can't bear the thought of life without her. The only thing that makes it worse is thinking I'll never know what happened," Brittany whispers. She wipes her face. "I just can't believe the tribute video I made for her birthday is going to be shown at her memorial."

I think about that for a few seconds. "Can I have a copy of that video?"

"Why?"

"When I'm investigating a death, I like to have reminders of the person with me. I feel like I was getting to know Marlowe, but obviously, you knew her so much better. Getting that kind of personal insight could be really valuable for the investigation."

"Really?" she asks.

"Yes."

"I'll send it to you."

"Thank you. Oh, I wanted to ask. What do you think happened?"

"Me?" she asks.

"Like I said, you knew her better than anyone. You were her best friend. You likely knew things about her that no one else did. Like, was she dating anyone?"

"No. She wasn't seeing anyone. She hadn't in years. She was focused on her career. Always our career. Everybody wanted a piece of her, it seemed. But there were plenty of guys who were obsessed with her. Even stalker-ish, I would say. There was even one in particular. I can't remember what she called him, but I had a feeling that he was around a lot."

"Could it have been the guy in those pictures? The ones the news put up and said was her new love interest?"

"I doubt it. Those pictures didn't really show much. Obviously taken by somebody who doesn't know how to create a story," Brittany says.

"But you do," I intuit.

She nods. "I was the first one to ever say I wanted to be an actress, you know. She didn't say it until after I did. We were always Inseparable. From the minute we met, we wanted to spend every second together. She loved coming over to my house. Even when we were really small, we would sing and dance and do little shows. Then we got older and realized the internet was a thing and there was no stopping us from there.

"Especially Marlowe. Nobody could get enough of her. The whole world opened up to her. I understand it, though. She was beautiful and talented. Everything anybody would want. It was easy to get lost in a shadow when she was around."

"Is that how you felt? That you lived in her shadow?"

"Everybody did. Nothing was going to stop her. If she wanted something, she was going to have it. I couldn't wait for the world to find out what she was going to do next. She was going to shock everybody. And she would have been the perfect Vera. Now no one will get to see that performance."

"Can I ask you one more question?" I ask.

"Go ahead."

"What are you going to do now?"

I've watched the tribute video so many times I could close my eyes and see the images projecting on the back of my eyelids just as accurately as they show up on the screen. But I have to keep watching it. There's something in it I'm looking for, but I don't know what it is. I'll know it when I see it. It's in here. I know it is.

I focus on the section of the video that was playing when Meredith stopped it. She said it was embarrassing Marlowe, but I can't help but wonder if there was another reason behind her ending the tribute. I watch it again. Something I didn't notice before stands out to me. Maybe. I'm not completely sure.

I watch it again. And again. Then I know.

I stop the video and take a screenshot, then email it to myself so I can pull it up on my phone. Closing out the window with the video on it, I pull up a search bar and start researching. It takes a couple of hours, but by the time I am in the car and on my way to the apartment building, the gears are turning in the back of my mind.

She helped me. Even if she didn't know she did. She told me her story.

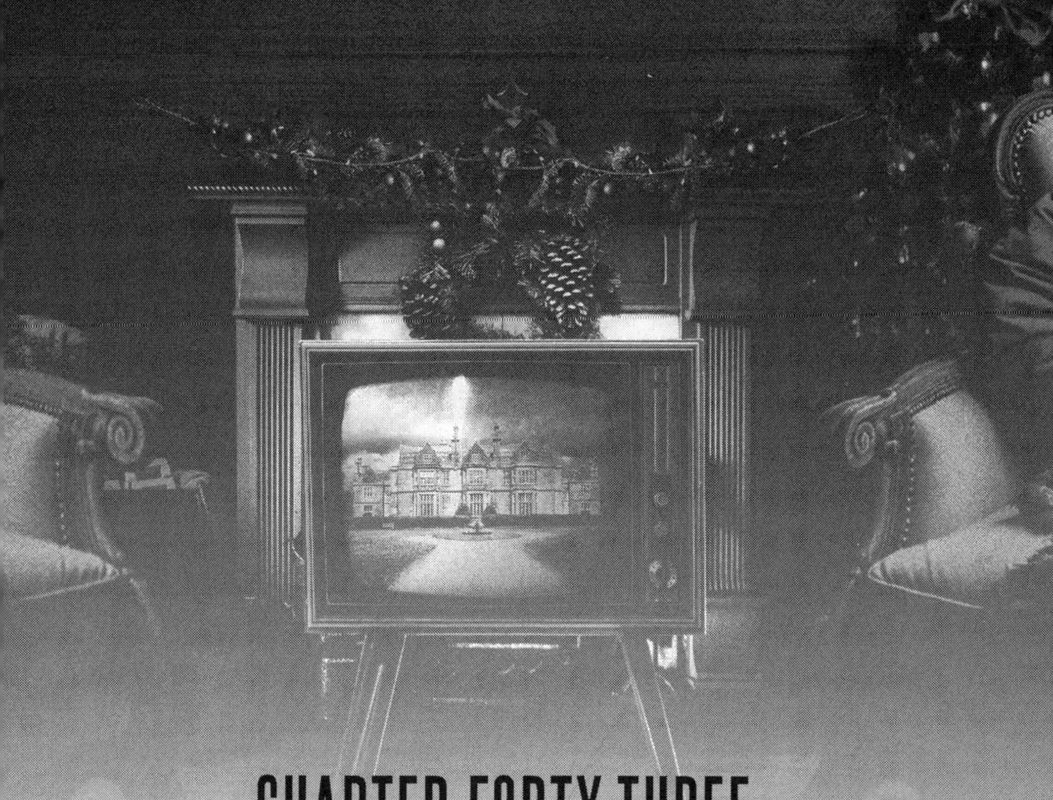

CHAPTER FORTY-THREE

BRANSON IS COMING DOWN THE STEPS TOWARD THE LOBBY OF THE apartment building as I come out of the manager's office. He pauses, pulling the dog he's walking to a stop beside him as he gives me a questioning look.

"Agent Griffin. What are you doing here?"

"Investigating. I'm trying to find out what happened to Marlowe Gray."

He nods, looking emotional. "Do you have any idea yet?"

"I have a few ideas, but I'm still gathering information. Maybe you could help me."

"I don't know what I could tell you, but I'll do anything I can," he says. "We weren't neighbors for very long."

"That's true. But you two moved in really close together. Just a couple of weeks. Did you know that?" I ask.

"I think we talked about that when we first met," he says. "We both thought it was interesting that the two apartments were empty at the same time. It's such a nice building and in such a good location."

"It is," I acknowledge. "And with those back entrances, it's perfect for if you don't want to be seen."

He nods silently, measuring his response before he gives it. "I'm sure that was something she appreciated."

"How much time did the two of you spend together?" I ask.

"We didn't spend time together. Not in any sort of formal sense. We ran into each other occasionally outside of the building. A couple of times she walked with me while I was walking Bruno because she was already out jogging. But we didn't make plans to see each other, if that's what you're asking."

"You seemed really shocked when we found her body. It hit you hard," I point out.

"Agent Griffin, I'm sure you're used to finding dead bodies and seeing people you know in that sort of condition. But I'm not. That's the first time I've seen anything like that. The only time I've ever seen somebody dead was my mother, and she was already stuffed, made up, and in a box. She was a nice kid. It isn't easy seeing something go bad like that."

"What do you mean go bad?"

"She slipped, didn't she? I just figured it had to be an accident. Out partying half a night like she was, she probably had a few too many and just went over. She was up on that balcony all the time. It was bound to happen."

The manager already told me Frederic was in Marlowe's apartment, so I'm not surprised when I go in and find him in the living room. But he does seem startled to see me.

"I thought the police already went through the apartment," he says.

"I'm not the police. But why would it matter if I was?" I ask.

"Marlowe died here. I would think you would understand it might need to be searched more than once."

"I do understand that. I only meant I was told I could remove items and it wouldn't cause a problem in the investigation. I wanted to make sure that was still the case."

"What are you removing? Financial records?"

"Among other things. It was my responsibility to manage her career and her personal affairs," he says. "Now there are things that will need to be settled as well as confidential information that needs to be kept out of the wrong hands."

"What kind of confidential information would Marlowe have?" I ask.

"That does go against the meaning of the word 'confidential', doesn't it?" he counters.

"I hope you aren't suggesting that whatever information a manager might have shared with an actor is protected by some sort of confidentiality that supersedes a death investigation," I say.

"Of course not," he answers. "But I do have to ask you to be discreet. I can't imagine any of this could have anything to do with her death, and as harsh as this might sound, my career does need to go on."

He holds out the papers he has in one hand.

"Scripts?" I ask.

"And treatments," he says. "She was on the shortlist for a variety of projects and was reviewing them. They aren't public knowledge at the moment and I don't want to be accused of letting sensitive information be leaked."

"Because that is certainly the most important issue right now," I comment.

I look over the scripts and notice the one she showed me is missing. The project she wanted to take. I don't ask about it. She didn't want Frederic to know about it, so it's likely she kept it somewhere else. I hand them back to him without mentioning the missing one.

"Is that all?" he asks.

"I'll need to see her financial records."

"Excuse me?"

"When someone with resources like she had dies unexpectedly, it's important to consider all of the different factors. Maybe it's not polite, but I'll put it in terms you could understand. I need to follow the money."

"That's not an option. It's my job to protect her and her best interests, even now. And I won't allow just anyone to dig through her private information. You'll have to come back with a warrant."

"And it's my job to find out why she's dead. You might have been her manager, her accountant, her gatekeeper, but none of those are protected by law. You didn't have power of attorney. Her financial information is hers. It isn't yours to protect, and you have no right to demand a warrant. You also don't have the right to take her private information now. Because while your devotion to her even in death is chivalrous, the fact that she's dead means she is no longer, in fact, your client."

He tosses the papers to the table in front of me and walks out of the apartment. I pick them up and put them into my bag, then head into Marlowe's bedroom to look for the script.

"Where the hell did he go?" I ask. I look around. "Seriously, where did he go? I can't see him."

Off to one side, a chunk of charcoal gray foam shoots up into the air.

"There he is," Dean says.

A few more chunks follow and soon I see the top of Xavier's head. He looks like he's somewhere between climbing up the foam and flailing like he's drowning. Dean goes to the side of the deep pit and reaches for his hand, eventually succeeding in dragging him up and out onto the side.

"How did that look?" Xavier calls over.

"Good," I tell him. "You definitely didn't go as far that time."

"What about the landing position?" he asks.

"It looked more accurate. I think you're right. There's no way she was facing forward when she went over the edge of the balcony. She wouldn't have landed that way or in that spot. But there was still something off about it."

"Alright. One more thing to check," he says.

Xavier scrambles in his socked feet around the edge of the foam-filled pit until he's standing beside me again. Around us, children continue to play on the various attractions and obstacles courses, totally unaffected by the grown man who has spent the better part of the last hour tossing himself into the main foam pit from different positions and at different velocities.

He turns around to face me.

"What now?" I ask.

"Watch," he says.

The last time he went into the foam, he toppled backward like he'd lost his footing, which made him not go as far as when Dean shoved him in last time. Now, he scoots his feet back so they dangle over the edge. He waits there for a tense second, then slips over. Right before disappearing completely, his hands grab onto the edge of the pit. His fingertips turn white with the force of holding himself in place. Slowly, they slide away and he falls into the foam chunks below.

"Xavier, that was perfect. Come on, I have to go see the medical examiner."

His hand pops up out of the foam in a fist. "My wristband is blue. I have fifteen more minutes."

CHAPTER FORTY-FOUR

"ARE YOU READY FOR THIS?" SAM ASKS.

"Yes. I might not have every answer yet. But I'm going to find them. And I do have some of them. If these people want drama, I'm going to give it to them."

Frederic and Brittany arrive at almost the same time. They come into the apartment looking confused and maybe just a little unnerved.

"What's going on here?" Brittany asks.

"Come on in. You'll find out."

"I was told to come here to answer questions," Frederic says. "I assumed that meant the police would be here."

"Oh, they are. Let me introduce you to my husband. Sheriff Sam Johnson. But if he's not enough for you, I also have a good friend of mine. Probably a name you'll recognize. Detective Noah White."

Noah comes into the room. He's wearing his uniform and the expression on his face could crack stone.

"Who called me?" Brittany asks. "It didn't sound like you. I thought it was the police, too."

"It's interesting how our minds can convince us of something because it's what we expect, or what we want it to be. But don't worry. I'll explain everything. Go on in and sit down. Make yourselves at home. After all, both of you are comfortable here. Right? You both spent plenty of time with Marlowe."

The door opens hyy again and Meredith comes in.

"Emma," she starts. "You said you needed to speak with me about Marlowe's estate."

"Come on in. We'll get to that. But I have a few things I want to talk about with all of you before we do," I tell her.

"All of us?" she asks. "What do you mean?"

I lead her into the living room and she sees Brittany and Frederic.

"Meredith, what's going on?" Brittany asks.

"I don't know. Emma called and told me she needed some information before the medical examiner will release Marlowe's death certificate."

"And you need that in order to file a claim against your life insurance, don't you?" I ask.

She looks at me with an offended expression. "Are you implying something?"

"What would I be implying?"

"That I murdered my daughter for her life insurance policy."

"Not at all," I insist. "Go ahead and have a seat and I'll explain why we're here." She goes to the couch and I wait for her to settle before starting up again. "I was just saying to Frederic and Brittany, but I find it fascinating how easily our minds can be manipulated. That we can convince ourselves of a truth or a reality simply by believing it enough.

"There is one reality here that none of us can argue. Marlowe is dead. But the question hanging over all of us is why? Was it an accident?

Did she kill herself? Was she murdered?" I look at each of them as I say this, letting the options sink in individually.

After several seconds, Frederic opens his hands toward me. "And? Which one was it?"

"I'm going to leave that to you to decide," I say.

"Then why are we here?" Brittany asks.

"Because whether Marlowe died at someone else's hands or her own, or because of an accident, I believe each one of you has something to answer for. I've heard in the entertainment industry they say there are no small roles. Well, each of you has one. Let's just see how they all play out."

"This is a waste of our time," Meredith huffs. "You're supposed to be this incredible FBI agent, but you don't even know what happened."

"That's not what I said. I said I was going to leave it to the three of you to decide for yourselves. Let you play me for a little while. But if you are really concerned about the time, I'll start with you."

"I don't have anything to do with Marlowe's death. I did nothing but take care of her and do everything I could to help her be as successful as possible."

"You know, Meredith, I think you actually believe that. Unfortunately, your idea of helping her be as successful as possible was telling a series of lies that tangled up around both of you. And she was done keeping them."

"You don't know what you're talking about."

"Who is Charles Gray?"

"Marlowe's father."

"And you met him in high school?"

"Yes. He was the love of my life. I was supposed to spend the rest of it with him, but he was tragically killed in the line of duty," Meredith says.

"It's interesting that you put it that way. Because before you used to say 'in the service'. Which most people would understand as being the military. I did some research. You could say I took a little walk down memory lane. Only, it wasn't my memories. It was yours. And I found something interesting. Or, I should say, I didn't find something interesting. No Charles. He went to your school. I'll give you that. But there was nothing that showed the two of you had anything to do with each other. No pictures together in the yearbook. No quotes from each other or about each other. There wasn't even a newspaper article about your engagement."

"We never got married," she replies. "We wanted to, but both of us wanted a nice wedding and we didn't have the money for it. But as it went on we were essentially living as husband and wife. I used his name and we figured eventually we would go ahead and do it, but it wasn't a priority anymore once we found out we were going to be parents."

"Most people are the opposite. Even if they haven't put a lot of thought into getting married, once they find out a baby is on the way, it changes their minds. But, that's not up to me to judge. I'm more interested in what you said about him finding out he was going to have a daughter."

"He was thrilled. I think a lot of men want sons, but he was already the perfect girl dad," Meredith says.

"I bet it was hard to go through the rest of your pregnancy without him," I tell her.

"It was. Those were some of the most difficult months of my life," she says.

"You mean days."

"What?"

"You've said before that you had months of your pregnancy without Charles, which would make sense if you found out you were having a girl around five months into your pregnancy like most people do. But if he died right after you found out that you were having a girl, it would only be a matter of days. You see, the Carlsbad Hotel hostage incident and fire happened in December. You would have been just about ready to give birth if he died then. As a matter of fact, the stress of it could have sent you into labor. That would have been a much better story. You should have gone with that."

"So, I made up how he died because I didn't want to admit he died in a drunk driving accident. That doesn't make me a terrible person," she snaps, an angry light flashing from her eyes.

I smile. "You came up with that one quickly. And it's plausible. Good job. And if that was your only lie, the only way you'd hurt Marlowe, maybe I'd let it go."

"I didn't hurt her," she insists.

I go into the kitchen and come back with Marlowe's prescription bottles. I set them on the table in front of Meredith.

CHAPTER FORTY-FIVE

Meredith

"WHAT THE FUCK WAS THAT, MARLOWE?" MEREDITH demanded.

"Be careful, mother. Your Shining Pines is showing," Marlowe replied.

"Stop that," Meredith said. "Someone is going to hear you. And you already made yet another mistake. Leaving your own birthday party? People are going to start asking questions, then what are you going to do?"

Marlowe whipped around to face her mother. She threw her arms out to the side and scoffed.

"I don't know, Mom. Maybe tell the truth. I know that's a revolutionary concept for you, but it could actually be just so crazy it works."

"You want to tell the truth?" Meredith asked with a cruel smile.

"You want to stand up in front of all the adoring fans who want to follow you, and the producers who want to give you jobs, and tell them you aren't a farm girl whose father was a hero? That you grew up in a trailer park and don't even know your daddy's name?"

"Maybe I do," Marlowe fired back. "I'm not the one who started the lie to begin with. You did. You came up with it because you've always been ashamed. It's the same reason you didn't let me have friends over when I was a kid. You made up that stupid story about my father and forced me to go along with it. You've been telling that one for so long I think you might actually believe it."

"You needed a father and I needed a fresh start," Meredith defended herself.

"Living in a rundown trailer park because it was the only thing that you could get after almost getting your ass sent to prison isn't my idea of a fresh start. But at least it's the truth."

"You think anyone would want to have anything to do with you if they knew that was actually where you came from? That you weren't working on a farm, you were kicking cans and barely getting by?"

"Why would it matter to any of them? And if they did decide they didn't want to work with me, who are you more worried about? Me because you don't think I'd have a career? Or yourself because you couldn't use me anymore?"

"I did everything for you, Marlowe."

"And now you're going to wring every drop out of me for it."

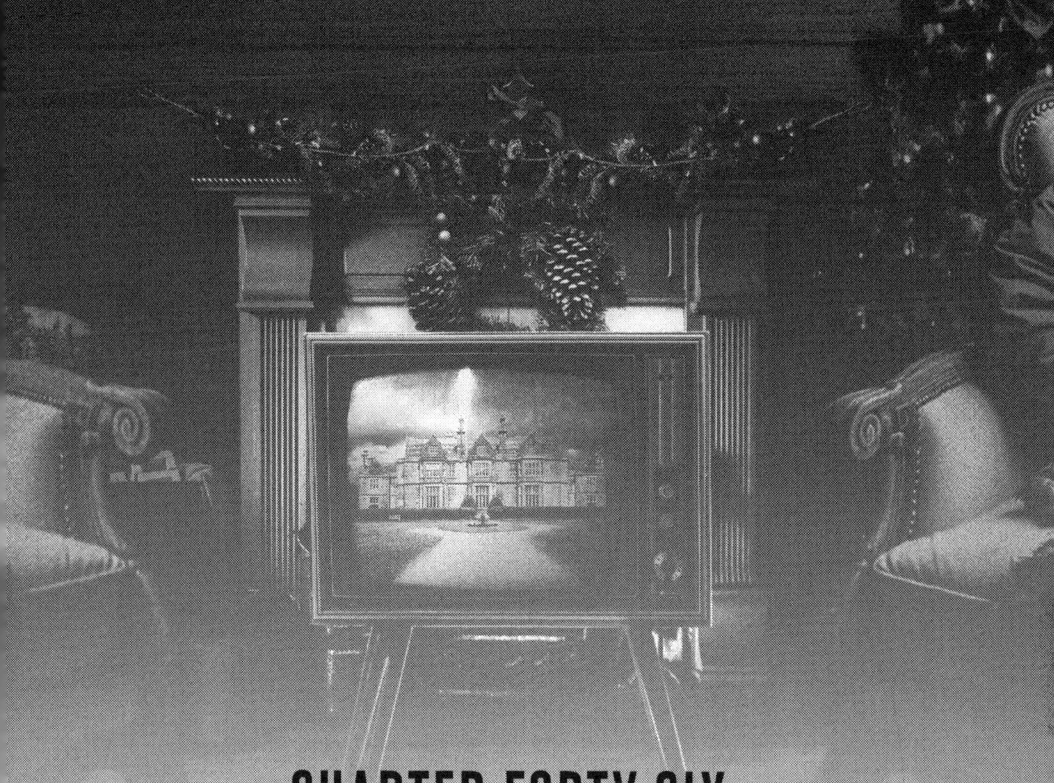

CHAPTER FORTY-SIX

Now

"WE ARGUED," MEREDITH SAYS. "EVERY MOTHER AND DAUGHTER argue."

"She was going to tell everyone the truth," I say.

"It would only have hurt her. She wouldn't have done that. Marlowe loved Marlowe above anyone else. She would do anything she could to protect what she had. What was she getting tired of, exactly? The adoration? The fame?"

"The blackmail," I say.

It ends her mocking laugh.

"The what?"

"Of course, I don't think that's what either one of them would call it. That isn't the nicest term in the world. But maybe he'll give us some insight."

I gesture at Sam, who goes to the front door and comes back with Branson. As soon as she sees him, her face drops.

"What are you doing here? You have no right to be here."

"I have every right to be here. She was my daughter. No matter how much you tried to keep her from me, I was her father."

"You weren't a father until she started making money, now were you?" Meredith spits.

"You wouldn't let me be. I didn't even know she existed until she was eight. Then I did everything I could to try to find her and be a part of her life."

"You didn't deserve to be. You were a worthless piece of trash headed into your next stint in prison. What was that for a baby?" Meredith rages at him.

Brittany and Frederic are watching silently, their eyes going back and forth like they're watching a tennis match.

"I cleaned up for her!" Branson growls.

"And then you came and took her money," Meredith snaps.

"I didn't ask for it. She offered it. When I approached her, I just wanted her to know who I was. That was it. I wanted her to know I didn't just walk away from her or ignore her. That I didn't know, and that when I did know, I couldn't be a part of her life. She was the one who asked me not to tell anybody. She offered to help me get a better life if I just kept the secret."

"All right, all right!" I bark, stopping this before it becomes an all-out brawl.

Their arguments stop and they turn back to me.

"But you did get used to the money, Brandon," I say. "She moved you in here because you followed her. You let her support you. And when she said she was going to come out with the truth, you wanted to stop her. You came over the night I was here with her. I didn't put it together at the time, but when she came back into the room, she was brushing off her arms. It was dog hair.

"When I first met you, you were carrying a dog leash. It was bright green, very distinctive. Then in the pictures of her that started going around, she was holding something bright green. I think she was with you. She was walking your dog. You said the two of you didn't spend much time together, but I don't think that's actually true. She was just very careful about being seen with you because she didn't want any rumors to start. They already had. People thought you were obsessed with her. Or that the two of you were dating.

"She was ready to admit to everything, but you didn't want to do that. And you were here the night she died to talk to her about it."

"I was nowhere near her the night she died. I was out with friends," he says. "It was hard knowing it was my daughter's birthday and I couldn't even spend time with her."

"That might be true. But you were near her. I looked through countless pictures of the nightclub from her birthday party. While she was dancing, she kept looking out over the crowd and I noticed she was focused on the same thing over and over. Last time I didn't realize what it was. But when I looked at the pictures, I saw somebody wearing a hat.

And it was funny because as soon as I looked at that, I saw the resemblance between the two of you. I hadn't seen it before, but she always wore a hat and sunglasses to disguise herself. And when I saw you in it, I knew what I was seeing."

"So, I went by the nightclub. I just wanted to see her for her twenty-first birthday. I didn't hurt her."

"You were here. When we were talking about her death, you said she slipped. That was bound to happen because she was out on that balcony all the time. She told me she loved that balcony because it reminded her of the balance beam. She was up there all the time, just like you said. And you would know what it was like to watch her on the balance beam, because you did when she was young."

"How did you know that?"

"Brittany's tribute video. Meredith stopped it during the party and I couldn't figure out why. So I watched it over and over again and I realized she stopped it right when Marlowe was doing gymnastics. There's a man sitting by himself in the bleachers. He's much younger and has facial hair, but it's you. I looked up the company on the shirt you were wearing and found a picture of you."

"You stalked her?" Meredith demands.

"I watched my daughter the way any father should be allowed to," Branson defends himself. "I never talked to her. I never got near her. I didn't want to scare her. I just watched her."

"And you must have been watching her that night from her apartment," I point out. "You can't see her balcony from yours. So, unless you were in the courtyard or in her apartment, you couldn't have seen her up there. And she wasn't alone when she went home. Something happened while she was there that upset her. She looked like she felt sick and scared, and left without telling anybody. I think you followed her."

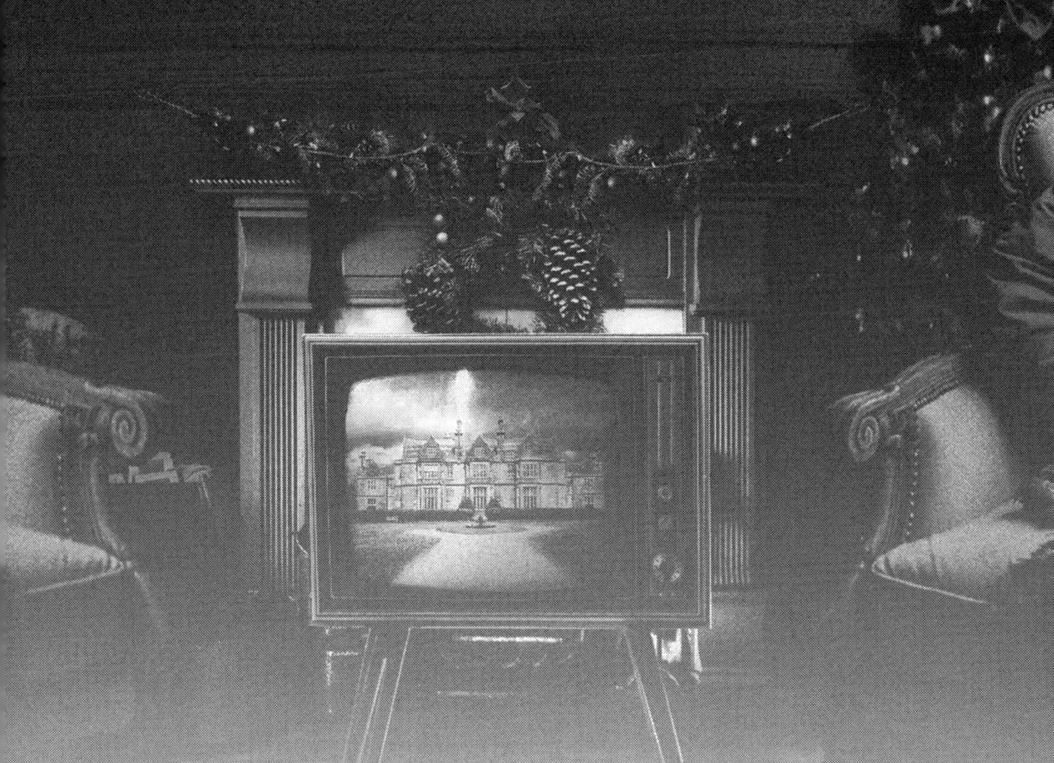

CHAPTER FORTY-SEVEN

Branson

"WHAT ARE YOU DOING HERE?" MARLOWE ASKED.

"I want to wish you a happy birthday," he said. "It's the first one that I've been able to see you."

"I really want to be alone."

"Marlowe, I know you told me you wanted to tell everyone the truth," he said. "But I'm asking you not to."

"I don't need your permission. That wasn't the deal. We got into this because I didn't want you to say anything and hurt Mom, but I can't take it anymore. I can't keep lying. I don't have to tell anyone who you are. You can leave and not be a part of it anymore."

"That's not what I want and you know it. I've wanted to be a part of your life since I found out about you. I don't want to start hiding again."

"You mean you don't want to be without the money."

"That's really all you think of me?" Branson asked.

"You didn't turn it down," she replied.

She walked out onto the balcony, drawing in deep breaths of the cold air to calm down.

"It helped me out. I'm not proud of my past, but at least I've been honest about it. I know who I am and what I've done. And I know how hard everything has been because of it. I haven't been able to get a good job. I've had to live in shit places. So, yes, it's been nice getting that leg up. And maybe I felt like it was owed to me a little. The one true thing Meredith ever told you was that you got your talent from your father."

"I've never had a father and I don't need one now if it means having another person capitalizing on me. Please leave."

CHAPTER FORTY-EIGHT

Now

"SHE WAS ALIVE WHEN I LEFT. I WAS UPSET AND I WAS ANGRY, but she was alive. She was already worked up when I got there and I might have made it worse, but I didn't lay a hand on her. And I know she was fine when I left because she was in different clothes when she was found. When I talked to her, she was still in her dress."

"There were two things that really stood out to me when I saw Marlowe's body," I tell the group. One was her toenails. A few of them were painted and a few of them weren't. But she was in her pajamas. Which tells me someone else came to the apartment. Someone she has known for a long time, but maybe not who she felt really comfortable with."

I look at Frederic and he gives me an incredulous gape. "Toenails? Somehow the fact that her toenails were chipped tells you I was there that night?"

"I didn't say they were chipped," I say. "I said some were painted and some weren't. Which you probably wouldn't have recognized as meaning anything. But I know what it meant. The first night I came over here to talk with Marlowe, she immediately changed into her comfortable clothes and started removing her toenail polish. She told me it was her routine. She did it every night as soon as she got home, and every morning she painted them again. She trusted me, so she was willing to do it with me there."

"So?" Frederic frowns. "What does that have to do with anything?"

"She was outside in her dress when Branson left, according to him. But she was found in her pajamas with her toenail polish partially removed. She changed clothes and sat down to remove the polish. She stopped when you got there, which was why it was only partially done. I went over those financial records. The ones you didn't want me to see. I bet you didn't think I'd understand what I was seeing."

"What were you seeing?" he asks with a sarcastic lilt.

"What did you give Marlowe for her birthday?" I ask.

"For her birthday?" he asks.

"Yes. At the party, you gave her a gift. What was it?" I ask.

"A bracelet," he shrugs. "With charms that represented each of the projects we've done together."

"From what company?" I ask.

"Francois."

"That's a really nice company," I note. "I'm sure it was beautiful. Why did she seem so uncomfortable about it?"

"She didn't. She loved it," he says. "She was just overwhelmed."

"I think it's because she knew you hadn't bought it for her. She bought it for herself. It was all the confirmation she needed. And you knew it. You could see the end coming."

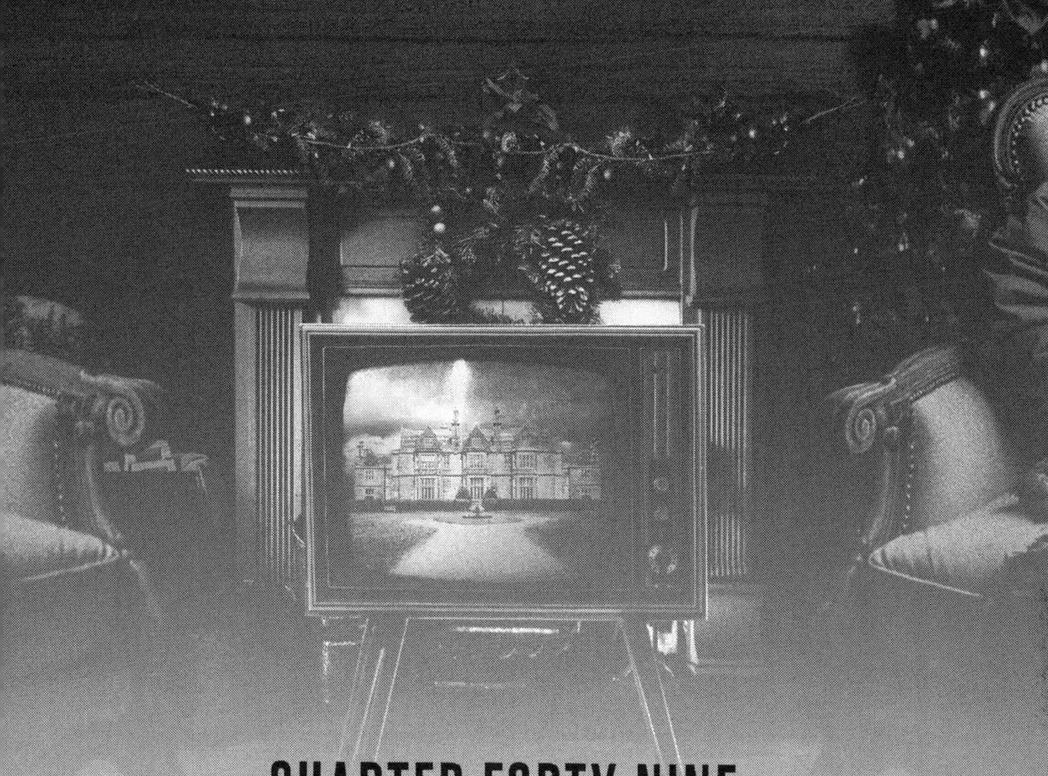

CHAPTER FORTY-NINE

Frederic

"I CAN EXPLAIN."

"Frederic, there's nothing left to explain," Marlowe said.

She walked away from the door, rolling her eyes. She just wanted to be alone. Just one more night. A little more time to enjoy this life before everyone found out all of her secrets and everything changed. This was the perfect example of why.

"But there is. It isn't what it looks like."

"It isn't?" she snapped. "So, you mean the charge at Francois I found on my credit card that I didn't make and that I disputed, but got rejected for, wasn't because you used my credit card to buy my birthday present?"

"I was going to pay you back."

"Frederic, listen to me. The bracelet is the absolute least of your worries. I honestly probably wouldn't have even noticed if I hadn't started wondering about the money disappearing from the charity fund. That's one of the main reasons I started looking through my own records. I needed to know what was happening. Imagine my surprise when I found out one of the most frequent recipients of funds from the subscriptions are all you. At least you got creative and came up with different names to help you steal the money more effectively."

"I wasn't stealing," Frederic protested.

"Oh, I'm sorry. Do you prefer skimming?" Marlowe asked. "Just get the hell out. I've already gotten in touch with a lawyer to find out how to press charges and make sure every cent of that money goes back where it should have been, to begin with."

"You can't do that, Marlowe. You'll ruin me," Frederic said.

"That's really not my problem," Marlowe said. "I didn't do this. I didn't tell you to steal money from me and from the people who actually need it."

"But you did refuse to pay me what I'm worth," he replied. "I came to you with a very reasonable request. I've been with you from the very beginning of your career. When you were nothing. And all I wanted was to be acknowledged for that work. But you just tossed me aside like I was nothing."

"You controlled my life, Frederic. You controlled what projects I even knew existed, much less did. You controlled where I went and who I could be seen with. You wouldn't let me be a part of negotiations. I couldn't live that like that. Every day I felt like I getting crushed. Like I didn't even know who I was anymore. I wasn't living my own life. I was doing what you told me so that you and my mother could benefit from it. Don't you think I knew you'd been stealing from me? There was no point in me giving you a raise because you weren't going to be employed by me anymore. Just like you aren't now."

"You will never be anyone again, Marlowe. You get rid of me and there isn't anyone who will pay you more than slave wages because you're too stupid and too dysfunctional to handle any of it on your own."

Marlowe was starting to feel like she couldn't breathe. The anxiety was building up inside her so much she was struggling to even think straight. She couldn't do this anymore. She couldn't keep fighting like this. Her pills were in the other room, but she didn't even want them. She just wanted to be outside.

"Leave," she managed to say.

She got outside and took a long breath.

"Don't walk away from me when I'm talking to you. Do you know what I could do to your reputation?"

She pressed her hands to the rough stone of the balcony and felt the urge to climb up. Her feet balanced on the edge and she teetered between safety and oblivion. Maybe if she just closed her eyes, the universe would decide for her.

"Marlowe, stop acting like a child. Get down," Frederic said. But his voice was far away, like it wasn't real. The only thing that was real was the wind on her face and the open air of the night.

"Leave me alone," she said.

"You're being ridiculous."

She turned slowly in a circle. She didn't know which way she was facing. She didn't know how far her feet were venturing to either side of the barrier. It didn't matter. Sudden wind made her lose her balance and she felt like the universe had decided. But hands grabbed onto her.

"Open your eyes. Look at me, Marlowe. I want to see you look into my eyes and tell me you're going to throw me away."

CHAPTER FIFTY

Now

"I TRIED TO STOP HER," FREDERIC SAYS. "I GRABBED HER SO THAT she wouldn't fall."

"There was a bruise on her arm," I admit.

"Because I took hold of her to stop her from hurting herself. I was mad at her. I hated her in that moment. But what good would it have done to kill her?"

"She wasn't going to be any good to you anymore," I counter.

"And you wouldn't have charges brought up against you," Brittany mutters. "Now you sound like the next of Delta's projects."

"The thought of that excites you, doesn't it, Brittany?" I ask, cutting a sudden glance over to her.

She looks at me with widened eyes and lifted brows. "Me? What do you mean?"

"Delta could do a tribute to Marlowe and tell the story of her tragic loss. And who better to play the role of the titular character than her best friend?" I ask.

"That's sick," Brittany says. "She was my best friend. I loved her."

"So much that you wanted to be her," I point out. "You told me yourself you were the one who always wanted to perform. You were the one who said you wanted to be in the entertainment industry. But she's the one who got the attention. Beautiful, special Marlowe."

"I was proud of her," Brittany said. "I might have wanted some of that for myself, but it was just because she was such an inspiration. I saw how far she had gone and I knew I could do the same thing. It just hadn't happened for me yet."

"Not for want of trying, though, right? You tried to get role after role and nothing ever came to you. Then you found out Marlowe was getting the parts, and it drove you crazy."

"This is ridiculous. I wasn't even at her house that night. I went home so I could get ready to leave for my grandparents' early the next morning. There are a lot of people in this world who want to be in show business. It doesn't mean they go around killing their best friends so they can get the good roles."

"And you just got one, didn't you?' I ask.

"Yes," Brittany says.

"I heard that. There was an article about it. What's your character's name again? Sylvia?"

"Yes," she says.

"Marlowe told me about a role that she really wanted and had told the producers she was going to take, behind Frederic's and her mother's back." At this mention, both of them look at each other, but I continue on. "It was originally Amber. Then Sylvia. But they changed it again for her. Tell me, how did you find out about the role?"

"I saw the script and thought it was interesting, so I did an audition."

"Where did you see the script?"

"It was sent with a stack to Frederic. I was waiting for Marlowe one day and I happened on it."

I shake my head. "No. The script wasn't sent through Frederic. They went directly to Marlowe herself. And the scripts were only given to the people who were in very serious contention for the roles. Right after her death, you told me that she would be a perfect Vera. How would you have any way of knowing that's what they were going to call her character, that when it was only put in her script and no one else saw it?"

"She showed me."

"No," I shake my head. "She didn't show anyone because she knew it wasn't the kind of role Frederic would ever negotiate for her. That script is now missing. The only way you could have known that name is if you were there that night and took hers."

"And you can't imagine that someone might have noticed me for me?" she asks. "I'm not invisible. Marlowe got all the attention, but she wasn't everything."

"You made sure people knew you existed, didn't you?" I ask. "During the tribute video, I heard the song and couldn't place the singer, but knew I'd heard it before. That's because it was you singing. I'd heard it on her social media before. You started doing that a lot over the last couple of months. And right after she died, you started posting pictures and videos of the two of you, then just of you. You were talking about how much you missed her and how hard life was going to be without her, but you weren't mourning. You were auditioning.

"You'd heard about the project from other people and you wanted to do it badly. Then you heard they wanted Marlowe and you were furious. You came here that night to confront her about taking another role you wanted."

"I didn't understand why she wouldn't help me. She could have given me a leg up. Put in a good word for me. Anything. But instead, she just went and took everything for herself."

"But you have it all now, don't you?" I say.

"You can't blame me for that. I never touched her."

"You're right, Brittany. You never even touched her. I said there were two things that stood out about her. The toenail polish, and the blood on her fingertips."

CHAPTER FIFTY-ONE

Brittany

BRITTANY STOOD WITH HER EYES CLOSED, HER FACE TURNED UP TO the sky as the wind brushed over it.

"I don't know what I'm going to do without her. She was my best friend. The most beautiful person I'd ever known. The world lost such a bright star."

She whispered it again and again until it flowed off her tongue naturally. The loud music around her made it harder to concentrate on the words, but she was going to have to get used to it. She'd need to know her lines. At least it also softened the sound of the cries.

She opened her eyes to check the fingertips clinging to the edge of the balcony. By now Marlowe's voice was getting scratchy and quiet. She'd lost much of it during her party and it was getting weaker now. She stayed back from the edge. She hated heights. Almost as much as she hated watching Marlowe walk along the edge of the balcony. She was tempting fate. Maybe that was what she wanted.

In the distance, she heard voices start counting down. She counted along with them waiting for the New Year.

10

9

8

7

6

5

4

3

2

1

Her fingertips left only a little bit of blood behind. Brittany could only see it in the sparkle of the fireworks overhead. She hummed in her throat as she listened to the first moments of all that came next.

Should auld acquaintance be forgot, and never brought to mind?
Should auld acquaintance be forgot, and days of auld lang syne…

AUTHOR'S NOTE

Dear Reader,

I hope you enjoyed *The Girl and the Silent Night*. Thank you for your continued support with the Emma Griffin series. This is my favorite time of the year and I hope you loved reading this book as much as I loved writing it! If you can please continue to leave your reviews for these books, I would appreciate that enormously. Your reviews allow me to get the validation I need to keep going as an indie author. Just a moment of your time is all that is needed.

My promise to you is to always do my best to bring you thrilling adventures. I wish you and your family a Merry Christmas and Happy Holidays from the bottom of my heart!!

Yours,
A.J. Rivers

P.S. If for some reason you didn't like this book or found typos or other errors, please let me know personally. I do my best to read and respond to every email at mailto:aj@riversthrillers.com

ALSO BY
A.J. RIVERS

Emma Griffin FBI Mysteries by AJ Rivers

Season One

*Book One—The Girl in Cabin 13**

*Book Two—The Girl Who Vanished**

*Book Three—The Girl in the Manor**

*Book Four—The Girl Next Door**

*Book Five—The Girl and the Deadly Express**

*Book Six—The Girl and the Hunt**

*Book Seven—The Girl and the Deadly End**

Season Two

*Book Eight—The Girl in Dangerous Waters**

*Book Nine—The Girl and Secret Society**

*Book Ten—The Girl and the Field of Bones**

*Book Eleven—The Girl and the Black Christmas**

*Book Twelve—The Girl and the Cursed Lake**

*Book Thirteen—The Girl and The Unlucky 13**

*Book Fourteen—The Girl and the Dragon's Island**

Season Three

*Book Fifteen—The Girl in the Woods**

Book Sixteen—The Girl and the Midnight Murder

Book Seventeen— The Girl and the Silent Night

Other Standalone Novels

*Gone Woman**

* *Also available in audio*

Made in the USA
Middletown, DE
09 August 2022